Her mother had been nearly incoherent with distress. Was something going on she wasn't aware of? She was seventy-one now. Maybe looking after a rambunctious five-year-old was too much for her.

No. She shook her head to reject the disloyal thought. Dr. Campbell was the one who was wrong.

"I know my mother. She didn't do this. It was an accident."

"We'll soon find out. Sharon is questioning Ava now."

Julia stared at the door. "She'll be scared, all by herself."

"Sharon's very good at what she does. She has a way of making kids feel comfortable."

Julia turned on him, the anger and despair she'd been holding inside spilling out. "And you? Do you enjoy upsetting five-year-olds and turning families' lives upside down? Does it make you feel powerful to sic the authorities on us?"

"Look, Mrs. Stewart, I take no pleasure in bringing in the authorities. But I've seen child abuse, up close and personal, and I can tell you it's damn ugly. The things parents and caregivers are capable of doing to defenseless children…"

He stopped abruptly, his chest heaving. Closing his eyes, he averted his face and took a deep breath. When he turned back to her, his steely control was back in place. "So yeah, if I have even the smallest suspicion that a child has been abused, I'm going to ask questions. And I'm not going to apologize for it."

Praise for Jana Richards

"Richards has a knack of developing characters with real depth, something which the genre often fails to do."

~Belinda Williams, Belinda Williams Books

~*~

"Jana Richards is a new to me author and if this is the norm for her I will definitely be on the lookout for more works by her."

~Dianthus, Long and Short Reviews

~*~

"Ms. Richards knows how to keep a reader turning page after page. Her characters are strong, passionate, and each has their faults."

~Liadan, Coffee Time Romance

One More Second Chance

by

Jana Richards

The Lobster Cove Series

This is a work of fiction. Names, characters, places, and incidents are either the product of the author's imagination or are used fictitiously, and any resemblance to actual persons living or dead, business establishments, events, or locales, is entirely coincidental.

One More Second Chance

Contact Information: info@thewildrosepress.com

Cover Art by *Tina Lynn Stout*

The Wild Rose Press, Inc.
PO Box 708
Adams Basin, NY 14410-0708
Visit us at www.thewildrosepress.com

Publishing History
First Champagne Rose Edition, 2015
Print ISBN 978-1-62830-705-4
Digital ISBN 978-1-62830-706-1

The Lobster Cove Series
Published in the United States of America

Dedication

To my editor Nan Swanson for her infinite patience.
Glad to be working with you again, Nan.

Chapter One

"I'm sorry to barge in, Principal Stewart, but there's a phone call for you on line one that I think you should take. It sounds urgent."

Julia Stewart knew Beth, long-time secretary at Lobster Cove High School, wouldn't interrupt mid-reprimand unless it was important. She gave her a slight nod, then turned her attention to the two teenage boys sitting on the other side of her desk.

"Looks like you've been saved by the bell. For now. We'll schedule another little chat about smoking on school property later. Go with Mrs. Anderson."

They couldn't leave fast enough. Beth threw her a worried look as she closed the door behind them. Julia picked up her phone. "Hello, Principal Stewart speaking."

"Julia, I'm sorry. It wasn't my fault. I didn't know. I'm so sorry." Her mother sobbed, her words nearly incomprehensible.

She gripped the handset. "Mom? What's going on?"

"She fell. I'm so sorry, so sorry."

Julia's heart thumped painfully. "You mean Ava fell? Where did she fall? Is she okay?"

"She was in the basement. I didn't know. It was an accident. I'm so sorry."

"Mom! What's going on? Is Ava all right?"

There was a thud, as if her mother had dropped the phone. Julia jumped to her feet, alarmed. What was going on at her parents' house? Where was her daughter?

"Mom? Mom!"

She heard voices but couldn't make out what was being said. Finally she heard her father's voice on the line.

"It's all right, Julia. Ava had an accident. She fell part way down the basement steps."

"Oh, my God!" Her heart lodged in her throat. "Is she all right? Is she conscious?"

"Yes, yes, she's banged up, but she's alert. I think she needs to go to the hospital, though. Her arm may be broken."

Julia brought her trembling hand to her mouth to cover a sob. *Dear God. My poor baby.*

"I'll meet you at the hospital."

"I think it's best if you pick Ava up and take her there yourself. She's very upset and she wants her mother."

"But it would be faster if you took her. By the time I drive to your house—"

"Don't argue with me, Julia!" he said sharply. "Your daughter needs you. Get over here, now!"

For a second, she couldn't speak. Her father rarely raised his voice. For him to do so now told her the situation was very serious.

"I'll be right there."

She slammed down the receiver, grabbed her purse and jacket, and ran out of her office.

"Ava's had an accident. I've got to go," she said to Beth on her way out. Pushing her arms into the sleeves of her jacket, she shoved open the door and dashed to the parking lot. A steady April rain chilled her to the bone by the time she reached her car. Of all the days to forget her umbrella.

Careening off with a squeal of tires, she headed for her parents' house. The weather forecast had called for heavy fog to roll in off the Atlantic and blanket Mount Desert Island, the little corner of Maine Julia called home. For once, they'd gotten it right. Her windshield wipers worked overtime to take away the moisture, but they could do nothing to help her see through the misty soup. She pressed on, gripping the steering wheel, knowing she was driving faster than prudent. But she desperately needed to get to her five-year-old to see for herself that she was okay.

Finally she pulled into her parents' driveway and ran from the car, not bothering to turn off the ignition. As soon as she opened the back door, she could hear Ava crying.

"Mommy! I want Mommy!"

Julia found her in the kitchen, sitting in her grandfather's lap, her right arm cradled protectively against her chest. Tears streamed down her face. Julia kneeled by her father's chair.

"I'm here, baby. It's all right now." She kissed Ava's forehead and noticed a bruise above her right eye.

"It hurts, Mommy!"

"I know, sweetheart. We're going to make it better." She turned to her father. "I'll put you in the back seat of my car. You can hold Ava on your lap."

"You'll have to take her," he said, not meeting her eyes. "Your mother's upset. I need to stay with her."

She couldn't believe he wouldn't help her take Ava to the hospital. "Dad, you have to come with us."

"I'm sorry, Julia. Your mother needs me."

What the hell was going on? Until today, she'd believed her father would do anything for Ava. How could he abandon them both like this?

She didn't have time to argue. Scooping Ava into her arms, she wordlessly followed her father to the back door. He opened it for her, then ran ahead to open the passenger door of her car. Julia carefully placed Ava on the seat and closed the door. When she lifted her head, she met her father's eyes and read the pain in them before he turned away.

"Let us know how you make out," he said, his voice cracking.

Julia nodded and got in the car. Once Ava's injuries had been addressed, she'd find out exactly what had happened and why her father refused to come with her. But for now, all she wanted was to ease her daughter's pain.

The hospital emergency room was busy for a Tuesday afternoon. After being seen by a triage nurse, they were ushered into an examining room. Julia held Ava on her lap, trying not to touch her injured arm. Even the smallest jostle made her howl. Julia wanted to howl herself, but instead she whispered soft, reassuring words and choked back her own distress.

Her daughter's sobs wrenched her heart. How had this happened? Ava knew she wasn't supposed to play on the stairs. It was an old house, with steep, uncarpeted basement stairs. She'd told Ava to stay out of the basement when she was at her grandparents' house. But she was only five; why hadn't her parents kept her safe?

Finally the door to the examining room opened and a tall, dark-haired man wearing a white lab coat entered, followed by a nurse. Julia's heart fell. She'd hoped Dr. Willson would see them. She'd known Henry Willson since she was Ava's age, and she trusted him. She wasn't keen on entrusting her daughter's care to someone she'd never met and had only heard rumors about.

He smiled at Ava and knelt to look at her at eye level. He touched her knee gently.

"Hi, Ava. I'm Dr. Campbell. Can you tell me what happened?"

She snuggled closer to Julia. "I fell."

"Where did you fall?"

"Down the basement stairs at Grandma and Grandpa's house."

"I explained all this to the triage nurse," Julia said impatiently. "Is Dr. Willson on duty today? He's Ava's doctor."

Eyes the color of deepest, darkest chocolate flashed at her from an unsmiling face. "Dr. Willson is off today. I'm the only doctor in the ER." He turned his attention back to Ava. "Would it be okay if your mom puts you on the examining table? I'm going to take a look at your arm."

Ava nodded, her chin trembling. He rose, and Julia tried to do likewise, but her arm had fallen asleep while holding Ava, and she simply didn't have the strength to raise her. Seeing she was unable to move, the doctor lifted Ava from her arms and gently placed her on the table, turning her so she was lying on her back with her head on the pillow. Julia rubbed the pins and needles from her arm.

He touched the bump on Ava's forehead that Julia had noticed, then ran his fingers through her blonde hair, likely checking for more abrasions. He lifted her left arm and examined the scrapes that were visible below the sleeve of her T-shirt. Then he gently probed her right arm, but when Ava cried out, he retreated.

"I'm sorry. Your arm really hurts, doesn't it?"

"Yes," she said. Her chin wobbled, and Julia had to look away, afraid she was going to cry, too.

"Does it hurt anywhere else?"

"On my legs."

Dr. Campbell carefully pushed up Ava's jeans to reveal her shins and knees. They were badly scraped, the skin rubbed raw in some places and beginning to bruise in others. He looked over his shoulder and spoke to the nurse.

"Let's get Ava into x-ray as soon as possible. I want pictures of that arm." He turned to Ava and gently fingered the bump on her head once more. "And I want a skeletal survey."

"What's a skeletal survey?" Julia asked.

"It's a series of x-rays of all the bones in the body, or most of them, anyway. It's commonly used in a trauma such as this to check for broken bones." He spoke to the nurse once more. "In the meantime, let's give Ava something for the pain and get a splint on that arm to keep it in place."

"Yes, Doctor."

Ava looked up at Dr. Campbell, her eyes shiny with tears. "Is it going to hurt?"

"The x-rays? No, I promise they won't hurt. It's sort of like getting your picture taken, only it's a picture of your insides." He smoothed her wayward curls with a gentle hand. "We're going to take a lot of x-rays, so it's going to take a long time, maybe an hour or more. Do you think you can be brave for that long?"

She nodded solemnly. "Yes."

"I knew you could," he said with a grin.

Despite her pain, Ava grinned back at him. The expression on her face told Julia she had complete trust in him.

Ava was given a dose of children's strength ibuprofen and fitted with a splint that kept her right arm immobile. Dr. Campbell touched her good arm.

"I have to go look after some of my other patients now, but I'll be back after your x-rays are done."

"Promise?"

"I promise. I might bring someone with me to talk to you. Is that okay?"

"Okay."

Julia wondered who he was talking about. And why was he asking Ava rather than her?

With a curt nod in her direction, he left the room. Shortly after that, an orderly arrived to wheel Ava to the x-ray department. The doctor had been right about the x-rays; they took over an hour to complete. Ava was required to stand, sit, lie down, and flip over so that every angle of her body could be x-rayed. By the end, she was cranky and uncomfortable, but true to her promise to Dr. Campbell, she didn't cry once. The fact that the painkillers had kicked in by then helped, too.

Finally the x-ray technician was satisfied they'd taken enough pictures, and they were sent back to the examining room. Fifteen minutes went by, then a half hour, then an hour. Where the hell was Dr. Campbell?

"I wanna go home," Ava wailed.

Julia knew exactly how she felt. Both of them were exhausted, hungry, and close to their breaking points. Ava grew restless. Too uncomfortable to sit on Julia's lap any longer, she stretched out on the floor.

"Honey, why don't you lie down on the table? You might be more comfortable."

"No!" she cried. "I wanna go home."

She kicked at Julia's chair, then cried out when her shin connected with a chair leg, probably hitting one of her many bruises. She started to cry, her high-pitched wails growing increasingly more distraught with each passing moment. Julia got down on her knees beside her and tried to soothe her, hoping to avoid a total meltdown.

"It's going to be okay, baby. We'll get you fixed up soon. I promise."

"I wanna go home!"

Dr. Campbell chose that moment to enter the room. To Julia's complete and utter shock, Ava scrambled to her feet and ran to him, throwing her good arm around his legs.

"Can I go home now?" she whimpered.

He seemed taken aback. So was Julia. Ava was normally shy around people she didn't know, especially men. But somehow she'd come to believe she could trust the doctor.

Julia wasn't so sure if she trusted him, especially when she noticed a woman in a business suit entering the room behind the doctor and Nurse Linda. She closed the door behind her.

Dr. Campbell quickly regained his equilibrium. He picked Ava up in his arms, being careful not to hurt her, and set her on the examining table.

"Hey, what's going on? I thought you were being a brave girl."

Tears slipped down Ava's cheeks. "My arm hurts."

Julia couldn't stand it any longer. She pulled herself to her full height and glared at the doctor. "If you hadn't made us wait here for so long, Ava might have been able to endure. But she's tired and she's hungry and she's in pain. When are you going to do something about it?"

Dr. Campbell regarded her with cold eyes. "We're going to cast Ava's arm right away. But first we have some questions."

"What questions?" Julia was as baffled as she was angry. She wanted to shout at him, tell him where he could stick his questions, but held back because of Ava.

The woman in the business suit spoke up. "My name is Sharon. I'm with Child Protective Services. I'd like to have a few words alone with Ava."

Julia stared mutely at the woman. Child Protective Services? Her stomach lurched. Dear God, did they think this was something more than an accident?

"Can I speak to you in the hallway for a moment, Mrs. Stewart?" Dr. Campbell said.

Ava looked up at Julia, her lower lip trembling. "Don't go, Mommy."

"It's only for a minute, baby, I promise. I'll be right outside the door, and I'll come back as soon as I can. Okay?"

"I promise it will only take a minute," Dr. Campbell said, his tone quiet and reassuring. "Sharon and Nurse Linda will stay with you, and Sharon's going to talk with you for a minute. Is that all right?"

A tear slipped down Ava's cheek, and Julia nearly told the doctor she wasn't going anywhere. But then Ava nodded slowly. "Okay."

Dr. Campbell gave Ava a warm smile and patted her knee. "I knew you were a brave girl. We won't be long." When he turned to Julia, the smile was gone.

She followed him out of the examining room and stepped to one side as he closed the door. His jaw clenched as he turned to look at her, and fear wrapped itself around her heart and squeezed.

"What did the x-ray find?" she asked.

"A spiral fracture of the right arm." He paused for a moment and took a deep breath as if trying to control his emotions. "I've seen this kind of injury before. A fracture like this can be the result of a fall, but it can also be an indication of child abuse. An arm as small as Ava's will break like a twig if it's twisted hard enough. I'm obligated to contact the authorities if I suspect abuse."

Julia stared at him in shock, her brain struggling to process his words, as if trying to translate some unintelligible language. The words *child abuse* rang in her ears. Finally she found her voice.

"You think someone deliberately hurt her?"

"Her injuries are consistent with abuse."

"I don't give a damn what they're consistent with. Ava has not been mistreated. My mother said she fell down the stairs, and if that's what she said, then that's what happened."

"I believe there's more to the story than a simple fall."

"If it comes down to believing you or believing my mother, I'm going with my mother."

"Perhaps you don't know your mother as well as you think you do."

Julia sucked in a breath and stared into Dr. Campbell's dark, accusing eyes. The idea that her mother would hurt Ava was ridiculous. She adored Ava, would do anything for her…

She blinked and looked away, remembering an incident the other day. She'd heard her yelling at Ava about the milk she'd spilled on the kitchen floor, making such a huge deal of it that Ava had cried. It had struck her as strange, since she couldn't remember her mother yelling at anyone, ever. She wasn't as patient as she used to be. And how did she explain her strange phone call telling her Ava had been hurt? Of course she'd been upset, but her mother had been nearly incoherent with distress. Was something going on she wasn't aware of? She was seventy-one now. Maybe looking after a rambunctious five-year-old was too much for her.

No. She shook her head to reject the disloyal thought. Dr. Campbell was the one who was wrong.

"I know my mother. She didn't do this. It was an accident."

"We'll soon find out. Sharon is questioning Ava now."

Julia stared at the door. "She'll be scared, all by herself."

"Sharon's very good at what she does. She has a way of making kids feel comfortable."

Julia turned on him, the anger and despair she'd been holding inside spilling out. "And you? Do you enjoy upsetting five-year-olds and turning families' lives upside down? Does it make you feel powerful to sic the authorities on us?"

"Look, Mrs. Stewart, I take no pleasure in bringing in the authorities. But I've seen child abuse, up close and personal, and I can tell you it's damn ugly. The things parents and caregivers are capable of doing to defenseless children..."

He stopped abruptly, his chest heaving. Closing his eyes, he averted his face and took a deep breath. When he turned back to her, his steely control was back in place. "So yeah, if I have even the smallest suspicion that a child has been abused, I'm going to ask questions. And I'm not going to apologize for it."

It was Julia's turn to look away. How had it come to this? What was going on with her parents?

Sharon emerged from the examining room and closed the door. "Apparently, Ava went down the stairs to get her teddy bear and tripped on a box of laundry detergent that had been left on the stairs."

"Mr. Fizz," Julia said with a moan. This was all because of a teddy bear?

"Excuse me?" Sharon asked.

Julia swallowed the sob that wanted to escape. "Mr. Fizz is the bear. Ava's had him since she was a baby. She takes him everywhere." How had Mr. Fizz ended up in the basement?

"Does your mother normally watch Ava while you're at work, Mrs. Stewart?" Sharon asked.

"No. My regular babysitter had an appointment today. Ava's in kindergarten part-time. She only goes to the sitter when she's not at school."

Sharon turned to Dr. Campbell. "What were the results of the skeletal survey?"

"There were no broken bones aside from her right

arm, and no indication of any previous breaks. Her medical records show no history of trips to the ER for any sort of similar trauma."

Sharon nodded. "Good. Given what Ava has told me, I think we can safely conclude that her injuries were the result of an unfortunate accident. Mrs. Stewart, I'm sorry we put you through the wringer. I hope you understand that whenever there's any question about a child's safety, we need to look into it."

As an educator, Julia understood. She'd asked questions about a student's bruises a few times during her career. She knew it was important not to turn a blind eye. But as a parent, it was devastating to be on the other end of those questions. She'd never felt more helpless in her life.

She managed a simple nod. "Can I go to Ava now?"

"Of course."

The doctor followed her into the examining room. The nurse had cleaned Ava's scrapes, bandaging one on her left elbow with a Band-Aid emblazoned with the face of a cartoon character.

"You're almost done, Ava," Dr. Campbell said. "We're going to send you to the cast room now. What's your favorite color?"

"Pink," she said without hesitation.

The doctor grinned, the smile transforming his face from intense to carefree. "I think we can arrange for you to have a cast in that color." He turned to Julia, all business once more. "Fortunately, even though the fracture is a spiral, it has clean edges that fit together well, so we can cast it without Ava having to undergo surgery. I'm going to use a fiberglass cast so we can take some x-rays while it's in place and make sure the arm is healing properly."

Julia took a deep breath and pushed down the tears of stress and exhaustion that wanted to fall. "How long will she have to wear the cast?"

"About a month. Please make a follow-up appointment so we can check on Ava in a week."

She nodded, too tired and upset to do much else. The doctor smiled at Ava.

"I've got to go now, but I know our cast technician will take real good care of you. You've been a very brave girl, Ava. I'll see you at your next appointment."

Like hell he will. Julia would make damn sure they saw Dr. Willson next time. She didn't want to see Dr. Campbell ever again.

But in a town as small as Lobster Cove, Maine, that likely wasn't an option.

Chapter Two

The emergency room buzzed with people, noise, and activity. Just the way he liked it.

A rush of adrenalin surged through Alex Campbell's veins as he dealt with patient after patient. A car accident on the main highway just outside of Lobster Cove had kept him busy most of the afternoon. Thankfully, the injuries were limited to broken bones, cuts, and abrasions, with only one admission. There was all the usual stuff for a Friday night—a couple of drunks who'd gotten into a bar fight, a baby with croup, a toddler who'd stuck a button up her nose. Fortunately for the citizens of the Lobster Cove area, he rarely saw the injuries he'd dealt with as a resident in the ER of the San Diego hospital where he'd worked before coming here, things like gunshot wounds and stabbings. The only GSW he'd treated in the fourteen months so far at the Lobster Cove Hospital was during hunting season, when a trigger-happy hunter shot his buddy in the rear end. He'd spent a good hour picking buckshot out of the unfortunate fellow's ass.

There was nothing more exhilarating than a busy ER. The only thing missing tonight was a heart attack. But the night was still young.

Nurse Novak hurried toward him, her ponytail bobbing. "Dr. Campbell, we've got a suspected heart attack in examining room one. Can you come quickly?"

Be careful what you wish for, Alex. He fell into step beside her. Tracy Novak was his favorite nurse in the ER. Her calm demeanor put patients at ease, and he could always count on her common sense, efficiency, and excellent nursing skills. But at the moment, tension flowed off her in waves.

"What's going on?"

"My best friend's father is the suspected heart attack," she said with a frown. "Occupational hazard of working the ER in the same community you grew up in."

"I'll bet." It must be tough. He'd been too busy to get to know a lot of people outside of the hospital, so he'd been able to maintain a professional distance with his patients. Distance was important. He never wanted to get so close that he lost objectivity. That was why when his contract expired in ten more months he was heading back to San Diego.

That, and the warm weather in San Diego. One winter in Maine was plenty; two would be more than enough. Why people willingly endured that horror year after year he had no idea.

Tracy pushed open the door of the examining room, and Alex followed her, grabbing the chart off the front of the door as he entered. When he looked up, he saw a familiar pair of blue eyes. Blue eyes that narrowed in dismay when they recognized him.

"Mrs. Stewart. How's Ava? I haven't seen her since she broke her arm a couple of weeks ago."

She lifted her chin. "She's fine. She's seeing Dr. Willson."

Her message was clear. She didn't want him anywhere near her daughter, and if she had her druthers, she likely wouldn't want him treating her father, either.

Too bad for her. He was the only doctor in the ER tonight.

Tracy looked from her friend to him and back again before clearing her throat. "Dr. Campbell, this is Paul Dawson. He's seventy-five years old and has a history of stable angina. He's been experiencing chest pain, sweating, heart palpitations, and nausea on and off all evening."

"Let's take some blood to check for heart enzymes."

"Right. What about an EKG?"

"Yes, as soon as possible."

"I'm on it." She grabbed the phone and made a couple of quiet calls.

Alex lifted Mr. Dawson's hand and felt the pulse at his wrist. It was beating way too fast. He gentled his voice. "When we get the test results back, we'll have a better idea what we're dealing with. Do you take nitroglycerin for your angina, Mr. Dawson?"

The man avoided his gaze. "Usually."

"Did you take some tonight?"

He shook his head and stared at the ceiling. "No."

Before Alex could ask why not, Julia Stewart jumped in. "Why on earth didn't you take your nitro, Dad?"

Alex felt his patient's pulse jump. Paul Dawson took a deep breath and looked at his daughter. "I ran out and forgot to refill the prescription. It's no big deal. I told you it was just the angina. We didn't need to come here."

She tenderly smoothed his hair. "You should have

told me. I could have gone to the pharmacy for you."

"You're too busy to be bothering with my prescriptions. You've got all your responsibilities at the school, not to mention you have Ava to look after by yourself."

"Dad—"

He lifted his head from the pillow, his face turning red. "I want to go home. We have to go home and look after Ava."

"Ava's fine with Mom. You need to stay here and let the doctor treat you."

"No!" Sweat broke out on his forehead, and his pulse raced. "We need to go home!"

"Okay, Dad, okay," she soothed. She rubbed his shoulder in gentle circles. "If that's what you want, I'll go home and check on Mom and Ava."

Mr. Dawson let out a long, shaky exhalation, rested his head on the pillow once more, and closed his eyes. "That's good. You should go now. Stay with your mother. I'll be all right."

She looked up at Alex, her eyes full of confusion. She didn't understand, but he was beginning to.

"Mr. Dawson, these bouts of angina you've been experiencing this evening, how long do they last?"

"Maybe ten, fifteen minutes, if I lie quietly and let them pass. Then in a little while they start up again."

"But in between, all the symptoms disappear?"

He considered the question for a moment. "Yes."

"How's your wife, Mr. Dawson?"

Paul Dawson opened his eyes. Alex watched his body tense, his free hand clenching at his side. "Dora hasn't been feeling well. It's best if Ava stays with someone else."

Julia frowned at her father. "Mom is sick? She didn't say anything earlier. What's wrong with her?"

"Just a cold, but you know she doesn't like to complain." He gripped her arm, sweat breaking out on his forehead once more. "Go, Julia. Please."

She got to her feet, clearly reluctant to leave him. "Okay, Dad, I'm leaving."

Tracy put her hand on Mr. Dawson's shoulder. "How about if I see if my brother Logan is busy tonight? He could check on Dora and Ava. Ava adores him."

"That's because he feeds her junk food," Julia said, trying to smile for her father.

"Yes, Logan's good with Ava." He closed his eyes, clearly exhausted. "I guess that would be okay. But just for a short time. Just till we get home."

"I'll make a quick call to Logan and see if he's available, and if he's not, I know Edie's home tonight. I'm sure she could look after Ava." Tracy headed to the door. "I'll be right back."

"Oh, sure," Julia said in a bright voice that sounded forced to Alex. "Edie's little girl is the same age as Ava. Maybe they can have a sleepover."

"Maybe." Mr. Dawson kept his eyes closed. He seemed to be resting for the moment, now that he knew someone he trusted would be checking in on Ava and his wife.

The question was why was it so important to him that Ava not be alone with Dora Dawson? Had his suspicions about Mrs. Dawson abusing her granddaughter been right after all? Two weeks ago when she'd presented at the hospital, Ava herself told him she'd fallen. There'd been nothing to indicate a history of abuse, and her injuries were consistent with a fall down the stairs. He and Sharon from Child Protective Services had backed off, satisfied it had been an accident, just as the child said.

Now he wasn't so sure. Did Julia's father believe Mrs. Dawson was a danger to the five-year-old? Ava was a fragile little girl. She needed their protection. Anger filled his chest, and he had to take a deep breath to calm himself.

Distance, he told himself. *Objectivity.*

Tracy re-entered the room. "Logan's on his way to your house, Paul. He'll be there in a couple of minutes."

He closed his eyes and let out a relieved breath. "That's good. Thank you."

With a squeeze to Mr. Dawson's shoulder, Tracy smiled.

"You're welcome. For now, just try to relax."

A moment later, a technician with a portable electrocardiogram machine knocked once before entering, and Alex took the opportunity to make his exit.

"Mr. Dawson, I'll be back when your test results are in. You just relax for now. We're going to take good care of both you and Ava tonight."

He raised his head from the pillow. "But you're not going to keep me here, are you?"

"That depends on what your test results say, but I have a feeling you're going to sleep in your own bed tonight."

Mr. Dawson sighed deeply. "Thank you, Doctor."

"You're welcome." He caught Julia's eye. "Can I speak to you for a moment, Mrs. Stewart?"

She nodded and rose to her feet. Alex held open the door for her, and they walked together to an empty examining room at the end of the hall. Julia sat in the chair next to the examining table, her blue eyes ringed with dark circles of fatigue, her shoulders slumped in weariness. Alex pulled another chair close and leaned toward her, their knees almost touching. She looked small and fragile and very vulnerable. The urge to pull her into his arms, to soothe her, protect her, came out of nowhere. He blinked and sat up straight in an attempt to put some space between them, both figuratively and literally.

"Mrs. Stewart, your father's test results will be ready shortly, and I think they'll confirm my suspicion that he hasn't suffered a heart attack."

She sagged in relief, her eyes filling with tears. "Thank God."

Alex had to stop himself from touching her. He clasped his hands together. "I believe what he's experiencing is a series of panic attacks."

She looked at him in confusion. "Panic attacks? Why? What would cause that?"

"Anxiety, extreme stress. Can you think of any source of stress in his life that might cause this?"

Two vertical lines of worry formed between her brows, marring the perfect, pale skin. "No…I don't know. He's been retired for almost ten years. He and Mom lead a quiet life. They go to church, see their friends, work in the garden. I can't understand where any stress would be coming from."

He took a deep breath before pushing on, knowing he was heading into dangerous territory with his next question. "Two weeks ago, when you brought Ava here, she had been hurt while staying at your parents' house. Tonight your father was adamant that Ava not be alone with your mother. Do you think he could be upset because he's afraid she hurt Ava last time and she might hurt her again?"

Julia inhaled sharply, her eyes widening. "No! Are we back to that again? I told you before, it's not possible."

"Then how do you explain your father's vehemence?"

"He's sick, and he's upset. He doesn't want them to be alone."

"Mrs. Stewart—"

She got to her feet so quickly her chair scraped backwards on the linoleum floor. "I want to be with my father."

"Of course."

Alex stood and moved his chair out of the way. Julia slung her purse over her shoulder and started for the door. He stopped her with a hand on her arm. She stared at his hand, and then lifted her gaze to look into his face, her eyes ablaze in blue fire.

"Something's going on with your parents, particularly with your mother. For Ava's sake, you need to find out what. I can help you—"

"Thank you for your concern." She moved her arm out of his grasp. "We'll be fine. If my father's test results show he hasn't had a heart attack, are we free to go?"

"Yes, but I want you to make a follow-up appointment for him. Have him see Dr. Willson or Dr. Rob Sato as soon as possible. We need to treat his anxiety, or the next time he really could have a heart attack. He may need medication to help him relieve the symptoms." He knew there was no point asking her to bring her father to see him.

She took a deep breath and nodded. "All right."

An hour later, he returned to Mr. Dawson's examining room. Tracy had the results of the blood work and the EKG. Just as he thought, Mr. Dawson's symptoms had not been caused by a heart attack. He watched as Julia helped her father from the examining table. Together they walked slowly down the hall to the exit. As they got to the door, she turned to hold it open for her father, and her gaze met his. In her eyes he read her uncertainty and fear.

Alex's gut twisted. He stepped toward her, though what he planned to do or say once he reached her, he had no idea. But Julia and her father left before he could get to her.

He turned on his heel and headed toward his next patient, disgusted with himself. *So much for professional distance.*

Chapter Three

Julia picked up her ringing phone and heard the school secretary's voice in her ear.

"Superintendent Perkins is on line one. Do you want me to tell him you're out of the office?"

"No, that's okay, Beth. I'll take it." Rob Perkins was a decent guy, but she had a feeling he had bad news for her. *Might as well face the music.*

"Good luck, Boss," Beth said before disconnecting.

She punched line one. "Hi, Rob."

"Hey, Julia. How's it going?"

"Depends on why you're calling."

"Can't a superintendent call one of his principals just to say hi?"

"Right. And the tooth fairy left a gold brick under my daughter's pillow last night. What's up?"

"I just wanted to give you a heads-up. The school board is holding a closed meeting tonight to discuss your proposal for the daycare at your high school."

"Can I attend, make a presentation?"

"No. I already asked. They want to discuss the proposal in private."

Julia could feel her blood heating. "They want to kill the proposal in private, you mean."

"We don't know that for sure."

"Call it an educated guess. We need that daycare, Rob. Five girls from this high school had babies this past year, and one more is due this summer. So far only one of them has come back to classes. If they don't graduate from high school, what kind of chance do they or their babies have for a secure future?"

The daycare was the first step in her plan to make sure her students had the tools they needed to succeed in life. The second step was to give them the information they needed about sex and birth control so they wouldn't get pregnant in the first place. She knew that was a long shot, at best.

"Hey, you don't have to convince me. I'm behind you, remember?"

"Yeah, I remember. And I appreciate your support." Rob had made the initial presentation about the daycare to the school board, and had come up with ways to fund its creation and continued operation. Julia knew she had an ally in him.

But she also had a powerful enemy on the school board.

"Don't tell me, let me guess. Wyatt Stewart called the special meeting."

She heard his long sigh. "As a matter of fact, he did."

Wyatt Stewart, her former father-in-law and chairman of the school board, hated her and everything she stood for. He blamed her for the divorce from his son and for Russ's departure to the other side of the world. She closed her eyes and massaged her temple. As if she'd been happy when her husband left her. As if she hadn't been crushed by his desertion and his determination to sever all ties to his old life, including his ties to his daughter. She took a deep breath. One disaster at a time.

"What about my proposal to add a sex education component to the health curriculum? Are they going to discuss that, too?"

"They didn't mention it, but my guess is that it's bound to come up in their discussions tonight."

"So what can we do?"

"It's out of our hands, Julia. We'll have to abide by their decision."

"Great. So all we can do is sit around and wait?"

"'Fraid so."

"Thanks for letting me know, Rob. You'll call me as soon as you hear their decision?"

"Of course."

"Okay. I'll talk to you soon."

"Bye."

Julia carefully put down the phone. She'd been fighting with the board, with a few of the parents, and even some of her teachers, over one thing or another ever since she'd been hired as principal of Lobster Cove High School just over three years ago. Sometimes she felt like chucking it all and taking Ava to live someplace else, maybe to a city, where things were a little more progressive and she could put her ideas into action without so much opposition. Or maybe she'd go back to being a plain old high school English literature teacher with fewer responsibilities. Both ideas were appealing on a day like today.

But then she thought of her students, about girls like Sarah Keyser who were pregnant at sixteen and didn't know where to turn. And her parents who were aging and needed her. How could she abandon them?

Thinking of her parents caused a ripple of unease to skitter down her back. Something was going on with them, in particular with her mother, but every time she questioned them about it, she was told everything was fine. She didn't believe it for a minute, but her father became upset whenever she asked about her mother's health, so she let it drop. In truth, she was almost too afraid to know.

She cursed herself for her cowardice.

Her thoughts inevitably turned to Alex Campbell, as they had ever since Ava's broken arm. He'd been pretty hard on her and her family that night. At the time she'd been angry beyond words, but she'd come to understand he was only trying to protect her daughter. And she had her own doubts…

Every time she closed her eyes, the accusation in his dark eyes haunted her. She remembered their conversation the night she brought her father to the emergency room. He still believed her mother had something to do with Ava's injury. What hurt the most was that he believed she would knowingly put Ava in harm's way.

Why did his opinion matter to her? She barely knew the man.

Perhaps it was her own sense of guilt. Sometimes the sole responsibility for Ava's care weighed heavily on her. She wondered if she was doing the right thing by raising her in Lobster Cove. Was she limiting her daughter's choices because she wanted to live here?

Once, after a glass of wine—or three, too many—she'd confessed her fears to her friend Edie, herself a mother of three. Edie said every mother worried about messing up her kid's life. It came with the territory. All she could do was love her daughter, and protect her, and follow her best instincts.

The hell with Dr. Campbell. What did he know about her family, or her life? She didn't need some sanctimonious do-gooder from California judging her abilities, or inabilities, as a mother.

She was already her own harshest critic.

****

Alex dragged his suitcases out of the trunk and slammed the lid. Removing his sunglasses, he took a good look at the house he was going to live in for the next ten months.

Home, sweet home.

It wasn't much to look at: a modest bungalow with white clapboard siding and grey asphalt shingles, a carport attached to the side, and wide concrete steps leading to a red front door. He'd been told it had three bedrooms, that the interior had just been repainted, and the carpets and furniture were new. The house was similar to the other 1950s-era houses on this block in Lobster Cove. Except that this one was coming to him rent-free, courtesy of the Island Health Board Recruitment and Retention Committee.

He'd been perfectly happy with the one-bedroom apartment he'd been living in, also rent-free, in Bar Harbor, located a few miles down the highway from Lobster Cove. He'd also been perfectly happy to work full-time in the ER at the Lobster Cove Hospital. But with the departure of one of the physicians from the Lobster Cove Family Health Clinic, his services were now needed there. He'd still work two days a week in the ER, but the rest of his duties would be at the clinic. During his training, he'd completed rotations in family medicine, and he liked it well enough, but emergency medicine was his passion. However, the health board had been adamant, and he wasn't in much of a position to argue.

He hauled his suitcases to the front door and pulled the key from his pocket. The door opened to a decent-sized L-shaped living room and dining room, furnished with a new sofa and chair and a dining table with four chairs. He slipped off his shoes, not wanting to drag dirt onto the new carpet, and then carried his suitcases to the biggest of the three small bedrooms. The bathroom and kitchen, while not new, were pristinely clean and perfectly functional.

"Honey, I'm home," he said aloud to the four walls.

At least for now.

He knew the committee hoped that by giving him bigger accommodations they'd sweeten the pot enough to entice him to stay. It was a nice gesture, but it wasn't going to work. He'd signed a contract with the health board in which he promised to work a minimum of two years on the island in exchange for them paying off a portion of his massive student debt. Rural hospitals all over America were making similar deals in an effort to bring health professionals into their communities. His contract had a provision stating he could extend his contract for an additional two years. If he did that, another large chunk of his debt would be paid. Though the offer was tempting, Alex had no intention of staying past the two-year mark. He was a California boy, born and bred. He'd kill for his grandmother's Mexican cooking, sell his soul for sushi from his favorite Japanese restaurant. He missed the heat. He missed his friends. He really missed his grandmother. And though he'd never thought it possible, he actually missed his mother.

With its ocean vistas, quaint and colorful main street shops, and mountain and forest views, Lobster Cove was a beautiful place to live. But it wasn't home.

As he walked back to his car to pick up more boxes, he saw Julia Stewart and her daughter heading toward him on the sidewalk. He knew the instant she recognized him—she hesitated slightly, as if thinking about turning around and walking in the other direction. She might have done so, too, if Ava hadn't waved and run to him.

"Dr. Campbell! Hi!" She held up her neon-pink cast. "Isn't my cast pretty?"

"The prettiest I've ever seen. Seems fitting for a pretty girl."

She grinned, revealing a gap-toothed smile. He kneeled in front of her, pretending to inspect her teeth. The bruising on her face and arms was either gone or faded, and her sunny smile told him she bore no ill effects from her ordeal. It was good to see her so happy and healthy, almost fully recovered. It occurred to him that before he came to Maine he rarely, if ever, saw his patients outside of the ER. Now someone he treated in the ER might be the same person who waited on him at one of the restaurants, or was his teller at the bank. His patients were becoming people for him rather than an assortment of maladies.

He wasn't sure how he felt about that.

"You know, all my special patients call me Alex."

She nodded solemnly, as if she were being initiated into an exclusive club. "Okay. I can do that."

"I see you lost your two front teeth. I thought you were too little to be losing teeth."

She glared at him indignantly. "I'm not little. I'm turning six next week. I'm having a birthday party."

"I'm sorry, I didn't realize. Happy birthday, Ava."

She seemed mollified by his apology. She pointed to her missing front teeth. "The tooth fairy left five dollars for each one."

"Really? When I was your age, the tooth fairy only left me a quarter."

"I don't think the tooth fairy liked you very much. Were you bad?"

Alex hid his grin. "Probably."

Julia reached them, pulling Ava close and laying a protective hand over her blonde curls. "Even the tooth fairy has been hit by inflation. There's not much a kid can buy these days with twenty-five cents."

"I guess that's true."

He rose and stared into her clear blue eyes. Two spots of pink colored her cheeks in the otherwise alabaster perfection of her complexion. He'd thought about her a lot the last couple of weeks and wondered how she and her family were doing. He'd even gone so far as to speak with Dr. Willson to ask if Julia's father had visited him. He had, and Dr. Willson had prescribed an anti-depressant. He'd wanted Paul to see a therapist in order to get at the root of the anxiety. But he'd refused, so the doctor had no choice but to try to treat his panic attacks medically.

"So what brings you to this neighborhood?" Julia asked. "I thought you lived in Bar Harbor."

"How did you know that?"

She lifted one small shoulder in a nonchalant shrug. "There's not much you can keep private in a community this small."

She was right. When he first arrived, he'd been shocked by how much people he'd never met knew about his circumstances. They knew he'd gone to med school at UC San Diego, knew he was working in Maine to pay off his student debts, and also knew he was thirty-two and single. He was surprised they didn't know about the eagle tattooed on his right shoulder. The lack of privacy had been disconcerting for a city boy used to living in anonymity.

He explained the deal with the house and his new duties at the clinic in town. "So now I'm going to be living here." He indicated his new abode with a crook of his thumb.

"My Grandma and Grandpa Dawson live in that house right there," Ava said. She indicated the two-story house next door, then turned and pointed down the street. "And we live two blocks that way."

"We're practically neighbors." Turning to Julia, he asked, "How's your dad?"

"He's fine." She smiled, but it was forced. Julia Stewart didn't want to share any secrets with him.

Hell, she didn't want to be anywhere near him. He understood her reasons; he'd been witness to some unhappy moments for her family, and he'd made her look at some disturbing possibilities. What he didn't understand was why her distrust and dislike mattered to him so much.

"We should be going," Julia said to Ava as she took her hand, the one not in a cast. "Goodbye, Dr. Campbell."

"Goodbye, Mrs. Stewart. Bye, Ava."

He watched them make their way down the sidewalk. Ava turned in a circle and waved her bright pink cast at him as she skipped alongside her mother. Alex grinned, lifting his hand to wave back. To his surprise, Julia made a half turn, their gazes locking as she stared at him over her shoulder. She raised her hand in goodbye, then quickly turned and walked away. Mother and daughter soon disappeared around a corner.

He grabbed a couple of boxes from his car and brought them inside. As he placed his few belongings around the house—family photos, some mementos from California—he told himself to keep a safe distance from her and her daughter.

Julia Stewart didn't want anything to do with him.

****

Three nights later, Alex pulled into his carport at midnight. The ER had been relatively quiet, and his shift had dragged. He felt more tired than when he was run off his feet.

As he stepped from his car and walked toward the side door of the house, a figure appeared in the carport, startling him.

"Is Polly home?" she asked.

He took in the woman's long, graying hair and her petite stature. She was perhaps sixty or seventy, barefoot, and wearing what appeared to be a sleeveless nightgown.

What the hell? "Polly?"

"Yes, Polly," she said in irritation, as if he should know what she was talking about. "She's my friend. She lives here."

"I'm sorry. I'm the only person who lives here."

She shook her head emphatically. "No, Polly lives here."

"Where do you live?"

"Oh, you know."

Alex took a step closer to her. Did she have some form of dementia? Who was she? He was pretty sure he'd never seen her in the ER or at the family clinic. He pulled his cell phone from his pocket.

"Maybe I can call Polly for you. What's her number?"

She rattled off a series of meaningless numbers. Alex dialed nine-one-one. A dispatcher picked up immediately.

"Nine-one-one. What is your emergency?"

"This is Dr. Alex Campbell," he said softly into the phone, turning away so she wouldn't hear. "There's a woman on my doorstep who appears to have dementia. I think she may have wandered from her home, and I don't know who she is."

"I'll send a patrol car by. What's your address?"

He told her, and she said there'd be a car at his house within five minutes. He repocketed his phone and approached the woman.

"There, I've called. Someone will be by for you soon."

She shivered in the cool, damp night air, wrapping her arms around herself. Alex took off his jacket and placed it gently over her shoulders. Confusion filled her face.

"What am I doing here?"

"You said you were looking for your friend Polly."

"Polly?"

The utter bewilderment he saw in her eyes tore at his heart. He couldn't imagine how terrifying it must be to fall into the rabbit hole of dementia, to lose a sense of what was real and what wasn't.

"Don't worry," he said gently. "Someone will be by soon to help you find your way home. Can you tell me your name?"

She thought for a moment before answering in a whisper, "Dora."

A patrol car pulled into the driveway and a police officer got out. Dora shrank against his side as he approached, and Alex put his arm around her shoulders to reassure her.

"Don't worry. He won't hurt you. He's going to help you."

Alex was relieved to see that he'd previously met the policeman at the hospital. Officer Nate Harris had arrived in the ER to question a couple of his patients who'd been involved in a minor car accident. He'd been efficient without upsetting them, which was something Dora desperately needed right now.

"Dr. Campbell, good to see you," Officer Harris said quietly, his eyes on Dora. "How can I help you?"

Alex told him about finding Dora in his carport when he arrived home. "She doesn't remember where she lives. Can you help us out?"

"She told you her name was Dora?"

"Yes. She said she was looking for her friend Polly."

"She looks familiar, but I can't place her," Officer Harris said. He laid a gentle hand on Dora's shoulder. "Do you remember your last name?"

She looked at him blankly. He tried again.

"Who looks after you, Dora? They're going to be worried about you."

"Paul looks after me," she said in a tiny voice. "Is he going to be mad at me?"

"No, of course not," Alex soothed. "But I'm sure he wants you back home."

"I know who she is," Officer Harris suddenly said. "Dora Dawson. She taught me English literature in high school, or at least she tried to. Not my best subject."

"Is Paul Dawson her husband?" Alex asked.

"Yes, and I think they live next door," Officer Harris said, indicating with a nod of his head the same house Ava had pointed to as belonging to her grandparents. The pieces were beginning to fall into place.

The officer retrieved a blanket from the patrol car and, after removing Alex's jacket and handing it back to him, wrapped the blanket around Dora's shoulders. The large blanket engulfed her tiny frame and hung to her knees. She was no more than five foot three, and fragile looking.

Just like her daughter.

Alex watched as the policeman walked Dora across the lawn to the house next door. He knocked repeatedly, until finally a light came on over the front door and Paul Dawson opened it. Alex couldn't hear what was said, but eventually Paul took Dora's hand and led her inside.

He finally understood the reason for Paul Dawson's anxiety, and his fear of leaving Ava alone with his wife.

How much did Julia know about her mother's illness? If she didn't know, why not? And if she did, why would she leave her little girl in her mother's care?

Chapter Four

The next day, during the noon hour, Alex walked through the halls of Lobster Cove High School, looking for Julia Stewart's office. The curious glances of students and teachers followed his progress, and he was pretty sure his presence here would be the topic of conversation in every coffee shop in Lobster Cove within the hour. He knew they all wondered what he was doing at the school.

He was wondering that himself.

Why was he sticking his nose into Julia Stewart's family business? He'd never before felt so compelled to help a patient outside of the examining room, to delve into personal problems that were really none of his business. But when he thought of Ava, with her sweet gap-toothed smile and the neon pink cast on her arm, when he remembered the lost look on Dora Dawson's face, he had no choice but to get involved.

Finally, he found an open door with a sign that read Office. He peeked inside and saw a vacant desk strewn with papers and files, and mismatched filing cabinets lined up against the wall. A couple of open doors within this outer office appeared to lead to private offices. Knocking on the frame of the outside door, he called, "Hello?"

A moment later, Julia Stewart stuck her head through one of the doors, her eyes widening in surprise when she saw him.

"Dr. Campbell, what are you doing here?"

Alex took a step toward her. "I was hoping to speak with you in private. Do you have a moment?"

She blinked a few times. "I…okay, sure. Come in."

Julia stepped aside to allow him to enter, and then closed the door behind him. Her office was miniscule, more of a closet than an office befitting the head of a school. Her compact wooden desk was strewn with what looked like spreadsheets. Beside her open laptop, a half-eaten sandwich and an apple sat on top of a file.

"Do you always eat your lunch at your desk?" he asked.

"Not always. Only when I have a project to complete." She took her seat behind her desk and gestured for him sit also. "But I'm sure you didn't come here to lecture me on my eating habits. What can I do for you, Dr. Campbell?"

"Please, call me Alex."

Her brow furrowed with a combination of surprise and suspicion. "Okay. Alex. Why are you here?"

"Because I wanted to let you know I met your mother last night."

"Well, sure, my parents are your next-door neighbors. I knew you'd meet her eventually."

He exhaled a long breath. How did he explain this to her? "Last night, when I got home from the hospital sometime after midnight, your mother was in my carport. She was disoriented, barefoot, and wearing her nightclothes. She didn't remember her last name, Mrs. Stewart."

She stared at him for a few seconds, her mouth slightly open. Then she shook her head. "No, you're mistaken. That couldn't have been my mother."

"I didn't know who she was, so I had to call the police. The officer identified her as your mother and took her back to your father's house. I saw your dad take her inside. If you don't believe me, check with Officer Harris. Check with your father."

She continued to stare at him, then closed her eyes and sank back against the headrest of her chair. Bringing her hand to her face, she massaged the spot between her brows. Alex saw the tremor in her hand and the agitated rise and fall of her chest as she tried to keep her emotions in check. He wished he could say something, do something, to give her some comfort.

"I'm sorry, Julia."

She opened her eyes and blinked at him, sitting up a little straighter. Taking a deep breath, she let it out slowly before speaking again.

"So what does this mean?"

"I believe your mother could be experiencing some sort of dementia, perhaps Alzheimer's. Or maybe it's something totally unrelated. It's important to have her seen by a doctor. If it is Alzheimer's, there are drugs available that may delay some of the symptoms in the early stages. At the very least, your family needs to know what you're dealing with. I'm also concerned about your father's health."

"Yes, so am I." He saw her throat work, as if she was holding back tears. "Damn it, this is my fault. I should have seen it. I noticed in the last few months that my mom seemed forgetful, but I thought that was just because she was getting older." She took a shaky breath. "I also noticed she didn't have the patience with Ava she used to have. I should have visited them more, seen what was really going on with them, but I get so busy with school and with Ava. I live just a few blocks away, but sometimes days, even weeks go by and I don't see them. I should have known."

Alex couldn't stop himself. He came around the desk and knelt beside her chair, taking her hands in his. "It's not your fault. It's not anyone's fault. It just is. Don't beat yourself up."

Her eyes were shiny with tears, her long lashes starred into points. A tear rolled down her cheek. Without thinking, Alex gently wiped it away with the pad of his thumb.

"Don't cry. It's going to be all right."

She nodded and sat up straighter, as if trying to get herself under control. Finally she asked, "What happens now?"

"I guess you talk to your parents, convince them to have your mother seen by a doctor."

She swallowed. "All right. I'll do that today."

"Do you have any brothers or sisters, someone who can help you?"

"No. There's just me. I was born to my parents late in life, after my mother was told she'd never conceive."

"I'm sorry I had to dump this on you. I'm sure it was the last thing you wanted to hear, but you needed to know."

"Yes."

She carefully pulled her hand from his, signaling her wish for some space and an end to this conversation. Alex rose and headed to the door. "I'll let you get back to work. Good luck, Julia."

As he turned the doorknob, he heard her soft voice. "Alex?"

"Yes?"

"Thank you for telling me."

He gripped the doorknob to keep from going to her and comforting her once more. He barely knew Julia Stewart. Why should she matter so much to him?

With a brisk nod, he opened the door and left.

****

For several moments after Alex Campbell's departure, Julia sat motionless in her chair, her pulse thundering through her head. *Alzheimer's disease? Dear God.* She wanted to deny the possibility, to rage against him for telling her, but she knew he was right. She and her parents needed to face this thing, whatever it was. She could no longer stick her head in the sand and pretend nothing was wrong.

With a sigh, she reached for her phone and punched in Tracy's number, hoping she was home today. She nearly cried in relief when she heard her friend's voice on the line.

"Tracy, I don't know what to do."

"What's wrong, sweetie?"

Julia told her everything, from her mother's strange forgetfulness to the visit she'd just had from Alex Campbell. "He says I should talk to Mom and Dad, convince them to have Mom checked out by a doctor."

"He's right. If it really is Alzheimer's, you should know. You might need home care to step in to give your father a respite. His health could deteriorate if her care puts him under too much stress."

Tracy only confirmed what Alex had already told her, yet she'd needed her view. She'd needed to hear it from someone she trusted. Listening to Tracy corroborate Alex's opinion made it all the more real.

And frightening.

"I plan to see them this afternoon, after school. Can you look after Ava for a while? I don't want her to overhear this conversation."

"Sure, Ava can stay with me. I'm off today."

"Thanks. How 'bout I buy us dinner at Maggie's Diner later?"

"Sounds great."

"Good, good." She hesitated, unsure how to ask her next question. "Tracy, if my mother really does have Alzheimer's, do you think…I mean, is it possible she could have been responsible for Ava's injury?"

"I don't know, Julia. Only a small percentage of Alzheimer's patients become violent, but people with Alzheimer's often experience a big personality change. I wish I could give you a more definitive answer, but we just don't have enough information about your mother's health right now to be sure about anything."

Julia felt sick inside. How could she have missed what was going on with her parents? How could she have put Ava in harm's way? She felt stupid for some of the things she'd said to Dr. Campbell the day of Ava's injury. She could see now he was only concerned with her daughter's welfare.

"I'd better run. Thanks, hon. I'll see you later."

"Bye."

Julia set the receiver back on the phone, her gaze landing on her half-eaten sandwich. The smell of the tuna fish suddenly nauseated her. She wrapped the remains of the sandwich in the plastic wrap and tossed it in the garbage, and slipped the apple into her desk drawer, hoping she'd have an appetite for it later. With a sigh, she got back to work, forcing herself to concentrate on budgets and projections instead of her mother wandering in the dark in her nightgown.

Three hours later she finished her budget document. It was almost the end of the school day. She backed up her work and powered down her laptop. As soon as the bell rang, she'd pick up Ava at the elementary school and head over to Tracy's before speaking with her parents.

Her stomach knotted. Would this conversation turn into a confrontation? She loved her parents. They'd been supportive and loving all her life, and had gone well beyond the call of duty during her difficult separation and divorce. She couldn't have made it without them. Telling them of her suspicions felt like she was stabbing them in the back.

Julia had just put away her documents and pulled her purse from the bottom drawer of her desk when a knock sounded at her door. Reluctantly she said, "Come in."

Ralph Sykes stuck his head through the open door. "Can I see you for a minute?"

Her stomach clenched. Ralph Sykes was the last person she wanted to talk to right now. But she made herself smile instead. "Of course. I have an appointment I need to get to shortly, but I've got a couple of minutes. Have a seat."

He slipped into her office and closed the door. Instead of sitting, he paced the small area beside her desk.

"Ms. Stewart, you know my feelings about the daycare you're proposing. I believe it's wrong for our school and for our town."

Julia suppressed an impatient sigh. "Yes, you've

made your opinions well known, Ralph. I understand them, but I respectfully disagree."

"I wish you'd reconsider."

"I'm sorry, but I'm not going to do that. I believe the daycare is very necessary."

He narrowed his eyes at her. "There's opposition on the school board and in the community, you know. Some say we need a new direction at the head of the school."

She pressed her lips together to keep from telling Ralph what a sanctimonious asshole he was. A long time high school math teacher at Lobster Cove High School, he'd been a thorn in her side ever since she'd been hired as principal three years ago. He'd felt the job should have gone to him, and he had his supporters in the community. For the last three years, he'd done everything in his power to undermine her authority.

She measured her words carefully. "I'm aware of that, Ralph. I'll do everything I can to make parents more comfortable with having a daycare for the children of students at the school. But as I said, it *will* be in place in the fall."

For a few seconds, their gazes locked in a silent battle of wills. Julia wouldn't give the bastard the satisfaction of seeing her blink first. Finally Ralph looked away.

"I don't like the idea of my Chloe being exposed to talk of sex out of wedlock and everything your daycare implies."

Julia nodded. The news was hardly a surprise. Ralph's sixteen-year-old daughter Chloe was a good student, and a sweet kid. She often babysat Ava. But she was socially awkward, which made her a target for teasing that often bordered on bullying. Julia had stepped in on a couple of occasions when she'd witnessed Chloe being harassed in the hallways. Having a father who was a teacher at the school, one that most of the students thoroughly despised, didn't help her cause.

"I understand your opinion."

"I'm considering organizing a petition against the daycare. If we get enough votes, we can take our views to the school board."

Julia narrowed her eyes. *Bring it on.* She kept her voice calm.

"That's your prerogative, of course."

He gave her a small smirk. "I thought I should warn you."

She dipped her head. "I appreciate it. But perhaps I should remind you that the push to create a daycare in the school to encourage students with young children to continue their education didn't come from me initially. It came from parents and members of the community. And I'm sure they won't let it go without a fight."

The smirk disappeared. "I guess we'll find out."

"I guess we will." She hoisted her purse onto her shoulder. "Now, if there's nothing else, I really have to be going."

Ralph gave her a brisk nod and left her office. Julia exhaled slowly, closing her eyes and willing her heart rate to slow down. Just what she needed. Another battle to fight.

****

"Alejandro! *Mi querido!* How is life in the north country? Is there still a lot of snow?"

Alex grinned. His grandmother began every phone

conversation with a question about the weather. Having lived all her life in either Mexico or southern California, she was morbidly fascinated with snow and blizzards and temperatures below freezing, probably because she'd never experienced any of those phenomena herself.

"All the snow is gone, Nona, and has been for a while now. It's spring now. The grass has turned green and the tulips are blooming. And it's raining every other day."

He found the changing of the seasons in Maine fascinating, though he could have done without the changing from fall to winter. Not only the landscape changed, but people's attitudes. The coming of spring brought optimism and hope to the residents of Lobster Cove. Just when they were at the end of their endurance, just when they thought they couldn't stand another nor'easter, spring arrived with a warm breeze and the smell of warm, damp earth in the air.

"*Esto esta bien.* That's good." She cleared her throat. "I spoke with your mother yesterday. She said she hasn't heard from you in a while."

Alex sat up straighter, immediately on high alert. "I guess it's been a while since I called. She could call me, you know."

"She has. She says you never answer your phone."

"I'm busy, Nona. I've got a full slate of patients at the clinic, and I do two shifts a week at the ER. I don't always have time to chat."

"You're avoiding her."

"No, I'm not."

His protest was met with silence. He could almost see Nona's face. Her lips would be pursed in disapproval, her eyebrows raised in a 'Who do you think you're kidding' expression. The thought almost made him smile.

Almost, but not quite.

"All right, fine. I may have not picked up one time when I saw her number on my call display. But in my defense, I was really busy." He didn't add that he was busy doing laundry, not working. He just hadn't been in the mood to listen to a lecture.

"You need to talk to her, Alejandro. She misses you."

"Believe it or not, Nona, I miss her, too."

His mother had been upset with him for taking a posting so far from home when he'd had the opportunity to do basically the same job and work off the same amount of student debt closer to home in rural communities in New Mexico and Arizona. But after a visit to Mount Desert Island and the towns of Bar Harbor and Lobster Cove, he'd decided to accept their offer. The place was so different from southern California, so peaceful, so uncongested. There was no rush-hour traffic on the island; nothing on the island was in a rush, including the traffic. Being on the ocean, albeit the cold North Atlantic, was a point in Lobster Cove's favor, too. He didn't think he could live anyplace far from an ocean.

Of course he'd seriously questioned his decision after experiencing his first winter on the island. He'd managed to survive, but he wasn't keen to experience it again.

His mother had wanted him to stay in San Diego and had been disappointed that he hadn't gone into a specialty like cardiology or plastic surgery, something that really brought in the bucks. All his life she'd been obsessed with climbing social and economic ladders.

"Then you'll call her?"

"Yes, I'll call her soon. I promise."

"Good."

With that out of the way, they chatted about members of his extended family, events in the news, and other miscellany, until his grandmother declared it was nearly time for her weekly card game with her friends.

"I've got to run, Alejandro, but I'll call you soon. *Te quiero."*

"Te quiero, Nona. I love you, too."

Alex grabbed some clean towels and jumped in the shower. As the steaming water melted the stress of the day, he wondered how long he could postpone a conversation with his mother.

Chapter Five

After dropping Ava at Tracy's, Julia headed to her parents' house, her stomach feeling sicker the closer she got. She told herself she was speaking to her parents, not people she didn't know. They loved each other. They could work this out. She hoped.

She pulled into the driveway and walked to the side entrance. As she pushed open the door and stepped inside, she called, "Hello." Passing through the small mudroom and the kitchen, Julia followed voices into the living room at the front of the house. Her father was resting on the couch and her mother was in her favorite recliner, a half-knitted sweater on her lap, her knitting needles in her hands. She looked up and smiled at Julia.

"Hi, honey."

Julia bent to kiss her cheek and breathed in the scent of her mother's favorite perfume. The fragrance took her immediately back to warm memories of childhood and being tucked safely into bed with a goodnight kiss. It occurred to her that their roles were slowly reversing. She would soon have to parent her mother.

"I wanted to see both of you, to talk to you." She perched on the edge of the armchair and faced them. "I had a visit from Dr. Campbell today. He told me he found you in his carport last night, Mom. You were in your nightgown and were disoriented. You didn't know your last name. Do you remember, Mom?"

Dora looked at her blankly. "I don't remember that."

"He had to call the police because he didn't know who you were." She turned to her father. "The police brought her home. He saw you open the door, Dad."

Paul slowly sat up. "She was walking in her sleep, that's all. She's all right now."

"Dr. Campbell and Tracy both feel Mom should see Dr. Willson for a checkup, see what's going on with her. I could make an appointment—"

"No!" Paul got to his feet. "I told you. She's fine."

"Dad, she was wandering in the middle of the night."

"It was nothing, just bad dreams. She's fine."

"Dad—"

"I said leave it alone, Julia."

His face had turned an alarming shade of red as they argued, and Julia was afraid he'd have another anxiety attack, or worse. "Okay, Dad. I'll leave it alone for now. But we'll talk again very soon."

She went to him then and put her arms around him in a hug. He felt bonier than he used to. Had he lost weight? She stepped back and looked into his face.

"Did you fill your nitro prescription?"

"I did." He gripped her forearms. "We're fine. We look after each other. You don't have to worry about us, sweetheart."

She dredged up a smile for him. "I like worrying about you. You're my favorite two people to worry about."

He chuckled. "You're just like your mother. She likes to worry about everyone, too."

Julia glanced at her mother. Dora was unraveling the row of knitting she had just completed. "Thanks, Dad. She's the most special person I know." She faced him again, her voice low. "But we are going to talk about this again. Soon."

He sighed and nodded. Julia kissed his cheek and then went to her mother once more.

"Bye Mom. I'll see you later."

Dora gave her a sunny smile. "Bye, honey."

Julia put her arms around her small shoulders and hugged, trying desperately to hold onto the mother she loved. "I love you."

"I love you, too."

As she left the house, she took a deep breath. What did she do now? Nothing had been settled. Nothing had even been discussed. Did she have to force her father to seek help for her mother? What if she upset her father so much he had a heart attack? She couldn't bear to distress him that way. But she couldn't sit back and do nothing, either.

Glancing toward the house next door, she saw Alex Campbell's car in the carport. On impulse, she headed across the lawn to his front door. She rang the doorbell once, then again, and was about to leave when he opened the door, his shirt wide open and his dark hair slick and dripping onto his shoulders.

"Mrs. Stewart, hi. Sorry I didn't answer the door right away. I just got out of the shower."

As Julia stared at the dusting of dark hair across his broad chest, down to a flat, muscled stomach, she had a sudden vision of him stepping naked and wet from the shower, all hard muscle and sleek, lean power. She had to blink a few times to dispel the scene in her head.

"I'm sorry to intrude on you at home. I was at my parents' house, and I saw that your car was home..." What was she doing here? Alex Campbell didn't want to hear her problems. She took a step back. "I'm sorry. I shouldn't have bothered you."

Alex stopped her with a hand on her arm. "You're not bothering me. Come inside and tell me how your meeting with your parents went."

She looked at his hand on her arm, at the contrast of his olive skin against the paleness of hers. She felt the warmth of his hand, the strength of it. She so desperately needed to borrow some of that strength, needed someone to talk to. Looking up into his dark eyes, she nodded her assent.

"Okay. Thank you."

She stepped inside the house, and he closed the door behind her. "I was just about to make some tea," he said as he buttoned his shirt. "Would you like a cup?"

"Sure, I'd love some."

She followed him to the kitchen and sat at the table while Alex filled a stainless steel kettle with water and set it on the stove to boil. His movements were economical and graceful as he moved around his kitchen in his bare feet. Reaching into a cupboard, he pulled out a china teapot in a flowery pattern. The idea of such a masculine man using an object so feminine-looking made her smile.

"I wouldn't have pegged you as a tea-drinking, flowered-teapot-owning kind of guy."

He grinned at her over his shoulder. "You can blame my grandmother. She's Mexican-American, but she has an obsession with all things English. She's a big fan of afternoon tea."

"My grandmother used to believe all problems could be solved over a hot cup of Earl Grey." Happy recollections flashed through her memory. "I was only twelve when she died, but I still miss her."

"I'm lucky. My grandmother is still alive, but I've been kind of blindsided by how much I've missed her since I've been here. It's tough not being able to drive across town to see her."

"I know what you mean. I missed my parents terribly when I lived in Thailand."

"You lived in Thailand?"

"Yes. My ex-husband and I taught English there for a few years after we finished college. It was a fun adventure, but I was homesick a lot of the time. I guess I'm not meant to be a world traveler."

Alex warmed the teapot with a bit of water from the kettle, swirling it for a moment before emptying it in the sink. Then he placed a couple of spoonfuls of loose tea into the pot and filled it with hot water, letting it steep while he brought teacups and milk and sugar to the table. Julia was comforted by the little ritual that reminded her so much of her grandmother and her mother.

After bringing the teapot to the table, along with a strainer to catch the loose tea, he sat across from Julia. "Tell me what happened with your parents."

He poured her tea, and Julia wrapped her hands around the cup, savoring the warmth. "My mother remembered nothing about talking to you or being outside in the middle of the night, and my father said she was sleepwalking. When I tried to tell him that we should take Mom to have her checked by a doctor, he became very agitated, so I dropped it. I was afraid he was going to get sick again. I don't know what to do."

"I'm no expert in this area either, but I understand it's not unusual for a spouse of an Alzheimer's patient to deny the symptoms. I'll talk to the hospital social worker tomorrow and have her get in touch with you. Maybe she's got some ideas."

"Okay." Relief flowed through her. At least she wouldn't have to face this problem on her own.

They drank their tea in silence, but the silence didn't feel awkward. Julia felt soothed, the stress slowly leaving her body. Perhaps her grandmother had been onto something. The tea seemed to be working.

She finished the last of it and set down the cup. "I should be going. I left Ava with Tracy, and she's probably hungry by now."

Julia got to her feet and headed to the front door, with Alex following her.

"Thanks for the tea, and for listening. I guess I needed both today."

"Anytime. Seriously, Julia, anytime you need to talk, about anything, give me a call."

She wondered if he was speaking as a doctor, as a friend, or as a man. Which one did she want him to be?

"Thank you."

"I'll try to keep an eye out for your folks, see if there's anything I can do for them."

She was touched by his offer. "I really appreciate that, but I know how busy you are."

He waved away her concern. "It's no big deal. I appreciate my grandmother's neighbors checking in on her, and I'd be happy to do the same."

He really did understand how she felt. "In that

case, thank you."

She opened the front door and stepped outside. Turning to Alex, she smiled. His thick hair had begun to dry, and the dark strands gleamed in the spring sunshine. Her breath caught in her throat at his beauty.

"Bye, Alex."

"Bye. Take care."

Julia hurried down the steps and across the lawn to her car. An appreciation for his looks was as far she could take any relationship with him. Her life was too complicated, too full already. And she would never get involved with a man who planned to leave Lobster Cove in only a few more months.

****

Julia picked up Tracy and Ava and headed to Maggie's Diner. Located in downtown Lobster Cove on Oak Avenue, the diner's reputation for excellent food had spread across the island, and, as usual, the place was packed. Luckily, her secretary Beth was seated alone at a large table and waved them over when they entered.

"Hey, Boss! I've got room here!"

They joined Beth at her table, and Maureen Bennett brought menus, along with glasses of water and cutlery wrapped in paper napkins. After taking their order, she turned to Julia.

"Ms. Stewart, do you have a minute? I'd like to speak to you."

Julia's stomach dropped into her shoes. What else did she have to deal with today? Maureen didn't appear upset, but it was difficult to be certain what she was thinking. Had there been problems with either her daughter or stepdaughter at the school lately? Nothing had been brought to her attention. Last year her stepdaughter Avery had been bullied, and her daughter Paige had landed in her office when she'd tried to take the matter into her own hands. Julia had worked very hard to deal with bullying in the school since then.

"Yes, of course."

After Maureen dropped off their order in the kitchen, Julia followed her into a small, cluttered office. As she closed the door, Maureen smiled. "I won't keep you from your dinner long. I haven't had a chance to talk to you, and I just wanted to tell you how pleased I am about Avery's experience at school this year. She's been so much happier. Thank you for taking the issue of bullying so seriously."

Maureen's speech caught Julia by surprise. In a day full of thunderstorms, this was a welcome rainbow.

"Thank you. My staff has been working very hard to instill a sense of empathy in our students. We want them to know that bullying of any kind won't be tolerated."

"They take their direction from you, and I believe you're leading them in the right direction."

She grimaced. "Not everyone feels that way."

"What do you mean?"

She told her about the problems with the daycare she was trying to set up. "It looks like I could be heading into a fight. Can I count on your support?"

"Of course," Maureen said without hesitation. "I believe the whole community has to work together to give our kids what they need."

"I appreciate that." She wished everyone in town felt that way. "I hear Paige is doing really well academically this year," Julia said.

Maureen's smile was wide and proud. "She is, especially in maths and sciences. She had some trouble with calculus at the beginning of the year, but we were able to find a tutor online who's helped her tremendously. She's determined to get top marks her last two years of high school so she can get into a veterinary medicine program."

"I'm sure she'll succeed." *Calculus. Ralph Sykes' subject.* It said a lot about his skill as a teacher, or lack thereof, that a talented, motivated student like Paige Bennett had to seek outside help to get her through the course. How did less academically gifted students fare in his class? She made a mental note to find out.

"Like I said, I don't want to keep you from your dinner, and I should probably get back to work myself. I just wanted to let you know how pleased I am about my girls' school experience this year."

Julia reached for her hand. "You have no idea how happy I am to hear it."

They went back into the restaurant, and Jill, Maggie's business partner, brought coffee for her and Tracy and a glass of milk for Ava. A few minutes later, the bell over the door tinkled to announce a new arrival, and Julia looked up to see Alex Campbell walk into the restaurant. Their gazes met across the room, and she felt a flutter of excitement in her stomach. She blinked and looked away, unwilling to acknowledge her reaction to him.

"Dr. Alex!"

Ava scrambled out of her chair and ran to Alex, launching herself at him. He scooped her up into his arms.

"Hey, here's my favorite patient."

"That's 'cause I'm special, right?"

He grinned and tugged gently on her blonde ponytail. "That's right, Sweet Pea."

"My name isn't Sweet Pea."

"Really? I could have sworn it was."

Julia was aware that this little exchange was being watched by everyone in the diner. She was also aware that every woman in the room, no matter how young or how old, had stopped talking to stare at Alex the moment he stepped into the diner. With his dark, exotic good looks, he was an extraordinarily handsome man who could command the attention of any woman without even being aware of it.

But right now she was only concerned with the attention he was getting from one female—her daughter. Ava's usual reserve didn't seem to apply to Alex. Since their night in the ER she'd known Ava trusted him, but had that trust turned into an attachment? Should she be worried?

Alex tipped his head in greeting, still holding Ava in his arms. "Hi, Tracy, Julia."

"Why don't you join us, Alex?" Tracy said.

His gaze met Julia's, and for a second she thought she saw a flicker of regret. He turned his attention back to Tracy. "Thanks for the offer. Maybe another time. I've got a shift at the clinic in Bar Harbor with Dr. Manning tonight. I just stopped by to pick us up some take-out food."

Jill appeared at his side with a large paper bag. "Here you go, Dr. Campbell. *Bon appétit*."

"Thanks, Jill." Alex turned to Ava, who rested her uninjured arm trustingly across his shoulders. "Sorry, Sweet Pea. I've got to run."

He set her carefully on the floor, and with another nod at Julia and Tracy, he took his bag from Jill and headed with her to the cash register to pay his bill. As he was leaving, Ava called, “Bye, Dr. Alex.”

He lifted his hand in a wave. “Bye, Ava.”

When he’d left the building, Julia turned to Tracy. “What was that about going to the clinic in Bar Harbor tonight?”

“He volunteers at the free clinic there once or twice a month.”

That was news to Julia. Like everyone else in town, she knew he was using his stint in Maine as an opportunity to help pay off his medical school loans. After four years of university to get her teaching degree, she knew how quickly student debt could add up, and how difficult it was to pay off. It was part of the reason she and Russ had gone to Thailand. She also knew how difficult it could be to attract doctors and other medical professionals to a small place like Lobster Cove. So she had no problem with the Island Health Board making their offer to him. What surprised her was that he would offer his services *gratis* at the free clinic.

Beth fanned herself with a napkin, giving an exaggerated sigh. “If only I was fifteen years younger and twenty pounds lighter, I’d be all over the good doctor.”

Julia laughed. “Aren’t you forgetting something? Or someone? You know, Marty? The guy you go home to every night?”

“Marty?” Beth pretended to think about the question. “The name does sound vaguely familiar.”

“It should. You’ve only been married to him for

the last twenty years."

"What can I say? A pretty face like Alex Campbell's can turn the head of even the most devoted wife. I hear women from all over the island are making up diseases just so they can be examined by him. Isn't that right, Tracy?"

Tracy hid her smile behind her coffee cup. "I don't know about that, but I do know he's well-liked and respected at the hospital. He's great with patients, especially kids."

"That's what I heard, too. His looks are just an extra added bonus."

"It's too bad he's only here temporarily," Tracy said. "We could really use another young, dynamic family doctor who was willing to stick around."

"I hear Alex only has about ten months left on his contract, and the chances of him staying beyond that are pretty slim." Beth winked broadly at Julia. "Unless, of course, he falls madly in love with a nice Lobster Cove girl and decides to chuck city life to stay with her here."

Julia stared at her in surprise. "Don't look at me. I hardly know him!"

"Ah, come on, Julia. Somebody's got to do it. I was going to volunteer, but as you're so fond of reminding me, I'm already married. So it's up to you. Take one for the team."

"The team's going to have to manage without my help."

She knew Beth was joking—sort of. But she had no intention of throwing herself into the dating pool any time soon. Her marriage had left her with plenty of wounds that hadn't entirely healed yet.

Perhaps they never would.

Chapter Six

It was truly astounding how much noise seven six-year-old girls could make.

Julia's head still pounded from the shrieks and giggles as she surveyed the remains of crumbled birthday cake and half eaten hotdogs littering her kitchen table. Brightly colored balloons and bits of wrapping paper were strewn across the floor. Thank God Ava's birthday only came around once a year.

Fortunately, the afternoon's festivities of games, prizes, opening presents, and excited squeals was over for another year, and the children had gone home, except for her friend Edie's daughter Natalie. She glanced out the open kitchen window and saw Ava and Natalie playing in the back yard on the swing set. They slid down the plastic slide in tandem, and Julia grinned at their excited laughter, induced, no doubt, from a lingering birthday cake sugar high.

Julia wondered what was keeping Edie. She'd said she needed to pick up her daughter early so she could head into Bar Harbor to do some shopping, but a half hour had passed since the other children left, and she still hadn't arrived. It didn't really matter; Ava and Natalie were best friends and enjoyed hanging out together. But it was odd for Edie not to phone if she was going to be late. She'd probably had to make an emergency diaper change before coming over. With two other children aside from Natalie, a boy a year older and a girl who'd just turned one, Edie had her hands full. She'd been run off her feet since the arrival of baby number three.

Julia began dumping paper plates and food remains into a garbage bag in an effort to bring some order to the kitchen. A minute later the girls ran into the house through the back door.

"Can we have a drink of water, Mommy?" Ava asked.

"Of course. What do you say?"

"Please!" they sang in unison.

Julia laughed as she filled two glasses with water at the tap. "Very good, my darlings. I have trained you well."

Natalie drank her fill before handing the glass back to Julia. "Is my Mommy coming for me soon?"

"Yes, I'm sure she'll be here soon, sweetie." Julia wondered if she should give Edie a call. She decided to wait another fifteen minutes before she officially started to worry.

The doorbell rang and Julia sighed in relief, sure it must be Edie at last. But when she opened the door, her former mother-in-law, Lily Stewart, stood on her front step, a large box wrapped in brightly colored paper in her arms. Lily smiled nervously, as if uncertain of her welcome.

"I hope you don't mind. I wanted to say happy birthday to Ava and drop off this gift for her."

Julia had always liked Russ's mother, but her relationship with her former father-in-law had deteriorated to the point that Lily obviously didn't feel welcome in her house. For Ava's sake, she wanted to amend that situation.

"Of course I don't mind. Why don't you come in, and we can have a cup of tea and what's left of the birthday cake? I'll have to shovel off a spot at the kitchen table before we sit down, though. It's a disaster zone in there."

Lily chuckled as she stepped inside. "Sounds like you had quite the celebration."

"Oh, yes. My ears are still ringing from all the happiness."

When they entered the kitchen, Ava ran to Lily as soon as she saw her. Lily bent over and held her tightly.

"How's my little birthday girl?"

"I got so many presents, Grandma. And we had balloons and played games, and everybody got a treat bag when they left."

"That's wonderful, Ava. I'm so glad you had a happy birthday."

Ava wrapped her arms around Lily's waist and looked up into her face. "I'm so glad to see you, Grandma. I haven't seen you in so long."

Lily brushed Ava's blonde curls from her forehead, her expression wistful. "I'm glad to see you too, darling."

As Julia watched them, a lump formed in her throat. It wasn't fair to Ava to deprive her of her grandmother's love and attention. But her relationship with Wyatt had grown so strained since her divorce that she'd avoided contact with Russ's parents. Unfortunately, Ava was the one who suffered most.

While Julia made tea, Lily gave Ava her present, and with giggles of delight, Ava and Natalie tore the wrapping paper from the box to reveal Barbie's dream house. They'd just taken the house out of the box and unwrapped the little plastic accoutrements that went with it when the doorbell rang again. Julia was relieved to see Edie this time when she opened the door.

"I'm so sorry I'm late," she said before Julia could say a word. "Believe it or not, I fell asleep."

"How did you manage to do that without the baby waking you up?"

"Aaron took the kids over to his mother's house for a while so I could have a nap. I curled up on my bed for twenty winks, and the next thing I knew it was four hours later. I'm sorry."

"Don't worry about it. It's not a problem." She glanced toward the kitchen where Lily now sat on the floor with the girls, examining Barbie's new abode with them. Julia lowered her voice. "Are you feeling okay? You're not sick, are you?"

Edie waved a hand in dismissal. "I'm fine. Just tired. The baby has been teething and hasn't been sleeping well. So I haven't been sleeping well either."

Julia noticed the dark circles under her friend's eyes that spoke of fatigue. "Tomorrow is Sunday. Why don't you bring the baby over here in the afternoon so you can have a rest?"

"That's really sweet, Julia, and I appreciate it, but Aaron's promised to take care of the kids tomorrow. I'll take you up on the offer another day."

"Make sure you do." Was it her imagination, or had Edie lost weight since she'd last seen her? She'd already lost all the weight she'd gained with her last pregnancy. She hoped she wasn't going overboard with the dieting.

When they walked into the kitchen, Edie said hello

to Lily and wished Ava a happy birthday before leaving with a now reluctant Natalie. After they'd gone, Julia finished cleaning the table and then poured hot water into the teapot along with a bag of Earl Grey tea and let it steep.

"You like milk in your tea, don't you, Lily?"

"Yes, I do." She grabbed the back of a chair to help haul herself to her feet, while Ava moved her new toy into the living room. "I'm surprised you remember. It's been a while since we had tea together."

Julia filled a small china creamer with milk and brought it to the table. "I know. I'm sorry about that. I should have invited you to Ava's birthday party, but I didn't know what Wyatt's reaction would be. It's been so long since I talked to either of you I was afraid he'd think I was only offering an invitation to get a present out of you."

"Did you honestly think that, Julia?"

She turned away, embarrassed. She *had* believed Lily and Wyatt would think an invitation from her would come with ulterior motives. And to be honest, she'd wanted to avoid a confrontation, especially on Ava's birthday. Family gatherings with the Stewarts had become more and more uncomfortable. Instead of time healing wounds, it had only succeeded in rubbing salt into the open sores.

For a moment, Lily watched Ava playing on the floor in the living room, then turned to Julia and spoke in a quiet voice. "I don't want to miss seeing Ava grow up. She's the only grandchild we have. Or at least, the only grandchild we're allowed to know."

Julia blinked at that statement. Did that mean Russ had fathered another child in Thailand? She wasn't sure she wanted to know. Or cared.

"I don't want you to miss seeing Ava grow up either. But with the way Wyatt feels about me, it's been difficult. I don't want her to see us arguing every time we're together."

She cringed when she thought about the previous Christmas. She and Ava had gone over to Wyatt and Lily's house on Christmas morning so Ava could open her presents from them there. They were supposed to stay for brunch, but Wyatt picked a fight with her about the school lunch program, which he'd opposed on budget grounds and she had fought to implement. She'd tried to avoid a confrontation; it was Christmas Day, after all. But Wyatt kept picking at her and goading her until she'd been forced to take Ava and leave before she said something she really regretted. Neither she nor Ava had been in their house since.

"Wyatt really misses her," Lily said with a sigh. "Do you think we could come to some sort of compromise?"

"What are you suggesting?"

"What if Ava spent a little time with us? Maybe an afternoon at our house once in a while? I could pick her up and bring her home so that you and Wyatt don't have to deal with each other."

Julia sipped her tea and watched as Ava moved Barbie and Ken into their house. She hoped the dolls' relationship would turn out better than hers. She and Russ had been happy once, but it had all started to unravel after they'd moved home to Lobster Cove and Ava had been born.

Or maybe she was kidding herself and their troubles had started long before that.

"I want Ava to know her grandparents. All her grandparents. I want her to spend time with you, I truly do. But I can't do that if I think Wyatt will bad-mouth me to her."

"That's not going to happen. We just want to spend time with her. I promise you, if I ever hear Wyatt say one unkind word about you in Ava's presence, I will stop him immediately. But I'm sure he's not going to do that. He's not a monster, Julia. He just misses his family."

"Okay, I'll trust you, Lily. We can start a week from this Monday, if you're free. I have an appointment after school I need to get to. Can you pick up Ava at the school? I can let her teacher know you'll be there. You could take her to your house and bring her back here after I get home."

Lily's eyes lit with excitement. "Yes, of course I can look after her. I'll be at the school to pick her up at three-thirty." She paused for a moment, setting her teacup back in its saucer. "You're sure about this? Maybe you'd feel more comfortable having your mother look after Ava."

Julia's stomach made an uncomfortable swoop, the way it did every time she thought about what was happening to her mother. "No, I'm sure I want Ava to be with you next Monday."

Lily smiled in happiness and relief. She reached across the table and grasped Julia's hand. "I can't tell you how happy this makes me. I won't let you down."

Julia squeezed her hand. "I know you won't." She vowed that from that day forward she wouldn't let the antagonism between her and Wyatt affect Ava's relationship with her grandmother.

****

Alex grabbed the chart off the back of the door and scanned it quickly before entering the examining room. *Melissa Maloney, thirty-four. Complaining of a urinary tract infection.* Upon entering, he found her sitting on the table with her legs crossed and her head bowed. She looked up and smiled, and when he extended his hand, she grasped it and gave it a hearty shake.

"I'm Melissa. I've heard a lot about you, Doc," she said before he had a chance to introduce himself. "All good things, mind you. I usually see Dr. Sato, not Mrs. Dr. Sato, the OB/GYN, I mean Dr. Rob Sato, the GP. I was relieved when I heard he was referring his patients to you while he was away on vacation. Like I said, I've heard good things."

The small town grapevine strikes again. He grinned. "Pleased to meet you, Melissa. I'm glad you feel comfortable seeing me in Dr. Sato's absence." He referred to the chart that Dr. Sato's office had sent over. "I see that you're complaining of a urinary tract infection. What makes you think you've got one?"

She rolled her eyes. "The usual—the urge to pee all the time, and the terrible burning when I do. I've had enough of them to know exactly what they're all about. Dr. Rob usually gives me an antibiotic and then I'm on my merry way."

Alex scanned the notes again. Rob Sato's cramped handwriting indicated she'd been in his office numerous times in the last year to seek treatment for urinary tract infections. The number seemed excessive. Aside from a simple test to check for bacteria in the urine, Dr. Sato had done no further testing. His notes indicated he'd wanted to investigate further, had warned her the UTIs could be a symptom of another problem, but Melissa had flatly refused.

"Well, according to your medical file, you're becoming quite the expert on UTIs. Will you indulge me for a moment and let me play doctor?"

"Will it take long? I need to use the bathroom again, and then I have to get back to work."

"I'll be as fast as possible."

"Okay then," she said reluctantly.

He took her blood pressure. It was slightly elevated but within the normal range. Her temperature was also a little above average, but according to her chart, both numbers seemed to be normal for her.

"Aside from the infections, how have you been feeling?"

"Oh, just terrific, Doc. I'm a working mom with two kids under six and a husband who's away working for weeks at a time. I think he spends more time with his buddies on that commercial fishing boat than he does with me. So, no surprise, I'm tired. I'm starting to get a little thick around my middle, and my scale is telling me to lay off the sugared donuts. To top it off, I'm beginning to find more hair in my brush than on my head. But aside from that, I'm great."

Alex tried not to laugh, but he couldn't suppress a smile. "You have what's commonly known as Busy Mom Syndrome. But I am concerned about the number of UTIs you've had in the last year. I'd like to send you for more testing. I want to do an ultrasound to see if there are any obstructions in the urethra or kidneys."

"Doc, I don't have time for that, and I definitely don't have the insurance. I can barely afford the antibiotics."

“I think it’s important to find a cause for your infections. There could be some underlying problem we need to treat.”

She shook her head as he spoke. “I can’t do it right now. Maybe later, when Davy gets home, if they’ve got themselves a good catch this time.”

“If cost is an issue, why don’t I arrange to meet you at the free clinic in Bar Harbor? I work there a couple of times a month.”

Melissa’s mouth was set in a straight, stubborn line. “I don’t take charity, Doc. Me and Davy and the kids, we pay our own way. Can’t you just give me the antibiotics for now?”

“Of course.” He wrote the script on his pad. There was no point arguing with her, or insulting her. “I’m giving you enough antibiotic for a week. I want you to come back to my office about seven days after you finish the medication. We’ll take another urine test and see if the antibiotic has truly cleared out the bugs. If not, we might need to try a different antibiotic for a longer term.”

“Is that really necessary? I have to take time off work, get my mother to sit with the kids—”

“Do you really want to keep getting these infections?”

She made a face. “No, I don’t. Okay, fine, I’ll be back in two weeks.”

“Good. In the meantime, drink plenty of water and keep your salt intake down. Try drinking cranberry juice. It helps some women with your problem.”

“All right.” She took the prescription. “Thanks, Doc.”

“You’re welcome. I’ll see you in two weeks. Don’t

forget to make an appointment on your way out."

She fluttered her eyelashes, a mischievous gleam in her eye. "If I didn't know better, Doc, I'd say you just want to get me in one of those cute little paper gowns, but I'm telling you, I'm not that kind of girl."

This time Alex did laugh. "Get out of here before I sic my nurse on you."

With a wink she left the room. Alex shook his head and laughed again.

Family medicine certainly had its moments.

****

A few days later, Julia stared out the window of her office to the beautiful spring day just beyond her four walls. She longed to be outside, to breathe in the fresh air with its slightly fishy, damp seaweed smell. It was the best smell in the world.

Perhaps what she needed was an afternoon off. Maybe she'd work in her neglected garden, or go for a walk. Or maybe she'd run. She hadn't gone for a good run in ages. It used to be a passion for her, but with her responsibilities at work and at home, running had fallen by the wayside.

With a sigh, she rose from her chair, giving up all pretense of working. For the last couple of days she'd been restless, unable to concentrate on her work. What the hell was the matter with her?

Her parents' health weighed heavily on her mind. She could hardly wait to meet the hospital social worker the following Monday, but meeting with her meant this thing with her mother was real and none of them could ignore it anymore. She and Ava had visited her parents every day after school, checking to see if they were okay. On the surface, all appeared normal, but Julia had picked up on some things she hadn't noticed before. Like the way her mother struggled to remember their names, and the way she'd ask the same question over and over. And the tension and sadness on her father's face. He was even less happy when she told him she was going to talk to a social worker about her mother.

Had her mother been sleepwalking as her father claimed? She prayed her mother didn't have Alzheimer's, and that the incident Alex witnessed had been some sort of aberration.

Alex. Why couldn't she get him out of her head? She didn't want to think about him, didn't want to remember the tender way he'd wiped the tears from her cheek, or the compassion she'd seen in his dark eyes. Nothing good could come from such remembrances.

The phone rang, saving her from her thoughts. She resumed her seat, and after exhaling deeply, picked up the receiver. Beth's voice came on the line.

"Superintendent Perkins on line one, Boss."

"Thanks, Beth."

A moment later she heard Rob Perkins's voice. "Hi, Julia. How's your day going?"

Crummy, lousy, depressing. "Very well, thank you. Do you have some news for me?"

"I do. Which do you want to hear first? The good news or the bad news?"

She sighed. "Hit me with the bad news."

"Okay, here it is. The school board will absolutely not consider any changes to the current health curriculum that includes a unit on sex education. They felt the money that would be needed to amend the curriculum could be better used elsewhere. And aside from the monetary issue, the board didn't like the message that sex education in the school would send, that it was okay for students to be sexually active. I'm sorry, Julia."

She closed her eyes and bowed her head. "It's not a big surprise. We knew going in it was a long shot." That didn't mean she wasn't disappointed.

"Yeah, it was. But it was still worth the effort. We can't win them all."

Julia massaged her temple with her index finger, unsure if she was angry at this development or just sad. Was she kidding herself? Would her ideas always be out of step with the community?

"I suppose not. So what's the good news?"

"They agreed to go ahead with setting up the daycare in the fall. It's going to be a pilot project, with funding for two years. To offset costs, we're going to allow children from other families in town to have their kids looked after at our daycare. We'll be setting up shop in two empty classrooms in the high school. So, what do you think?"

Julia was shocked. "I think that's amazing. I thought they were going to change their minds and rescind their approval."

"Rumor has it Wyatt Stewart argued for the daycare."

"Are you sure about that?" she asked incredulously. Why would Wyatt support any of her ideas? Would he soon change his mind and kill the project, just to spite her?

"I have my sources, and that's what they tell me. Congratulations, Julia!"

"Thanks, but I'm not popping any champagne

corks until I see babies in my school and their mothers in my classrooms."

"Hey, don't sound so pessimistic. This is a victory."

"Some people don't feel that way."

She told Rob about her conversation with Ralph Sykes and how he was planning to start a petition against the daycare. This time she heard him sigh, and she wondered if he had a headache as big as hers.

"I've heard that Sykes has political aspirations. He may use the daycare and any controversy he can work up about it as a springboard to get his name out in the community. A lot of the more conservative people in the area would support a stance like his."

"That's great. Meanwhile, I've got kids who don't have a clue about sex or birth control, and others who have babies and aren't coming back to school. Am I supposed to sit back and do nothing while they flounder?"

"We'll do all we can, Julia, but remember, we're educators, not parents. There are limits to what we can do."

"Yes, I know."

Privately, Julia swore she'd fight with everything she had for the daycare. And she wouldn't stop pushing to have sex education taught in her school. Her kids deserved it.

****

On Monday after school, Julia drove to the hospital to meet the social worker Alex had put her in touch with. Helen Murray was a middle-aged woman whose calm, efficient manner and quiet kindness put Julia immediately at ease. Julia told her about her concerns with her mother, and Helen promised to visit the Dawsons. She would encourage them to have Dora seen by her doctor. Once they had more information about Dora's health, they would be able to make informed decisions about her care. Maybe there was nothing seriously wrong with Dora, but they needed to know what had caused her bizarre behavior.

Julia's relief was profound. After speaking with Helen, she didn't feel so alone anymore. Someone else was on her side. Julia hoped for the best but prepared herself for the worst.

Chapter Seven

After supper, Julia and Ava walked to the ball diamonds at the school. The closer they got, the more Julia's spirits lifted. Today was the official beginning of softball season. She'd been playing in a co-ed recreational league for the last three years, and she'd been looking forward to this day for weeks. They were only practicing tonight, tossing and hitting a few balls to shake off the rust from a long, cold winter. But damn, it felt good to get her glove out of storage and be out in the early evening sunshine.

Ava skipped along beside her, as excited as she was. The children of the players attended practices and games, making them something of a family affair. They chased errant balls and played in the nearby park, having nearly as much fun as the adults.

"When my cast comes off, will you teach me how to pitch?"

"Sure, I'll try. But I'm not the greatest pitcher. I play shortstop, remember?"

"I remember. But I want to pitch."

"Okay," she said, giving Ava's pigtail a tug. "I'll give it a try. Maybe you should ask Edie to give you some pointers. She's the best pitcher on our team."

"How long till my cast comes off?"

"About another week or so. Dr. Willson's going to take another x-ray to see if your arm is completely healed, and if it is, it's outta there."

"How come I didn't see Dr. Alex again? I like him."

"Because Dr. Willson's been your doctor since you were a baby."

"Yeah, but I really like Dr. Alex. He's nice."

She decided to avoid the subject. "Hey, look. Devon and Tricia are already at the playground. Why don't you go join them? Remember, no wandering off where I can't see you. You have to be at either the playground or behind the fence at the ball diamond."

"Okay, Mom. See you!" She ran to join her friends.

Her daughter's attachment to Alex Campbell made her uneasy. Was Ava so starved for the attention of a father figure in her life that she'd latched on to him? How would she react when he left town in a few months? She couldn't let her get too close. It would be too painful. For both of them.

Julia made her way to the diamonds, greeting her friends as they arrived. Edie's husband Aaron showed up alone.

"Hey, Aaron. Where's Edie?"

He bent over to tie his shoes, avoiding her gaze. "She decided to stay home with the baby tonight. She said she had a headache. I brought Natalie and Michael so she could have a little break."

"Oh," Julia said in surprise. "That must be some headache. I don't think I've ever known her to miss a practice before." In fact, Edie had once completed pitching a game even though she'd had a hairline fracture of the tibia that gave her considerable pain, though she'd never let on at the time. Two seasons ago she'd been pregnant, only quitting at four months when

Aaron had forced her to after she slid headfirst into second base on a steal. Edie was competitive to her core.

"She just needs some rest."

It disturbed her that Aaron still hadn't looked her in the eye. "You'd tell me if something was really wrong, wouldn't you?"

Finally Aaron looked into her face and smiled. "Everything's fine. But with three kids, especially a fussy baby, she needs a break."

"I'll bet she does." She vowed to give Edie a call when she got home. She'd been neglecting her old friend. Their lives had become so busy lately, that they didn't spend as much time together as she would have liked.

She leaned over to tie her spikes, wondering if Tracy would make this practice or if she was working at the hospital tonight. She and Tracy and Edie had been inseparable as teenagers, sharing a love of sports and the outdoors. The three *amigas* they'd called themselves. Julia smiled at the thought. They were the best friends she'd ever had. Probably the best she'd ever have.

"Hi, Julia."

She hesitated at the sound of the familiar deep, male voice. Slowly, she lifted her head and looked up, her heart beating ridiculously fast.

"Alex. What are you doing here?"

He sat on the bench next to her. "I joined the team. Aaron told me about the league last winter, and I swore that if I lived through the cold, I'd join up in the spring. After being stuck indoors for so long, I need to get out."

She chuckled, charmed by him despite her

reservations. “You poor, sad, California boy. The temperature goes past the freezing point, and you wilt like a delicate flower.”

He grinned at her, and her breath caught in her throat. “That’s me. A definite hothouse flower. There’s no antifreeze running through my veins. How do you stand the cold?”

“It’s not that bad,” she said with a shrug. “You get used to it.”

He shot her a dubious glance. “I doubt I’d ever get used to it.”

He was probably right. Maine winters were an acquired taste.

“Have you played softball before?”

“Well, baseball, actually, but not for a few years. I’m hoping it’s like riding a bike and you never forget.”

“What position did you play?”

“Outfield, mostly, but I pitched sometimes, too.”

“Edie’s usually our pitcher, but she’s not here tonight. Maybe you can show us your stuff.”

“I don’t know. I’ve never pitched softball before. I don’t want to embarrass myself at my first practice. Exactly how competitive is this league?”

“Perhaps some of us take it a little more seriously than others.”

He grinned at her again. “By some of us, do you mean you?”

She couldn’t help smiling back at him. “Maybe. I’ve been known to be a bit intense on occasion.”

Aaron rallied the troops around home plate. “Listen up, everyone. We’re going to warm up with a little toss and catch, and then we’ll divide into two teams for a mock game so we can all get in some hitting and fielding practice. Let's go!"

Players broke off into groups of two to throw the ball to each other and loosen up. Alex approached her. "Care to be my partner?"

"Sure. Let's see what you're made of, California boy."

"Be gentle with me. It's my first time."

Julia suppressed her smile as Alex sprinted about ten yards into the outfield to take his place between two other players. When he was ready, she lobbed an easy ball at him.

"Anyone ever tell you that you throw like a girl?" he said as he easily caught the ball.

"Not unless they want to lose their teeth," she said pleasantly.

"Good to know."

She scrambled to catch his return throw, an overhand baseball pitch that dropped like a stone as it reached her. "Not bad, Campbell. Too bad there wasn't a lot of heat on it."

"You want more heat? You got it."

She caught his next throw against the palm of her hand instead of in the pocket of her glove, and felt the sting all the way up her arm. She resisted the urge to take her hand out of the glove and rub the sore spot.

"Nice. That one had a lot more mustard. When did you say you last played?"

"In college, as an undergrad."

She tossed the ball at him, and he caught it with an economical movement of his glove. "Why don't you try an underhand softball pitch, see how it feels."

"Okay. But get ready. I have no idea where this might go."

"I'm ready. Go for it."

He stood facing her, the ball in his right hand resting against his hip. Then, winding his arm in a windmill motion, he took a step forward at the same time, giving himself the momentum he needed as he released the pitch. The ball sailed high, and Julia had to make a vertical leap to catch it. She felt the speed of the pitch in her glove.

"Sorry about that," he said. "Nice snag."

"Thanks." She threw it back to him. "Try it again."

She crouched in the classic catcher position, her glove positioned in front of her at the strike zone level, as if there were a batter in place. "Right at the glove, Alex."

He wound up and released again. This time the ball hit the dirt about a yard in front of her and took a crazy bounce to the left, and she was unable to field it.

"Sorry about that."

"Not a problem."

One of the other players picked up the ball and threw it back to her. She tossed it to Alex and assumed the position once more.

"In the pocket, Alex."

This time the ball moved in a direct line from his hand to her glove. Julia was thrilled with the pitch, but she wasn't going to let him know. "Nice control," she said blandly as she threw it back to him. "See if you can add a little more speed."

Once more he wound up and let fly. The ball had more speed but sailed high, causing her to jump to her feet. Still, with an indulgent umpire, it might have had a chance to be called a strike.

By now all the other players had stopped throwing

to watch them. Aaron stuck his glove under his arm and clapped his hands.

"Come on, Alex. You can do it."

This time he threw a strike right down the middle. The crowd cheered. Aaron pumped his fist. "Looks like Edie may have some competition as pitcher this year."

Next they broke into two teams for an ad hoc game. Alex was put in as pitcher against her team, and he did a credible job, considering it was the first time he'd ever pitched underhand with a softball. He struck out a couple of players, getting them to swing at high strikes, but he also got smacked by Dave, one of the best hitters on their team. Dave cracked the ball into left field, the ball flying over the head of the fielder, who had to chase after it.

"You can't win 'em all, Doc," Dave chortled as he trotted around the bases.

Then it was her turn at bat. She dug her toe into the dirt next to home plate and raised her bat to shoulder height as she stared Alex down. His first pitch was high and inside, forcing her to jump back to avoid being hit. She saw him cringe.

"Sorry. That one got away on me."

"Not a problem. But do it again and you may find my bat where the sun don't shine."

He grinned. "I'll take that under consideration."

"Please do."

She watched his next pitch whiz across her strike zone. *Damn.* She really hated to lose. She dug her toe a little deeper in the dirt.

The next pitch was a fat one right down the middle. This time she was ready for it. She swung her bat, and with a satisfying crack it connected with the ball, sending it over the shortstop's outstretched arm to land safely in left field. She raced to first base and rounded the corner, but by then the ball had been thrown to second base. She trotted back to the bag.

The second base player tossed the ball to Alex. He gave her a look to ensure she wasn't trying to steal second before facing a new batter at the plate. He whizzed one across the plate. *Strike one.* Then a swing and a miss. *Strike two.* Julia started to get nervous. With two out already, she was in danger of being left stranded on base. She wasn't going down without a fight.

As Alex concentrated on his batter, she took a few tentative steps off the bag, then as soon as he let go of the ball she took off at full speed for second. She heard shouting, saw the shortstop race to second base. With one last burst of speed, she dove head first to the bag, her arms outstretched and reaching. Just before her hand touched the base, she felt the slap of a leather glove against her backside.

"Out!" Aaron called from home plate.

Damn. Julia got to her feet, and brushed the dirt from her clothes.

"Nice try, Jules. Better luck next time." Aaron clapped her on the back as she made her way back to the bench to pick up her glove. Alex grinned at her.

"Yeah, Jules. Better luck next time."

"Nobody likes a wiseass, Campbell."

She felt better than she had in days.

When Alex came to the plate, Julia went on full alert at her shortstop position. No way was she going to let a hit of his get past her.

She needn't have worried. The ball connected with

his bat with a loud crack and flew over her head—and over the left field player's head. Alex ambled around the bases, taking congratulations from players on both sides as he went.

Julia smiled. It was going to be a very interesting ball season.

****

Ava held Alex's hand as they walked home after practice. Julia wondered once more if she should be worried about her daughter's growing attachment to him. But she pushed the worry from her mind for tonight. For the first time in a very long time she'd had fun. It was springtime, and the sun was finally warm again. Couldn't she just enjoy the moment?

"You're great at shortstop," Alex said. "You're quick, and you've got a sure glove."

"Thanks, but I was actually a little rusty tonight. Hopefully I'll get up to speed after a couple of practices."

He chuckled. "If this is how you play rusty, it's going to be interesting to watch you when you're back in the groove. Are you always this aggressive when you play?"

Julia felt her smile disappear. Russ had always chastised her competitive nature. He'd had no interest in sports and had belittled her desire to win and play her hardest. He'd told her that recreational softball was hardly life and death and she should dial it down a notch. Why did she feel the need to make a spectacle of herself?

Julia suddenly felt self-conscious, as if Russ was beside her, whispering in her ear. Looking down at her filthy clothes, she saw that her T-shirt was stained with dirt from her slide into second. She knew her face was probably equally dirty, and her hair had mostly come loose from her ponytail. She lifted her hand to her hair and tucked a strand behind her ear.

"Yeah, I've been told it's a failing of mine. I can't seem to help it."

He gave her a quizzical look. "A failing? There's nothing wrong with playing hard. How can you succeed at anything if you don't give it your all?"

She stared at him, surprised. In his dark, smiling eyes, she saw no criticism or condescension. Just acceptance. And admiration. Her self-consciousness evaporated.

"I think I've got a couple of beers in my fridge. Would you like to stop by and have one?"

"Sure. That would be great. All I've got in my fridge right now is ketchup."

Julia laughed, feeling ridiculously happy and carefree, despite everything going on in her life at the moment. *Must be all the endorphins released during softball practice. What else could it be?*

When they reached her house, she told Alex to help himself to a beer from the fridge, and then excused herself to clean up. She changed into a clean T-shirt and jeans, then washed her hands and face and brushed her shoulder-length hair into some semblance of order.

When she returned to the kitchen, Alex and Ava were sitting at the kitchen table, Alex with a can of beer in front of him and her daughter with a glass of milk. Ava chattered about her day, about her teacher and the kids in her kindergarten class. He listened attentively, as if he were vitally interested in finger painting.

"My friend Natalie said her Mommy was sick,"

Ava said suddenly, her conversation abruptly veering away from the exploits of her kindergarten class. “That’s why she didn’t come to softball practice tonight.”

At the kitchen counter, Julia’s knife stilled as she cut cheddar cheese into cubes. She gave Ava a smile.

“Natalie’s dad said Edie had a headache, honey. That’s why she didn’t come out tonight.”

“Natalie said she was crying.”

She looked up sharply. “Edie was crying?”

Ava nodded solemnly. “Natalie didn’t feel like playing. She just sat on the swing.”

Alex placed his large hand on Ava’s tiny shoulder. “Sometimes a headache can feel very bad, Sweet Pea. It can make people cry.”

Julia set the plate of cheese on the table along with another containing raw vegetables and a small bowl of hummus dip, then grabbed a beer for herself from the fridge. She sat in one of the kitchen chairs, her appetite abandoning her. What was going on with Edie?

“Alex is right, honey. A migraine is a very bad headache. That’s probably what Edie has. It will go away soon.” At least she hoped so. She’d call her later and make sure she was okay.

A change of subject was in order. “You’re quite the ball player, Alex. You said you played in college?”

“Yeah. I played baseball from the time I was Ava’s age. I was crazy about it as a kid. In fact, at one point in my teens I even considered going pro.”

She could see him in the big leagues. He certainly had the height and the strength needed, along with a competitive nature that rivaled hers. “So what made you change your mind? Why did you go into medicine instead?"

He shrugged. "Getting to the big leagues was a long shot, at best. But then a couple of things happened. I hurt my knee and was out of commission for several months. And my grandfather had his first heart attack. I was impressed with the doctors and the medical staff who looked after him, and for the first time I thought seriously about doing something other than playing baseball. And my dad was a doctor. Maybe I wanted to follow in his footsteps."

"Well, baseball's loss is Lobster Cove's gain. The world needs doctors more than it needs professional baseball players. Do you ever regret it?"

"You mean not pursuing a baseball career? No, not really. For the most part, I love my work. Though sometimes I think it would be nice to make the money that players in the bigs make."

"Please, don't talk to me about money. Try being a teacher. Then you can complain about low wages."

He lifted his beer can and clinked it against hers. "*Touché*, Principal Stewart."

"You said your grandfather had his first heart attack. He had more?"

"Yes, one more. Unfortunately, it was fatal."

"I'm so sorry. Were you close?"

Alex took another sip of beer and then nodded. "Yeah, we were. When I was a little younger than Ava, my dad was killed in a car accident. My mother couldn't afford the mortgage payments on our house in La Jolla on one paycheck, so she sold the house, and we moved in with Nona and Tato in Chula Vista. I missed my dad a lot, but having my grandfather in my life eased the pain for me a little."

Julia reached for a carrot stick. “Does your grandmother still live in the same house?”

“Oh, yeah,” Alex said with a smile. “All her friends are in the neighborhood, her church is there, and with the exception of my mother, her children all live close by.”

“How many children does your grandmother have?”

“Two daughters and four sons. My mother is the youngest, and the only one who had less then four children. I’ve got twenty-four cousins, and most of them live in Chula Vista.”

Fascinating. “It must be fun, coming from a large family. My mother was an only child and my dad only has one sister. She lives in Boston. Her son, my only cousin, lives in Boston too, but I hardly know him.”

“It was great having so much family around when I was a kid. There was always a cousin or six to play with. Nona and Tato’s house always seemed to be full of people, and Nona was always cooking.”

“It sounds wonderful. So how come your mother doesn’t live in the same neighborhood where the rest of her family lives?”

He sighed and drained his beer can. “She works at UC San Diego in La Jolla, so it’s an easier commute to live there. She’s also in a more upscale neighborhood. She’s always been the kind of person who’s wanted more—more house, more clothes, more fancy vacations, you name it. You might have noticed that my last name isn’t exactly Hispanic sounding.”

She grinned. “Yes, I did notice that.”

“My mother has always found being of Mexican descent”—he glanced at Ava as if measuring his words

—"difficult. She went out of her way to get out of my grandparents' neighborhood and pass as anything but Mexican. She met my father when she first began working at the university. She was a secretary in the math department, and he was a medical student, on his way to a career in medicine."

"And it was love at first sight?"

"Pretty much, from what I've heard. Unfortunately, their happily ever after didn't last long. They were only married six years."

He'd suffered some terrible losses at a very young age. "I'm sorry, Alex."

He waved his hand and shrugged. "It was a long time ago."

"Do you get along with your mother now?"

Alex sighed, his mouth twisting. "It's… complicated. She was disappointed when I went into emergency medicine rather than specializing in something more lucrative. And I've never hit it off with her husband Tom. She remarried when I was eleven, and we moved back to La Jolla. But I missed my grandparents and my cousins. By the time I was fourteen I was taller than Tom, and I wasn't afraid to stand up to him anymore. We had a few"—he glanced at Ava again—"disagreements. I moved back in with Nona and Tato just before I turned fifteen. Unfortunately, my grandfather died later that year."

He stared at his beer can as if lost in thought, and Julia felt guilty for making him remember sad events in his life. Time to change the subject once again.

"So what's this I hear about you volunteering at the free clinic in Bar Harbor?"

"No big deal. Dr. Manning asked if I could help

out, and since I don't have much of a social life, I had the time to volunteer."

Julia winced at his comment. "You must think life is deadly dull in Maine."

"It's more like *I'm* deadly dull. I've been either going to school or working crazy shifts for so long, I've forgotten what a social life is. I'm going to try to remedy that this summer. Joining the ball team is a good first step."

"You'll like our team. They're a good bunch. You'll have fun."

"Then there's you."

Julia's breath caught in her throat at the look in his eyes. He looked *interested* in her, and not just in her skills as a softball player. She couldn't even manage to squeak out a response.

"What about me, Dr. Alex? I wanna be your friend, too," Ava said, kneeling on her chair to lay her hand on his shoulder.

He tore his eyes away from Julia to grin at her daughter. "You are absolutely my friend, Sweet Pea."

She launched herself into his arms, and Alex laughed as he caught her and set her on his lap.

"Whoa! Be careful, Ava. You almost fell. I don't want to have to put a cast on your other arm."

"But you caught me, right?"

Julia saw a range of emotions—surprise, tenderness, regret—cross his face as he cradled Ava in his arms. "Yeah, I caught you."

"I knew you would," she said confidently. She put her arms around his neck. Alex closed his eyes and kissed the top of her head. When he opened them again, his gaze met Julia's. He looked confused, concerned.

For the first time, it seemed, he understood that he was the object of Ava's adoration.

The good doctor had just been blindsided by the love of a child. The question was, what were they going to do about it?

****

When Alex got home, he picked up his phone. He couldn't put it off any longer. He had to call his mom. Talking about her with Julia and Ava had put her in the forefront of his thoughts.

He dialed her home number, and she answered after a couple of rings.

"Alex! It's good to finally connect with you. I was beginning to think you were avoiding me."

"Of course not. I've been very busy." He hoped his nose wouldn't grow from telling the half-truth. "How have you been?"

"I'm…umm…good."

Alex didn't like the hesitation in her voice. "You don't sound very convincing."

She laughed, but it didn't sound particularly happy to Alex. "I'm wonderful. I can't wait for my wonderful son to come home."

"That's not for several months, Mom," he warned.

"I know, but I've been doing some research. If you get your application in now, you can apply for training in one of the specialties and be ready to begin by July first of next year."

Not again. He tried to keep his voice level and calm. "Mom, we've talked about this before. I'm not interested in cardiology or surgery, or whatever other specialty has you so excited. I like emergency medicine, and I'm really starting to enjoy family medicine."

"But just think of the money you could make as a surgeon or cardiologist. And you wouldn't be working those wretched hours in the ER, trying to save gang-bangers intent on killing each other."

"It's not all about the money, Mom. It's about enjoying what I do, and being totally engaged by my work."

"How can you enjoy the stress of having someone's life in your hands?"

Alex sighed. "I hate to break it to you, Mom, but cardiologists and surgeons hold the lives of their patients in their hands, too. The more money you make, the more stress."

"What about dermatology? Nice and safe, good office hours."

"Dermatology? Mom, what are you talking about?"

He heard her sigh. "I just want you to be happy, Alex. And trust me, making good money is part of being happy."

They'd had this talk over and over again for years. It was time to put a stop to it. "Mom, listen to me. I'm not going back to school. I've already had years of education and training, and I'm happy with what I do. I've also got a mountain of debt I'm working really hard to pay off, and I don't want to add to it. So let's just drop the whole thing. I don't want to talk about it anymore."

"But Alex—"

"Enough! I told you, I don't want to talk about it anymore."

"You're making a mistake, Alejandro."

"Enough, Mom!" Could they not even have a five-minute conversation without it turning into a shouting match? “Look, I should probably get going. I’ll call you again soon.”

“All right.” She sounded resigned, sad even. Alex’s heart twisted with guilt.

“I love you, Mom.”

“I love you, too, honey. Goodbye.”

“Bye.”

He *did* love his mother. He just wished he could understand her.

Chapter Eight

The next morning Alex checked the particulars on the medical file before entering the examining room. Edie Cosgrove, thirty-three years old, three deliveries in seven years. Reason for visit today: lump in left breast.

He knocked lightly, and when he heard a muffled "Come in," he opened the door and stepped inside. Edie Cosgrove sat on the edge of the examining table wearing a paper gown tied in the front with a plastic ribbon. Alex extended his hand.

"Hi, Edie. I'm Alex Campbell."

Edie's grip was strong and her smile friendly. "I've been looking forward to meeting you. My husband Aaron has spoken highly of your softball skills."

The pieces clicked into place. "So you're the Edie I've heard so much about. I've been told you're quite the softball player."

Her smile disappeared. "I love playing ball. I'd hoped to meet you on the diamonds rather than here."

"That would have been my preference, too. Tell me what's going on."

Her hand went to her left breast. "I have a small lump, here. I breastfed all three of my children, so I was familiar with lumps that popped up and then quickly went away. But this one is different. It's hard, for one thing, and there's a little discomfort if I press on it. And it hasn't gone away."

"Are you breastfeeding now?"

"No, I finished weaning my youngest a couple of months ago. That's when I first noticed the lump. Actually Aaron was the one who first noticed the lump," she said, her cheeks turning pink. "I kept thinking it was going to go away like the others I'd had when I was nursing, but it hasn't."

"Let's figure out what's going on," Alex said. "I'm going to call in a nurse, and then I'll do a physical examination of the breast. Lie down on the table, and I'll be back in a minute. Try to relax."

Edie gave him a sardonic grin. "Sure, no problem."

He returned her smile. "I'll be right back."

A few minutes later he returned with Susan, his nurse. Alex smiled at Edie, trying to put her at ease. "Can you lift your arms overhead? I'm going to rip the gown a little so I can do the exam." He rubbed his hands together. "I'll apologize in advance for the cold hands."

"I won't hold it against you."

He chuckled, then ripped the gown so he could palpate each breast. He started with the right breast and, using the pads of his fingers, moved his hand in a circular motion, starting at the nipple and moving outward until he reached nearly to the collarbone and under the armpit. He felt nothing out of the ordinary. But when he moved to the left breast, he felt a hard lump below the aureole. Edie winced slightly.

"Is that the spot you were talking about?"

"Yes."

"It's uncomfortable to the touch?"

"Yes."

"Can you tell if it's gotten any bigger since you

first noticed it two months ago?"

"I don't think so." Edie bit her lip. "Is that a good thing?"

He smiled. "It's always a good thing. Have you noticed any other changes?"

"I've lost weight recently. No matter what I eat, I keep losing. And I'm tired, but that's probably because I've got three kids seven and under." She placed her hand over her left breast. "This breast seems to have become a little bigger than the other one."

Classic breast cancer symptoms. He tried to hide his concern with a smile. "Edie, I'm going to send you for some further testing. This lump is probably just a benign cyst of some sort, but I like to cover all my bases."

"As any good softball player would do."

He laughed at her comment on his unintended pun. He liked her. "Why don't you get dressed and wait here, and I'll come back after Susan sets you up with some appointments. Okay?"

"Okay."

Alex saw two more patients while Susan lined up appointments for Edie. He took the information she handed him and returned to Edie's room, knocking first before entering. She sat on the edge of her chair, her back straight and stiff. He took his seat at the desk.

"I'm sending you for a mammogram and a fine-needle biopsy. A technician will insert a very fine needle into the lump and withdraw material. Our pathologist will examine the material, and we'll go from there." He handed her the information about the times and places of her appointments.

She took the piece of paper and tucked it into her

purse. "Thank you. I'm not crazy about being poked with a needle, but at least I'll get some answers, one way or another."

"You will, but like I said, it's probably a benign cyst. I don't want you to worry."

"Too late for that," she said with a wan smile, "but I appreciate your concern. Tracy said you were a terrific doctor, and now I see she was right."

"You mean Tracy Novak?"

"Yes, we've been friends since we were kids. She and I and Julia Stewart. We're very close. Tracy mentioned you've been seeing Julia." Her eyes twinkled.

"No, not exactly seeing her. We've had a couple of beers after games, that's all." He shifted uncomfortably in his chair.

"Julia's a very special person. She deserves someone very special in her life." She took a deep breath and got to her feet. "So how long till I get the results of the mammogram and the fine-needle biopsy?"

"A few days after you have the procedures done. I'll have Susan call you when the results are in. If you need further testing, I'll get her to set up another appointment for you to see me again."

"You mean if the biopsy finds cancer."

There was no sugar-coating it. "Yes."

She took another deep breath, her face turning pale. Mention of the C-word tended to do that to people.

"In that case, I hope to never see you again, Dr. Campbell."

He laughed. "Me too. Unless it's on the ball diamond."

"Absolutely."

****

On Saturday morning, Chloe Sykes arrived to keep Ava amused while Julia worked on her proposed sex education unit of the health curriculum. Even though her proposal had been rejected, she wasn't ready to throw in the towel. She'd keep fighting for it, and if someone wanted to know what such a curriculum would look like, she'd be prepared to show them. Since there was no such curriculum in place in the area, she was going to adapt one already approved by the Maine Department of Education and used in other parts of the state.

A few weeks ago, she would have asked her parents to watch Ava. But her days of relying on them for child care were over. She simply couldn't take the chance of Ava getting hurt again.

Chloe took Ava to the playground for an hour, and after that they played quietly in the house and in the yard. At noon, Julia looked up from her laptop to glance out the window of the second floor spare bedroom she'd set up as an office. The girls were building a castle in the sandbox. Chloe looked as if she was having as much fun as Ava. She was sixteen, with a woman's body but the heart of a child.

Julia called them inside and made grilled cheese sandwiches and chicken noodle soup for the three of them. After lunch she paid Chloe and made a date for her to babysit again the following Saturday morning. With a smile and a hug for Ava, she left for home.

"So, what do you say we clean up the lunch dishes and then go see how Grandma and Grandpa Dawson are today?"

"Okay," Ava said. "But you're not going to leave

me there, are you?"

"No, sweetheart. We're just going to visit for a little while and then come home. Together. Okay?"

Ava appeared mollified. "Okay."

Ever since her accident, Ava had been reluctant to visit her grandparents. In fact, the night she'd taken her father to the hospital with chest pains, Ava had begged to go to the hospital with her instead of being left with her grandmother. Julia was ashamed now when she remembered her daughter's tear-streaked face.

At the time she'd been concerned about her father's health and thought her daughter was being unreasonable. She'd believed she would be fine with her mother. Of course that was before her father's reaction to leaving them alone together, and the "sleep-walking" incident at Alex's house. Even though there had been no further incidents, she hadn't left Ava alone with them since.

The social worker, Helen Murray, had visited with her parents, and her father had agreed to take her mother to Dr. Willson for testing. But he was dragging his feet, coming up with excuses to avoid making an appointment.

They walked the two blocks to her parents' house. Julia noticed that Alex's car was gone. He was likely at the hospital, or possibly at the free clinic. She couldn't seem to stop thinking about him, wondering what he was doing. Seeing him at softball practices had become the highlight of her week.

Stop it! Maybe Ava wasn't the only one who was becoming too attached to the temporary doctor.

She pushed open the door of her parents' house and stepped inside.

"Hello? Anybody home?" she called.

Her father appeared around the corner. "My two favorite girls. How are you?"

Julia gave her father a hug. "We're great. How are you and Mom?"

"We're fine. Come on in. Can I make you some tea?"

"Sure. Where's Mom?"

"She's in the bathroom, I think." He put the kettle on the stove to boil. "I'll let her know you're here."

Julia poured Ava a glass of milk, then pulled her mother's favorite teapot from the cupboard along with a container of teabags. She could hear her parents' hushed voices, but they hadn't re-emerged from upstairs. Was something wrong? If they hadn't come downstairs by the time the kettle boiled, she was going up after them.

Ava pointed to the window in the oven door. "Mommy, what's in the oven?"

"In the oven?" She crouched to take a look. There was definitely something in there, though the stove was cool to the touch. "I don't know, sweetheart. Let's take a look."

She opened the door and found the oven packed from top to bottom with canned goods of all kinds—soups, vegetables, fruit, meat. *What the hell?* The racks had been removed to allow the maximum number of cans to be stuffed in. Cans were sitting directly on the element. If someone turned on the oven, the labels could catch fire, or the cans explode. What was going on?

Her mother and father entered the kitchen at that moment. Dora smiled at Julia, her face lighting up when she saw her. She put her arms around her in a warm embrace.

"Julia! There's my girl! I haven't seen you in so long."

Julia hugged her back, surprised by her comment and the show of emotion since she'd been by the previous day to see her.

"Nice to see you too, Mom." She pulled herself from her mother's arms, and turned to face the open oven door. "Why is the oven full of canned goods? It could be dangerous if someone turns on the oven. Did you put them in there?"

Dora stared blankly at the oven. Paul put an arm around her shoulders.

"I put them in there."

"Why on earth would you do that?" Julia asked, incredulous.

"You know we don't have a lot of storage space in this kitchen. We used to keep extra supplies in the basement, but I got tired of going up and down those steep stairs. We hardly use the oven anymore, so I figured why not utilize the space."

It sounded plausible. Yet…

"How are you going to make sure no one turns on the oven by accident?"

"I'll take out the element. Then you won't have to worry about it."

Julia wondered why he hadn't done that before stuffing in all the cans. "Yes, that would be a good idea." She made herself smile, not wanting to upset them. "I could use a cup of tea. How about you?"

They sat at the kitchen table, the adults drinking tea and Ava having a glass of milk with her cookies. Julia's father played a card game with Ava.

"I planted red geraniums in the garden, didn't I, Paul?"

"You certainly did."

Dora toyed with her cup. "They're so pretty. Did I plant those geraniums?"

"Yes, you planted them, Dora," Julia's father said.

She drank some of her tea. "Did I plant those geraniums?"

Julia couldn't stand it any longer.

"Dad, when are you going to take Mom to see a doctor?"

Both parents stared at her, Dora in confusion and Paul in irritation. He pushed away from the table.

"Can't you get it through your head that we're fine?"

"Dad—"

"I think you should go, Julia. Your mother is tired. It's time for her nap."

"Come on, Dad. Can't we talk about this?"

He lifted his chin, his expression icy. "There's nothing to talk about."

"There's everything to talk about!"

"No!" His face turned red with anger. "It's bad enough you sent over a social worker to spy on us, as if we need a babysitter. *I* can look after us just fine! I've been doing it for years, and I intend to keep on doing it."

Julia looked from her mother's bewildered face to her daughter's frightened one, and then to her father's angry and hurt expression. She hadn't meant to upset all three of them like this, but it was obvious to her now that her mother wasn't well. Why was he fighting so hard to deny there was a problem?

It was pointless to continue arguing. It would only upset her father more and possibly make him ill.

“Okay Dad, I’m leaving.”

She put her arm around his neck and hugged, and to her relief he hugged her back. “I love you, Dad.”

“I love you too, baby.”

After kissing her mother goodbye, she and Ava walked home. Ava was quiet and held her hand tightly, as if she was afraid to let go.

Her mother’s health problems had a profound effect on all of them. She wished her father could see that.

****

As soon as the cast technician turned on the saw, Ava snatched her arm away, her eyes growing wide with fear.

“No!” she shouted.

The technician turned off the offending machine. “I promise it won’t hurt you. It only cuts the cast so we can take it off your arm. It won’t touch your skin.”

Ava was having none of it. As tears rolled down her cheeks, she cradled her cast with her good arm and turned her body away. Julia put her arm around her small shoulders.

“It’s okay, honey. It really isn’t going to hurt. You know I wouldn’t let anyone hurt you.”

“I want Dr. Alex,” Ava managed through her tears.

“Honey, Dr. Alex is busy. We don’t want to bother him. You’ll be fine, I promise.”

“Nooo! I want Dr. Alex.” Her cries took on a high-pitched edge that bordered on hysteria. Her body shook uncontrollably.

Julia rubbed her back, trying to think what to do. This was more than a temper tantrum. Ava was genuinely terrified. "Easy, honey, easy."

"I can call down to the ER and see if Dr. Campbell is in today," the technician offered with a kind smile. "If not, we'll reschedule for another time."

Julia hesitated. She didn't want to bother Alex at work. More importantly, she didn't want to acknowledge to him or anyone else how important he was to Ava.

But what choice did she have, with Ava making herself sick with fear?

She nodded at the technician, and the young woman picked up the phone and pushed a few buttons. After speaking to someone on the other end, she said, "Dr. Campbell will be up in a few minutes."

Julia swallowed. She didn't know whether to be relieved, embarrassed, grateful, or just plain worried. Alex was dropping everything to ease her daughter's distress. Word that he'd come to their rescue like a knight in shining armor was bound to spread through the hospital like a virus. Soon everyone from Lobster Cove to Bar Harbor would be talking about her. She could practically hear the rumors:

They're sleeping together.

Why shouldn't Dr. Campbell get a little action while he's in town?

She's using her kid to reel him in.

It won't last any longer than her marriage did.

Julia took a long, shaking breath. She couldn't bear to be the object of gossip. Not again. When her marriage ended so suddenly, people had talked. She'd found it humiliating to be gossiped about. And it hurt.

A lot.

Alex swept into the cast room, his eyes meeting hers as soon as he walked in. He quickly shifted his attention to Ava, who huddled against Julia's side, her body still trembling with hiccupping sobs. Alex gently lifted her cast-covered hand and squeezed her fingers.

"What's this I hear about you not liking the cast saw?"

"It's scary," Ava whimpered.

"Why is it so scary?"

"It's gonna hurt like when I broke my arm."

"No, it's not," he said patiently. "I promise it won't hurt. How 'bout if I hold you on my lap while Amanda is taking off the cast? I'll make sure she doesn't hurt you." This was said with an apologetic smile to the cast technician.

Ava took a shuddering intake of breath. "Promise you'll stay?"

"I promise, Sweet Pea."

"Okay," she said in a small voice.

"Good." He rapped her cast with his knuckles. "Let's get rid of this thing."

He scooped her into his arms and sat beside Julia on the examining table with Ava on his lap. Julia was very aware of him, of the solid strength of his thigh next to hers, of his clean, masculine scent, and the warmth of his body. A sudden desire assailed her. She wanted to bury her face into his chest just as Ava was doing, to let him hold her and look after her. But that wasn't possible.

Instead, she eased off the table and put a little distance between them.

Amanda started the vibrating saw once more. Alex

held Ava securely, bending over to whisper in her ear. Julia couldn't hear what he said, but whatever reassurances he offered seemed to work. Ava held her arm still as Amanda made two lengthwise cuts to either side of the fiberglass surface of the cast, then used spreaders to pry it open. After cutting open the inside netting and cotton padding with scissors, she removed the cast from Ava's arm. The whole procedure took no more than five minutes.

"That wasn't so bad, was it, Sweet Pea?" Alex said.

"Not so bad," Ava conceded.

"Good." He kissed the top of her head. "I've got to get back to work."

Setting her on the table, he hopped down and headed for the door. As he turned the doorknob, Julia finally found her voice.

"Thank you."

He looked up, and their gazes collided. She saw a flash of longing in his eyes, and she wondered if a similar emotion shone in her own eyes. With a curt nod, he opened the door and left the room.

Amanda washed the cast residue from Ava's arm and dried it with a towel. Finally it was over. Julia thanked her for her kindness, took Ava's hand, and hurried from the hospital.

Her stomach was tied up in knots as they drove home. She wondered if the cast technician would gossip about how Dr. Campbell held her daughter in his arms while she removed the cast. Even if she didn't, others in the hospital likely would. It didn't matter to the gossips that they hadn't slept together. There would still be talk.

And, once more, all her private fears and hopes

would be exposed for public display.

****

Melissa Maloney's face was taut with worry when Alex stepped into the examining room. She wore a bright red knitted hat over her head, which struck him as strange since it was at least seventy-five degrees outside. According to the chart, she was here to see him for another urinary tract infection. She looked like she was in serious discomfort.

"No offense, but I was hoping you wouldn't darken my examining room door with another UTI. It's pretty bad, isn't it?"

She nodded, and her lower lip quivered. "I thought I had it under control. I was drinking the cranberry juice like you said, and it seemed to work for a time, and then *bam*, it started again."

He looked over her chart. Was there something he was missing here?

"We'll try another antibiotic and see if works any better."

"Okay." She shifted uncomfortably. "Is forgetfulness a symptom of a urinary tract infection? I feel so foggy sometimes I can barely function. Yesterday at work I went down to the storeroom to get some supplies, but by the time I got there, for the life of me, I couldn't remember why I was there."

"Has this happened to you before?"

She nodded and looked away. "I'm so tired all the time. I thought it was just life, you know. Like you said, Busy Mom Syndrome. But some days I can barely get out of bed. I know I'm not giving my all at work, but I end up running out of gas before I run out of day. My boss has started to notice. I'm scared I'm going to lose my job." A tear trickled down her cheek.

"If you need me to write you a note for work, I can do that. Maybe it'll keep your boss off your back."

She nodded again. He composed a quick note on the clinic stationery, signed it, and handed it to her. Then he took her blood pressure and temperature. Like the last time, they were both in the high normal range. He wrote another script for antibiotics and handed it to her.

"We're going to figure this thing out. I don't think we have any choice but to do some more investigation, do you?"

Reluctantly, she nodded. "I guess you're right."

"Good." He began writing an order for the lab. "We're going to do a more thorough urine and blood workup, to start, and see what it shows us."

"Okay." Her lip quivered once more. "Do you know the worst of it?"

"What?"

Her face was full of anguish. "This."

She pulled off the knitted hat. Patches of hair had fallen out, leaving bald spots all over her scalp. Tears streamed down her face.

"I used to have such beautiful hair. My crowning glory, my mother called it. Now look at me!"

What the hell was going on?

He squeezed her shoulder. "We'll find out what's going on, Melissa. I promise."

She nodded, and wiped her eyes with her fingers, taking a deep breath to try to get herself under control. Alex handed her a tissue. She blew her nose, then pushed her arms into the sleeves of her sweater.

"That's a heavy sweater to be wearing on a warm

day like today," he said. "Are you cold?"

"Not really, but I've got some eczema on my elbows and I don't want people to see it." Another tear rolled down her cheek and she dabbed at it with the tissue. "I'm freaky-looking enough right now."

"Can I see your elbows?" Was this eczema related to her other symptoms?

"Sure." She removed her sweater and bent her arms so he could see. A red, scaly rash covered the entire area around both elbows. The lesions were thick and crusty. "Does it hurt or itch?"

"No, not really. Mostly it's just ugly. Do you think it's important?"

"I'm not sure. Have you always had problems with eczema?"

"No. It popped up about a year, maybe a year and half ago."

"A year and a half ago? So, around the time you started having trouble with urinary tract infections?"

Melissa blinked at him. "Yeah, I guess it was. Dr. Sato gave me some cream for it, and it went away for a while. It only came back again this spring."

"Did it get worse when you were out in the sunshine?"

"I suppose it did. I noticed it a few days after I planted some flowers in my garden." She shifted uncomfortably again. "Doc, are we done here? I really need to use the washroom."

"Yes, of course. We'll talk again once I get the results of your lab work. We *are* going to figure this out, Melissa."

Her eyes welled with tears once more. "Okay. Bye, Doc. Thanks."

When Melissa left the room, Alex made some notes in her file. He had a hunch that the rash on Melissa's elbows was the key to understanding what was going on inside her body.

Chapter Nine

The last day of school came as a relief. It had been a rocky school year, full of controversy, struggles, and failures, and Julia was glad to see it end.

But the tribulations weren't over yet. She needed the summer break to get ready for the storms that were sure to explode in the fall when the daycare opened. A couple of her teachers, like Ralph Sykes, adamantly opposed it. Fortunately, the majority of her teachers supported her, enough to ensure the daycare's success. She hoped.

She had a lot of work to do this summer, but right now all she wanted to do was have some fun. Tonight was their first actual softball game, against their arch rivals from Bar Harbor.

Julia held the bat high and scowled at the pitcher, doing her best to intimidate. She knew it likely had little effect on him. At five foot three and a hundred and ten pounds soaking wet, she didn't have the physical presence to intimidate anyone. Sometimes it was an advantage. Because of her diminutive size and because she was a woman, she was often underestimated. They soon discovered she was no pushover. In the classroom and the boardroom, she'd learned to use her brains and her quick wit to let people know they couldn't push her around.

But at the moment, all she wanted was a safe hit.

She let a couple of strikes pass by, hoping to lull the Bar Harbor pitcher into complacency. It wouldn't be the first time her hitting ability had been misjudged.

A fat strike rolled down the middle of the plate, and she saw her chance. She swung hard and connected with the ball, sending it over the second baseman's head. As she stood on first base, she gave the pitcher an innocent smile when he glared at her. He probably wouldn't underestimate her again.

The game ended with a satisfying score of six runs to four in favor of her team. Alex had hit a home run that brought in two runs, and had pitched, as well, since Edie had decided not to play this season. Julia had been shocked when Aaron announced she was staying home with the baby this summer instead of playing ball. She told herself that Edie had three kids now, and her priorities had shifted. But she couldn't quite accept it. The old Edie would have bundled baby number three into her stroller and brought her to the ball diamond the way she'd brought Michael and Natalie when they were that age. Sometimes, back then, Edie's mother came to their games and watched the kids while Edie and Aaron played, or sometimes she'd kept them at her house. Edie had always found a way to play. Julia couldn't stop worrying about her. She had a bad feeling that something was wrong, but whenever she called Edie she claimed everything was fine.

The only bright spot was that Tracy had been able to make tonight's game, and they'd had a lot of fun. Especially since they won.

"Would you like to come over for a beer?" she asked Tracy as they took off their cleats. "I've got some cold ones in the fridge."

"I'll have to take a rain check," Tracy said as she slipped on her sandals. "I'm working an early shift tomorrow. I've got to go home and do some laundry so I have a clean uniform to wear. Another time?"

"Of course. Talk to you later."

With a wave, Tracy headed to her car. Julia called to Ava, and she came running from the playground. She was dismayed to see her daughter's clothes were covered in sand and dirt, and she even had sand in her hair. Julia wiped at Ava's clothes with her hand.

"What on earth were you doing over there?"

"Tommy buried me in the sand. We were pretending we were at the beach. That's what you do at the beach."

"Oh, really?" Maybe she'd have a little chat with Tommy's mother.

She nodded solemnly. "Can we go to the beach?"

Julia gently ruffled her daughter's silky blonde hair, trying to brush away the sand. "Sure. The first nice hot day we'll go. But nobody's getting buried in the sand."

"Okay, Mommy."

She skipped ahead while Julia made sure her duffle bag contained all her equipment before she slung it over her shoulder. To her surprise, Alex came up behind her and slipped the bag from her shoulder.

"Let me carry that for you. It's heavy."

She blinked at him. "Oh. Okay. Thanks."

"Do you have time to come over to my place for a beer? I owe you."

She wanted to say yes, to throw caution to the wind. Alex was the first man who had stirred the cold embers of her libido since her divorce three years ago.

But she couldn't allow any relationship between them to go past the friendship stage.

"Thanks, but I need to get Ava home and throw her in the tub. She got a little carried away in the sandbox."

"Mind if I tag along?"

Warning bells went off in her head. Were they starting to make a habit of getting together after a game? "It's going to take a while to get her cleaned up. I need to wash her hair."

"That's fine. I should probably have a shower, too. I'll run back to my place and get cleaned up and grab some beer. By the time I get to your place, you'll have finished bathing Ava."

She scrambled for an excuse. "The house is kind of a mess."

"I'm not planning on critiquing your housekeeping skills." He paused, and she heard his sigh. "I'm sorry. I didn't mean to impose. It's just that I enjoy talking with you after our games, and I thought… That's okay. Forget about it."

Now she felt like she'd kicked a puppy. "Alex, I do want you to come over for a beer, especially if you're supplying them. I'm just a little worried, that's all."

"What do you mean? What are you worried about?"

She took a furtive look behind her to make sure no one could hear them. "This is a small town, you know. People talk."

"Yeah, so?"

"I'm the principal of the school. That means I have to maintain a spotless reputation."

"What are they going to talk about? We're having a couple of beers. Not much excitement in that."

"In reality, no, but on the gossip grapevine having a beer together after a game translates to having a steamy affair. If they see you coming to my house once, maybe even twice, it might be overlooked. But if it gets to be a habit, they're going to think something's going on between us. It's like playing with fire."

He gave her an incredulous look. "Seriously, Julia? How would anyone even know I went to your house? Are you under surveillance or something?"

"The next best thing—nosy neighbors." He deserved to know the rest of her concerns. She lowered her voice, not wanting her daughter to hear. "My reputation is a real concern for me, but it's not the only thing I'm worried about. I'm worried about Ava. She's becoming very attached to you. What happens when you leave in a few months? If I let this bond between the two of you flourish, she's going to be devastated when you go. She's barely six. She doesn't understand."

Alex didn't reply for several long minutes. Behind the frantic beating of her heart, Julia was aware of the sound of their footsteps against the cement sidewalk, the call of a crow in a nearby tree. Someone was barbecuing, and the smell made her hungry. She heard Alex's steady breath as he walked beside her.

"The last thing I want to do is to upset Ava. Or you. I guess I'll see you at the next game."

He took her duffle bag from his shoulder and held it out to her. Julia stared at it. She should pick up the bag, say thank you and goodnight, and walk away. Quickly.

She should. She really should.

"Listen," she heard herself say, "just don't call her

Sweet Pea anymore, you know?"

Don't make my daughter fall in love with you. Don't break her heart.

He seemed to understand. Nodding, he placed the bag back on his shoulder. "I'll be careful with her."

"Good. That's good."

They walked in silence until they reached her house. Alex handed her the bag and this time she took it from him. "So I'll see you in a little while?"

"In about a half hour or so. Is that all right?"

"It's great. See you then."

Julia and Ava walked to their front door. After letting Ava inside, she stood on the step for a moment and watched Alex walk down the sidewalk. A curious mixture of trepidation and excitement filled her chest. She hoped that by inviting him back to her house today she hadn't just made the biggest future regret of her life.

****

Forty minutes later, Alex arrived at Julia's house, a six-pack of cold beer in one hand. His knock was answered by Ava, who wore a charming gap-toothed smile along with her yellow cotton pajamas. Her damp hair was beginning to curl in ringlets as it dried.

"Hi, Dr. Alex!" she said holding the door open wide. "My Mommy said to tell you to sit down in the kitchen. We made sandwiches. She said to help yourself. She's having a shower."

An instant visual flashed through his head. Julia smiling in pleasure as she turned her beautiful face to the warm spray, her slim, naked body dripping with water. Blinking, he struggled to dispel the vision, focusing his attention instead on Ava.

"Thanks, Swe—Ava."

He followed her into the kitchen and, taking a can of beer for himself, placed the rest on the table. Ava opened the fridge and pulled out a plate, placing it in front of him.

"Mommy made this for you."

Alex pulled the plastic wrap from the sandwich and found ham and cheese on rye. "Thanks. I'm starved."

While he ate, Ava munched on carrot sticks and chattered about her friends at the playground. "My friend Tommy went to Disneyland at spring break this year."

"Oh, yeah?"

"That's in California, you know," she said sagely.

"So I've heard. Would you like to go to Disneyland?"

She gave an enthusiastic nod. "Tommy said it was fun. He went on lots of rides. And then they went to Sea World and saw the dolphins and whales."

"That's in San Diego, where I'm from."

"Is California far away?"

"Yes, very far. I wish it was closer so I could visit my mom and my grandmother."

"Did you go to Disneyland when you were little?"

"No, I didn't. I've never been to Disneyland." His mother hadn't had the time or money for frivolities like Disneyland. "Did you know that in San Diego, where I grew up, it never snows and it's almost always warm?"

Ava's blue eyes grew round with wonder. "Maybe Mommy will take me to California."

"I hope you get to go. You'd like it." Alex could imagine taking Julia and Ava for a walk on the beach along the bay. He'd love to show them around his world, introduce them to his grandmother—

Stop.

What was he doing? He'd only known Julia Stewart a short time, and during part of that time they'd had some serious misgivings about each other. They hadn't even gone on a date, or kissed. Why would he be thinking about taking her home to meet his grandmother?

Because Julia was the kind of woman who made a man think about family and forever. He already knew her life was here, and he had no intention of staying in Lobster Cove. So what was he doing in her kitchen?

Julia walked into the kitchen, her blonde hair still wet from her shower. She'd changed into a white T-shirt and pink shorts that showed off shapely, toned legs. She smiled at him, and Alex realized he was in her kitchen because he didn't want to be anywhere else.

"Thanks for the sandwich. It was delicious."

"I'm glad you liked it." She helped herself to a beer. "I'm not the greatest cook, but I can usually manage not to mess up a sandwich. Thanks for the beer, by the way."

"You're welcome. You don't like cooking?"

"Day-to-day cooking feels more like a chore to me than a pleasure. But strangely, I do enjoy cooking a holiday meal, or having people over for a barbecue. Unfortunately, I only have a few recipes that I do well."

"My grandmother is the greatest cook. She taught me how to make some simple Mexican dishes like fish tacos and guacamole. Someday I'm going to learn how to make Chicken Mole the way she does."

"Any time you need someone to test your efforts, Ava and I will be happy to volunteer."

He grinned. "I'll keep that in mind."

She opened a bag of potato chips and put them in a bowl. "You've talked about your mother's side of the family. What about your relatives on your Campbell side—your father's family? Have you kept in touch with them?"

"My dad's parents lived somewhere in northern California, I'm not even sure where. I only remember seeing them once, maybe twice. After Dad died, we lost contact with them. I don't know if my mother didn't make the effort, or if they just weren't interested."

"Have you ever thought about looking them up? Your grandparents might be gone now, but maybe there's other family," Julia said.

"Yeah, I've thought of it. I know my dad had two brothers, and I've always wanted to meet them. It's something I hope to do someday." He paused and took a sip of beer, the memories flowing. "As much as I loved my grandparents, my life was never the same after my father died. I don't remember much about him, other than little fragments of memories. I remember he was always smiling or laughing, and even my mother smiled more when she was around him. We were happy together."

Julia covered his hand with hers in a gesture of silent support. He was surprised at the memories that were pouring out of him. He hadn't thought of his father, and about losing him, in a long time, couldn't remember the last time he'd talked about him. All he knew was that Julia was easy to talk to. She listened without judgment, like a trusted friend he'd known for years instead of just a few months.

Ava laid her small hand on his arm, her skin pale

against his. "I don't have a daddy either. Mine lives far away now, and I don't see him."

Though she spoke in a matter-of-fact way, with little emotion, Alex saw the stricken look on Julia's face at her daughter's words. Didn't Ava's father visit her? He placed his hand over hers. "Do you miss your dad?"

She shrugged, her blue eyes solemn. "I don't know. I don't remember him."

Alex stroked her hair. How could any man abandon his child, especially one as sweet as this little girl? He fought the urge to pick her up and comfort her in his arms, knowing Julia wouldn't want him to do that. She was already worried about Ava becoming too attached to him.

He wondered if that ship had sailed. Maybe he was already in too deep.

He made himself smile. "Living with my grandparents was wonderful. I had lots of cousins to play with, and aunts and uncles who looked out for me. I had a wonderful childhood."

"I wish I had cousins," Ava said with a wistful sigh.

"Ava, you have lots of friends here in Lobster Cove, and people who love you," Julia said. He heard the hitch in her voice that she tried to cover with a smile. "You've got your grandparents, and Edie and Aaron and their kids, and Tracy and her brother Logan. You've got all your friends from school. Lots of people love you, baby."

"I know." She glanced at Alex and looked away.

Julia gently smoothed the blonde curls from her forehead. "I think it's time for you to hit the sack. Run upstairs and brush your teeth. I'll be up in a few minutes to tuck you in."

"Aw, do I have to?"

"Yes, you have to. Say goodnight and go upstairs."

Reluctantly, Ava slid off her chair and headed for the door.

"Goodnight, Dr. Alex."

"Goodnight. Sleep tight."

"You sleep tight, too."

Alex grinned, and she gave him a mischievous smile before running up the stairs. When he looked at Julia, his grin faded. Her brows were knit together in concern, the corners of her mouth pulled down in a frown. He held up his hands in mock surrender.

"Hey, I didn't call her Sweet Pea once."

She let out a long, tired sigh. "No, you didn't. I'm just surprised, I guess. I've never seen her take to someone like she has to you. She's usually pretty shy."

"It's probably because I looked after her when she broke her arm. She feels comfortable with me."

"She trusts you, you mean."

"Maybe." He knew a strong bond had developed between them. He hadn't meant for it to happen. He wasn't sure when it had happened, or why, just that it was there.

She rose from her chair. "I hate to rush you, but I should make sure Ava gets to bed."

Alex got to his feet, too. "No problem. Thanks again for the sandwich. I guess I'll see you at the next game."

"Sure."

"How are your mom and dad?"

"About the same, I guess. Dad's still deep in

denial. He's taken her to Dr. Willson for some initial medical tests, but he's been putting off making an appointment with the neurologist Dr. Willson wants her to see. And my mom is still…"

She looked away, on the verge of tears. Alex closed the distance between them and pulled her into his arms.

"It's okay. It's going to be okay."

Holding her securely with one hand around her waist, he tucked her head under his chin. She held her breath as if to keep from crying, her hands clutching the front of his T-shirt, her body tense. He slid his hand up and down her back, trying to soothe.

"It's okay if you want to cry, Julia."

"I'm afraid if I start crying I won't be able to stop," she said, sniffing.

"You don't have to be strong all the time."

She sighed and relaxed against him. "Sometimes I feel about as strong as a wet noodle. Superwoman I'm not."

He held her a little closer, burying his smile in her silky hair.

"I don't know. With a cape and some tights, you could definitely pass for a superhero. You could be Super Principal, defender of defenseless students."

He heard her chuckle. She looked up into his face, her eyes smiling into his, even though they were wet with tears.

"I couldn't be Super Principal. I look terrible in a cape."

He laughed softly. "You couldn't look terrible if you tried."

"Thank you," she said softly.

“For what?”

“For making me laugh when I felt like crying.”

“My pleasure.”

Alex’s heart thudded against his chest as she stared into his eyes. He couldn’t look away. He lifted his hand and gently trailed his fingers across her full lips, her eyes, her cheekbones.

Slowly, he lowered his mouth to hers, sighing at the feel of the softness of her lips. Her scent, something floral and sweet, surrounded him, intoxicated him. Need pulsed through his veins, but he held back, keeping his kisses light and tender when he wanted to mould her against him and explore every inch of her body with his hands and his tongue.

She made a little sound of pleasure deep in her throat and, straining upward to wrap her arms around his neck, flattened herself against him, breast to chest, sex to sex. Restraint snapped. He wrapped his arms around her, holding her close. She opened her mouth to him and his tongue swept every corner, mating and dancing with her tongue. Placing his hand on her buttocks, he pulled her against his growing erection, rubbing against her mound. She moaned in response, moving against him.

“Mommy, are you going to tuck me in?”

Julia pushed away from him at Ava’s plaintive call from the top of the stairs. Shock registered in her eyes as she stared at him, her chest heaving with her labored breath. Arousal, exhilaration, and complete and utter surprise pounded through his blood. He hadn’t expected fire to ignite between them, hadn’t expected her response. Hell, he hadn’t even expected his own response. He knew he was attracted to her, but the need he'd felt, the all-consuming desire, had completely blindsided him.

"I…I…should see to Ava," Julia stammered, her eyes still wide with shock. Her hair was tousled, her lip gloss smudged. The taste of her was still in his mouth. He still wanted her, but instead he took a step away.

"I should go." But he couldn't make his feet move any further.

"Yes," she whispered. She stayed rooted to her spot.

He wanted to touch her again, to kiss her, but he knew if he did he wouldn't be able to leave. They were both on the edge, and it wouldn't take more than a touch to set the flames ablaze once more. And this time he didn't think either of them could stop.

He closed his eyes, his hands clenched at his sides. That might be okay for him, but he knew Julia wasn't ready. She'd hate herself if she lost control and had sex with him now. Worse, she'd hate him.

"Go see to Ava." He heard the husky note in his voice, the unmet need.

"Yes." Still, she didn't move.

Their eyes met, desire dancing between them. It took every ounce of strength Alex possessed to turn away and walk out of her house. To walk away from her.

****

The damp night air did nothing to cool his overheated libido. He walked into his house and went straight to the fridge for another beer. Twisting off the cap and tossing it aside, he guzzled half the bottle before stopping, as if it could put out the flames of desire roaring through him.

He held the cold bottle to his forehead. *That kiss*. Just thinking about the way Julia had pressed herself against him, held him, opened her mouth for him, caused the heat to explode inside him once more. It was all he could do to keep from running back to her house and begging her to let him make love to her.

He took a deep breath. *Enough.* He needed to think about something else.

Carrying his beer with him, he walked into the small bedroom he used as an office and turned on his laptop. He brought up one of his favorite medical websites and punched in some of Melissa Maloney's symptoms, such as the urinary problems and the fatigue. Some possible explanations came up, such as Type One diabetes or kidney infection. But the blood and urine work had already ruled those out.

He tried a different angle. What about the rash on Melissa's elbows? He did a search on skin rashes. A long list of conditions and diseases popped up. He scrolled through the list until one name caught his eye: Lupus, called The Great Imitator because it could often mimic other diseases. It was notoriously hard to diagnose because no two patients' symptoms were exactly alike and symptoms sometimes came and went. But most of Melissa's symptoms were consistent with known symptoms of lupus.

After doing some more research on how best to diagnose the condition, he looked up Melissa's phone number online and gave her a call. Her husband answered and handed the phone to her.

"Doc? Don't tell me you're still at work. It's kind of late, isn't it?"

Alex checked his watch, surprised to discover it

was nearly ten p.m.

"Sorry, I didn't realize it was so late. I've been doing some research, and I think I might know what's causing your problems, but we need to do more testing before I can be sure. Can you see me at the clinic tomorrow? I can stay a little later if you want to come after work."

She burst into tears. "Thank you, Doc. If you can help me, I'd be so grateful. Davy and I have decided that no matter how much money it takes, we have to find out what's wrong with me. I can't go on like this."

"I know. Call my office tomorrow. Bring Davy if he's available. We're going to beat this thing, Melissa."

"Thank you, Doc, thank you so much. I'll see you tomorrow."

Alex turned off his phone. He hoped his hunch was right. With treatment, lupus could be controlled and Melissa's quality of life much improved.

With one mystery potentially solved, his thoughts immediately returned to the kiss he'd shared tonight with Julia. He had a feeling she would always be on his mind, no matter what he was doing or where he went.

Chapter Ten

Sometimes he loved his job, like when he made a breakthrough in a patient's case, as he'd done with Melissa Maloney. Additional testing confirmed his lupus diagnosis, and they'd already begun treatment.

But sometimes he hated his job. Like today, when he had to deliver bad news. The worst kind of bad news.

Alex paused and took a deep breath before plucking Edie Cosgrove's medical file from the rack on the door of the examining room and going inside. Edie sat on the examining table, and Aaron stood beside her, holding her hand. They both looked up when he entered the room, their anxiety palpable, a living, breathing terror.

"Hi," he said, as he closed the door.

"Hi." Aaron cleared his throat. "You have the test results back?"

"Yes."

Alex opened the file and laid it on the small desk in the corner, before turning to face them again. "Edie, the biopsy we took of the lump in your left breast tested positive for cancer cells."

Aaron shook his head. "No, that's not possible. For Christ's sake, Alex, she's only thirty-three."

"I know, but unfortunately, that's what we're dealing with." He turned to Edie, who was pale with shock. "I've made arrangements for you to see an oncologist in Bangor. He'll want to run more tests, and you'll likely need another biopsy that removes more fluid and tissue so it can be tested to determine what kind of cancer we're dealing with, and whether it's still contained inside the left breast. Once all those things have been determined, he'll discuss the best course of action with you."

She lifted her chin and looked directly at him. "What are my options?"

"In the best-case scenario, you'll undergo a form of breast-conserving surgery like a lumpectomy to remove the tumor in your left breast, which will leave a minimal amount of scarring. That may be followed with a course of radiation or chemo treatments, or both."

"And the worst-case scenario?" she asked.

"Depending on the stage at which we've caught the cancer, and whether it has spread to the lymph nodes or the chest wall, it could mean a radical mastectomy followed by chemotherapy, and possibly radiation."

Aaron closed his eyes, his face twisted in anguish. "Jesus."

"What do you think, Alex? What's my prognosis?"

He didn't want to scare her, or Aaron, but he wanted to be honest. They needed to brace themselves for what could be coming. "We don't have enough information yet to make a prognosis. That's why I want you to see an oncologist as soon as possible. You're young and fit, and you're in good health aside from the cancer. That's in your favor. But there's going to be a surgery of some kind in your future, and I'm reasonably sure your doctor will order a course of radiation or chemo to make sure we kill any cancer cells left behind after the surgery. Your surgery will be in Bangor, but we can do most of your treatments at the hospital in Bar Harbor. But you'll likely have to see your oncologist in Bangor at regular intervals, so you have to be prepared to make that trip often."

"What about side effects from the chemo or the radiation? I've heard they can make people sick," she said.

"Yeah, that's a possibility. It all depends on the drugs used, the amount used, and the length of the chemo treatment, but some of the most common side effects are hair loss, mouth sores, either loss of appetite or increased appetite, and nausea and vomiting. There's also an increased chance of fatigue, bruising, and infection. The main short-term side effects of radiation therapy are swelling and heaviness in the breast, sunburn-like skin changes in the treated area, and fatigue, but most of those symptoms go away in a few months."

She lifted a hand to her hair and smiled ruefully. "I think I can cope with the other stuff, but I'm just vain enough to be worried about losing my hair. Silly, isn't it?"

"No, I don't think it's silly at all," Alex said. He couldn't help but think of Melissa Maloney.

Aaron moaned in agony. Edie wrapped an arm around his shoulders and drew him close.

"It's okay, sweetheart," she whispered. "It's going to be okay."

Alex took a shaky breath as he watched them. How the hell was he supposed to remain objective and calm? How could doctors working in small communities cope with the emotional stress of treating people they knew and cared about? Since he'd joined the ball team, Aaron had become a friend. He was a good guy, someone he liked and respected. He didn't know Edie as well, but he liked her. Judging from the way she was comforting her husband now, she had an inner core of strength. She'd need to tap into that strength in the months ahead.

And she was a lifelong friend of Julia's. He grimaced and briefly closed his eyes. She'd be devastated to learn that Edie was seriously ill.

Aaron pulled himself together, pinching his eyes shut with his thumb and forefinger to stem the flow of tears. Edie faced Alex, one hand still rubbing her husband's back.

"So what happens now?"

"I'm sending you to see Dr. Collins in Bangor immediately. He's the oncologist I was telling you about. I've referred other patients to him, and I know he's an excellent doctor. Like I said, he'll want to do more testing, and then he'll be able to figure out how he's going to treat the cancer. My nurse has the details about your appointment with him." Alex took a deep breath and let it out slowly. "Edie, we're going to hit this thing hard. We'll do everything in our power to get you well again."

Her mouth quirked in a brief smile. "Thanks."

He took a sticky note from the desk and wrote down his home and cell phone numbers. Handing it to Edie, he said, "If you have any questions about any part of your treatment, feel free to call me, anytime. I know how confusing this is, and I know you'll probably have questions when you leave here."

It occurred to him that he'd never offered his home

number to a patient before, but somehow, in this situation, it seemed like the right thing to do.

****

Alex hit some fly balls into the outfield in preparation for tonight's game. Aaron was in Bangor this week with Edie while she underwent more testing. Softball was the last thing on his mind.

So in Aaron's absence he'd stepped in to fill his role of manager and chief organizer. In order to make it to the remaining games of the season, he'd had to trade shifts in the ER and make promises to work holidays and weekends until nearly the end of his time in Lobster Cove. But it was worth it to be able to help out Aaron and Edie. And to spend his evenings with Julia.

Alex grinned as he watched her take batting practice, her bat held high and a "don't mess with me" look on her face. She played ball like she kissed—with everything she had.

Memories of kissing Julia flooded back, arousing him all over again. The thought of her soft skin against his hands, the taste of her kiss, the scent of vanilla and roses that was so unique to her, caused his cock to twitch to attention. He winced in discomfort. Getting a hard on while wearing an athletic cup was damn uncomfortable. He looked away from Julia in an effort to get his body back under control. What could he concentrate on to take his mind off the mind-blowing kiss he'd shared with her? Algebra? The periodic table? World peace? Nothing worked until he turned his thoughts to winter in Lobster Cove. Remembering frigid temperatures, mile-high snowbanks, and icy roads managed to cool him down.

Their game against another team from Lobster

Cove ended in a draw after three extra innings, when they were forced to call it because of darkness. As Alex packed up the equipment, he said goodnight to his friends, keeping one eye on Julia. When she started to leave the ball park with her daughter, he followed her.

"Hey, Julia, can you wait up a minute?" he called.

Both she and Ava turned to face him. Ava's face lit with excitement. "Dr. Alex! Are you coming to our house for a beer?"

He couldn't help noticing the way Julia flinched and looked around to see if anyone had heard Ava's question. Her discomfort at having anyone know he came to her house after games jabbed him in the heart. Was she that concerned about people talking about them? Or was it more personal? Would she have objected to the town gossiping about any man she might invite to her home, or just him?

He focused his attention on Julia. "I don't know, Ava. That depends on your mom. Maybe you should ask her."

"Mommy, can Dr. Alex come to our house? Please?"

She sent him an annoyed glance. "I don't know, honey. It's pretty late."

"Please? I want to show him my new kitten."

"You got a kitten?" he asked in surprise.

Julia shrugged. "One of my teachers took in a stray cat she called Fred. It turns out Fred was a Frederica and was with child. Or with eight kittens, as it turned out. She was desperate to find homes for them, so we are now officially pet owners."

"She's beautiful," Ava said, vibrating with excitement. "Please, Mommy, can Dr. Alex come see her?"

Alex saw a flicker of annoyance cross Julia's face, mostly directed at him, he was sure. But he also saw a touch of fear, and it gave him pause. What was she so afraid of? Was she afraid he'd kiss her again? Was she afraid he wouldn't?

"Julia—"

"Come see our new addition," she said. She looked up into his face, her blue eyes steady, as if she'd made a decision.

"Okay." There wasn't anywhere else he wanted to be.

Ava grabbed his hand. "Come on, let's go!"

Alex laughed. "Hold on a minute. I've got my car here tonight because I brought the team's equipment. Do you want to ride with me?"

"Yes!" Ava said, still holding his hand. He looked for confirmation from Julia. She gave a wan smile.

"Sure, why not?"

Alex put the equipment bags containing bats and balls and back catcher paraphernalia into the trunk of his car. Julia buckled Ava into the back seat, then slipped into the passenger seat beside him.

"So how come you're looking after the equipment? Where's Aaron been the last couple of games?"

He couldn't tell her what was really going on with her friends. It was up to them when, and if, they told her about Edie's cancer.

"He's been busy. He asked me to help out for a while."

Julia turned to look at him, a puzzled look on her face. She obviously expected more of an explanation. He didn't like avoiding the truth, but the short account he gave her was all he could provide. He was grateful she didn't press for more.

In a couple of minutes they reached Julia's house. Ava ran up the walk and opened the door, anxious to see her kitten.

"Didn't you lock your door?"

Julia shrugged. "I guess I forgot. It's not a big deal."

"Not a big deal? Aren't you worried about being robbed?"

"In Lobster Cove? I can't remember the last time we had a robbery. Besides, I don't have anything much worth stealing."

"Tell me you lock your doors at night when you and Ava are sleeping."

She rolled her eyes. "I promise you I lock my doors at night, mainly because I don't want to be found in my nightgown if someone comes over for a surprise visit late at night."

"Geez, Julia."

"Like I said, it's not a big deal."

He thought she was being naïve, but he let the subject drop, for now. Bad things could happen anywhere, even in a small town like Lobster Cove. The illnesses of patients like Melissa and Edie proved it.

He followed her into the house. When they went into the living room, he saw that a corner had been blocked off with cardboard boxes, a plastic filing cabinet, and a baby gate to create a corral of sorts. Ava sat inside the corral, a fluffy white kitten cradled gently in her arms. Alex moved the baby gate and ventured inside. Julia stayed on the outside, watching.

He got down on his knees beside Ava and ran a

finger over the soft fur of the kitten's back. "So this is your new friend. What's her name?"

"Snowball," Ava replied. "Because she's as white as snow."

"Good name. How old is she?"

Julia answered. "Four months. We had her at the vet clinic today, and she got some shots."

"She didn't like it," Ava said.

"Neither did I," Julia said. "Veterinary care doesn't come cheap. And it's just the beginning. Our vet says that if we don't want Snowball to have a bunch of little Snowballs in the future, we should have her spayed when she's about six months old."

She looked worried, and for the first time Alex wondered about her finances. She'd remarked once about the low pay of a teacher. Was it really that tough? Being a single parent couldn't be easy financially. Was she getting any child support from her ex-husband?

"Snowball learned to use the litter box all by herself," Ava said proudly, pointing to a low-sided plastic box in the corner. "She hasn't peed on the floor once. Mommy says that once she gets a little older, we won't keep her cooped up in here anymore."

"That's probably a good idea," he said. "When she gets a little older, she'll be able to jump out of here anyway."

"Have you ever had a kitten, Dr. Alex?"

"No, I'm more of a dog person. When I was a little older than you, I had dog when I lived in my grandmother's house. I like cats, but my mom wouldn't let one in the house. Too much cat hair messing up her house, she said."

"She was right about that." Julia moved the baby

gate aside and stepped into the corral. She stooped to stroke the kitten, a smile on her face. “You’re going to be a lot of extra work for me, aren’t you, Snowball?”

Despite her words, Alex saw the affection in her touch. She straightened and went to the litter box, grimacing as she looked inside.

“The good news is that she’s using the box, and the bad news is that I have to clean it. I swear, Ava, you’re going to be doing this soon.”

“I will, Mommy. I promise.” Ava probably would have agreed to do anything to keep the kitten.

Julia smiled fondly. “I know you will. Someday. But for now, it’s my job. I’m going to take this out to the garbage can. Ava, a couple more minutes with Snowball and then you have to get in the tub.”

“Okay, Mommy.”

She took the litter box outside to dispose of the contents. A few minutes later, she returned to the living room and refilled the box with clean litter, settling it on some newspapers.

“Would you like that beer now?” she asked Alex.

“Sure.”

Alex gave the purring Snowball a couple of pets before getting to his feet and following Julia into the kitchen. She thoroughly washed her hands at the sink before retrieving two bottles from the fridge. She twisted the cap from her bottle.

“Did Aaron say anything to you about what’s keeping him so busy?” she asked.

Alex shifted uncomfortably. “I didn’t ask.”

“I tried phoning Edie today, but there was no answer. Same thing yesterday. She didn’t say a word about going on vacation. I’m sure she would have mentioned if they were planning to take a holiday."

Lifting the bottle to his lips, he drank deeply, deciding it was best to say nothing in case he inadvertently let something slip. He didn't like keeping her in the dark, but he had no choice.

Ava ran into the room, diverting Julia's attention, for which Alex was grateful.

"Wash your hands, sweetheart, and then you can have a snack. Would you like something to eat, Alex?"

His stomach chose that moment to let out a loud growl, and she laughed. "I'll take that as a yes. Would you like a sandwich?"

"I'd love one." He'd missed dinner, having run straight from the clinic to the ball diamond. "But you don't have to wait on me. I can fix it myself."

"Sure, go ahead. Everything you need should be in the fridge. Help yourself."

"You want me to make you one?"

"No, that's fine. I'll have an apple."

They worked side by side at the kitchen counter as he made a ham and cheese sandwich slathered with mustard and topped with lettuce and pickle slices, and she cut up pieces of apple and cheese for herself and Ava.

They took their food to the table and ate in silence for a few moments. When Ava had finished her snack, Julia affectionately ruffled her hair.

"Time to get ready for your bath, sweetheart. Go upstairs and pick out some clean pajamas, and I'll be up in a couple of minutes to run your bath."

"Ah, do I have to?"

"Yes, you have to. Say goodnight to Alex and run upstairs."

Ava slid from her chair and rounded the table to him. She held up her arms.

"Can I give you a goodnight kiss?"

Alex's heart tripped over itself. He glanced at Julia, but her stoic expression gave away none of her feelings. He bent to put his arms around Ava's tiny body, as her delicate hands wound around his neck.

"Goodnight, Dr. Alex."

"Goodnight, Ava."

He felt her feather-light kiss on his cheek. Then she let him go and ran out of the room, singing to herself as she raced up the stairs. When she was out of earshot, Julia lifted her gaze to his.

"I'm not doing a very good job at keeping the two of you apart."

"Why do you have to?"

"I told you before, it's not good for her to get so attached to you when you'll be leaving Lobster Cove in a few months. I don't want her to be hurt again."

"Again?"

"She was only three when her father left. She says she doesn't remember him, but at the time she asked for him over and over. She couldn't understand why he suddenly disappeared from her life."

He remembered what Ava had said about her father living far away. "Doesn't he ever visit her?"

She looked away. "No."

She said nothing more, making him wonder what Julia's feelings were for her ex-husband. Was she still in love with him? Was that the reason she kept her heart so guarded?

"I'd never hurt her on purpose. You know that, don't you?"

She lowered her gaze and stared at her clasped hands in her lap. “It’s easy to hurt someone, especially a child. You don’t even have to try very hard.”

He didn’t know what to say to that. She was right. Ava had become attached to him, and he to her. He had a hard time imagining leaving her behind when he returned to San Diego. The feeling was almost as strong as his inability to imagine leaving Julia behind. But he couldn’t imagine staying in Lobster Cove, either.

So where did that leave them?

“The other night, when you…when we…when we kissed, I…”

Her voice drifted off. She looked at him, confusion in her eyes. He leaned forward and grasped her hands.

“It was the most amazing kiss I’ve ever experienced,” he said truthfully.

“We can’t do it again,” she whispered.

“Why not?” He wanted to kiss her over and over again, and strip away her clothes to press his lips to every inch of her body. He wanted to kiss her right now.

Agony filled her eyes. “You know why. I told you. I don’t want Ava hurt.”

“Is that the only reason?”

Would she care if he left? Would she think of him when he was gone? He hoped so, because he was pretty sure she’d be on his mind.

“No,” she admitted. “People will talk.”

“I don’t give a damn what people say!”

“I do! I have to live here. You’ll leave and never give this place a backward glance.”

“Is that what you think? That I could forget you so easily?”

"Yes… Oh, I don't know." She took a shaky breath. "I wish I were the kind of person who could have a casual affair, but I'm not. And I've got Ava to consider."

"So you want me to leave."

She closed her eyes, but when she reopened them, they were free of tears and determined.

"Yes. I think it would be best for all of us if you didn't come over after games."

He nodded. He knew she was right, but if it was the right thing to do, why did it hurt so much?

He got to his feet and walked to the front door. Julia followed him. Stopping, he turned to look at her. She didn't look any happier than he felt. At least that gave him some comfort.

"Will I see you at the next game?"

"At the ball diamond, yes. But not after."

"What will you tell Ava?"

"That you have your life, and we have ours. Your life isn't here with us."

"I don't want her to hate me." The thought of Ava disliking him or being disappointed in him hurt far more than he expected.

"She won't, at least not for long. She'll be okay."

Alex wondered if she really believed that. He wasn't sure if he was going to be okay.

"Goodbye, Julia."

He reached out his hand to cup her cheek, needing to touch her one last time. He thought she might pull away, but instead she closed her eyes and leaned into his hand, turning her face to press a kiss into his palm. Then she backed away.

"You should go."

He opened the door and stepped through, not wanting to prolong the agony any longer. The soft click of the lock behind him signaled she'd closed the door.

He wished he could close off his feelings just as easily. He was pretty sure this was going to hurt for a long, long time.

Chapter Eleven

A week later, Julia had just put Ava to bed when the phone rang. When she picked up her cordless phone and saw Edie's number, she eagerly pressed the button.

"Edie?"

"Hi, Jules."

"Hi yourself. Where have you been? I've been trying to reach you for days. Your mother-in-law said she was looking after the kids while you and Aaron were out of town for a few days. Did you two go away for a second honeymoon, a little love fest?"

Edie laughed, but the sound was brittle. "I wish. I had some things I had to take care of. We were in Bangor."

"In Bangor? All week?"

"Yeah. Dr. Campbell sent me to have some tests done at the hospital."

Julia's whole body went cold, and her stomach clenched. She put a hand over her abdomen. "What kind of tests?"

She heard Edie sigh and take a deep breath before continuing. "A breast biopsy, among other things. I have stage three breast cancer, Jules."

For a moment Julia thought she might faint. She had to grip the edge of the kitchen counter to help her stand.

"That can't be possible, Edie. You're too young."

"I keep saying that, but apparently cancer doesn't care how young or old a person is."

Julia struggled to keep the panic out of her voice. "Alex is your doctor?"

"Yes. He found the cancer initially, and then he sent me to a specialist in the city right away."

Thank God Alex had found the cancer. But did he find it in time? "What are they going to do? How do we fight this thing?"

Edie sounded surprisingly calm. "I'm going to have surgery in a couple of days, and then after that my oncologist wants me to have a round of chemo, followed by a course of radiation to make sure we zap all the nasty little cancer cells in my body."

"Damn right we're going to zap the little bastards!"

Edie chuckled. "That's the spirit."

"What can I do to help?"

"I don't know. Aaron's mom is taking time off work to babysit the kids while we're away, but I'm sure she could use a hand with my little hellions. Maybe you could give her a break?"

"Of course. How's Aaron?"

"He's…he's taking it hard, Jules. He's really trying to be strong for me, but he's scared. I'm worried about him." It was so like Edie to worry about the people she loved instead of herself.

"Don't worry, sweetheart. We'll look after him. And we'll look after you, too. Okay?"

"Okay. Listen, we'll talk more later, but right now I need to phone Tracy and give her the news, too. I'm sorry to dump this on you, Jules."

"Don't worry about me. Just concentrate on getting better."

"I will. I love you."

Julia could barely speak. "I love you, too."

"I've got to go. Bye."

"Bye."

She set the phone on the counter, the numbness that had hit her when she'd first heard the word "cancer" now giving way to pain. Feeling blindly for one of the kitchen chairs, she sank into it, her legs unable to support her any longer. The tears came then, and she cried until she had nothing left except the fear that she was about to lose one of her dearest friends.

****

Alex's cell phone woke him from the first decent sleep he'd had in a week. Groaning, he fumbled for the phone on his bedside table. When he saw Julia's name on the screen, he sat up quickly and hit the talk button.

"Julia?"

"Alex, I'm sorry to be calling you so late." She sounded tired, upset, and more than a little shaky. "Edie called me tonight to tell me about…about her cancer."

He closed his eyes and bent his head. "I'm sorry, Julia."

"She said you were her doctor, that you found the cancer."

"I'm her GP. After she found a lump, I made the initial diagnosis and sent her to the cancer specialist in Bangor. It was important to find out what kind of cancer we're dealing with so we can treat it properly."

There was silence on the line, but he heard her erratic breath, as if she was holding back a torrent of tears. Finally she spoke.

"I know you can't give me any details about her condition, but I need to understand. Edie said her cancer is at stage three. What does that mean?"

He chose his words carefully, not wanting to divulge any patient information, and not wanting to scare her.

"It means that her tumor is bigger than five centimeters across and that some of the lymph nodes are affected. But it hasn't penetrated into the chest wall or the skin, and it hasn't spread to any other organs."

"What are her chances?" she asked quietly.

"Her odds are good," he said, hoping to reassure her. "Someone with her symptoms is thought to have a seventy-two percent chance of survival over five years."

"That's pretty good, isn't it?"

"Yes. It's very good."

Another pause. "Why did she get this, Alex? Why her?"

"I wish I could answer that question, but I can't. Nobody can."

"Edie is like a sister to me. She's a good person. She's never hurt anyone in her life." Her voice cracked. "She has a husband and three kids who need her."

"I know, sweetheart."

"I'm so scared she's going to die."

"We're going to do everything we can for her, Julia."

"Please don't let her suffer. I couldn't stand for her to be in pain."

"We'll do everything we can to make her comfortable during her treatments, but I'm not going to lie to you. She's got a struggle ahead of her."

She sniffed. "Thank you for being honest with me."

"Edie is young and strong, and she's got the support of wonderful friends like you. She's got a great chance of beating this, sweetheart. I want you to believe me."

"I want to believe you. I really do."

The pain he heard in her voice tore at his heart. He squeezed his eyes shut. "I know this is hard. But we're going to get through this, I promise."

He heard her muffled sob. "I should go. I'm sorry I woke you. Good night, Alex." The line went dead.

He stared at the phone in his hand for a few moments before clicking the Off button. She was trying to deal with the news about her friend all alone, trying to be strong. Both Ava and Julia's mother already needed her to be strong for them. How much more could she take?

Who was going to be strong for Julia?

Alex jumped out of bed and found his discarded clothes on a chair in the corner of his room. He dressed quickly and ran to the back door, where he'd left his shoes. Grabbing a jacket, his wallet, and a set of house keys, he locked the door and sprinted the two blocks to Julia's house.

The likelihood of a neighbor seeing him enter her house at that time of the night was remote, but knowing how Julia felt about maintaining her reputation, he kept to the darkness, slipping around the side of the house to the back door. He knocked softly on the wooden door, once, twice, and then a third time, a little louder. Finally a light came on in the back door hallway, and Julia opened the door as far the chain would allow.

"Alex? What are you doing here?"

"I wanted to make sure you're okay. Can you let

me in?"

He saw her swallow. "I appreciate your concern, but I don't think that's a good idea."

"Julia." He leaned his forehead against the door frame. "You're upset. I don't want you to be alone right now."

She stared at him, her blue eyes swimming with tears. Then she closed the door in his face. He held his breath, not sure whether she was shutting him out or closing the door to remove the chain. His heart pounded with uncertainty, the wait interminable.

Finally, she opened the door and stepped aside to let him in. They stood staring at each other in the tiny vestibule. Then she laid her hand against his heart, and a tear streaked down her cheek.

"You're right. I don't want to be alone tonight."

He wiped the tear with the pad of his thumb. "You don't have to be. I'm right here."

He lowered his mouth to hers and softly kissed her lips. She moaned against his mouth, her hand caressing his face. The light touch was all it took to set his blood on fire. He wanted to wrap her in his arms, touch every sweet inch of her skin. He wanted to be inside her, to empty himself in her, to make her shout his name as she orgasmed around him.

But she was too vulnerable tonight. If he took advantage of her weakened state, she'd hate him. He ended the kiss and took a step away from her, keeping her at arm's length.

"Alex," she whispered. "Make love to me. Please. I need you."

"Julia—"

She pressed herself against him once more and

kissed him until any protest he was about to make was overwhelmed by his need for her. Her tongue swept his mouth, tangling with his in a delicious duel that left him breathless and so hard he ached with wanting her. Ending the kiss, she wordlessly took his hand and led him up the stairs to her room. She slipped off her robe and threw it on a chair. A bedside lamp provided the only light in the room, just enough to reveal her short, white nightgown, the creamy length of her thighs, and the hard peaks of her nipples beneath the silky fabric.

She pushed the thin straps of her nightgown from her shoulders, and it skimmed down her body to pool at her feet. He stared at her, taking in her small, high breasts, her slender waist, the generous flare of her hips. Only a pair of skimpy panties covered her. Alex was seized with a desire to rip them from her body and sink himself into her.

He reached for her just as she reached for him. In a frenzy of kisses and touches, she helped him remove his clothes. He had just enough sanity left to find the condom he kept in his wallet and slip it on. Then they were on the bed, though he didn't remember exactly how they got there. His body and mind had spiraled out of control in a way he'd never experienced before. Nothing mattered but Julia. Nothing mattered but her pleasure, her touch. He needed her like he needed his next breath.

Alex inserted his finger inside her, withdrawing and plunging until she convulsed around him, her body bowing, her head thrown back. Kissing her again, he swallowed the cries that ripped from her mouth. She writhed under him, lifting her hips, rubbing her mound against his cock. He struggled to prolong the pleasure for both of them, but felt himself slipping into the abyss.

He couldn't wait any longer. Positioning himself at the entrance to her body, he gradually eased himself inside her. Trembling with the effort to take it slow, he pushed a little further. Julia's heavy-lidded eyes opened, her face pale in the dim light.

"Alex, please. I need you. Please."

Her soft hands kneaded his buttocks, her hips lifting to take him in deeper. Something inside him went wild. He thrust inside her, hard and deep, over and over, unable to stop. She met him thrust for thrust, her hands gripping him, her legs wrapping around him, spurring him on. His orgasm burst from his body with a sudden force that left him trembling and weak and unable to move from Julia's arms. She held him tightly, their bodies still joined, and her face nuzzled against his neck.

"I'm crushing you," he managed to whisper. "I should move."

"Shh." She kissed his neck. "Not yet. Stay."

She smoothed her soft hands over his back and shoulders, and Alex relaxed against her. He couldn't remember ever feeling this way after sex before, so sated, and so at peace. Being here with her felt so completely right.

Finally, he rolled off her and slipped across the hall to the bathroom to dispose of the condom. When he came back to the bed she was asleep, one hand under her cheek and her blonde hair mussed.

A beautiful mess.

Smiling, he climbed into bed and pulled her close. As he listened to the sound of her breathing, he wondered if this was the beginning of something for them, or if it was only the shock of learning about her friend's illness that had prompted her to let him into her bed.

****

She was in a small boat on a lake. It was a perfect day. The gentle breeze cooled her skin from the heat of the sun without marring the glasslike finish of the water. Her two best friends were in the boat with her. Tracy and Edie laughed as they threw their fishing lines into the water.

Something tugged at Edie's line, and she stood up, struggling to reel in her catch. But whatever was on the other end of the line was too strong, and it pulled her over the side of the boat and into the water. She disappeared under the surface. Tracy immediately dove in after her. Over and over, she came to the surface, gasping for air, then dove below the surface again to search for Edie. And then Tracy didn't come back up to the surface for air. She was gone. They were both gone, and she was alone.

"No!" she screamed. "No! Don't go! Don't leave me!"

"It's okay, sweetheart. It's okay."

Strong arms held her securely. *Alex.* She woke in an instant and wrapped her arms around him as tightly as she could. Snuggling against his chest, she breathed in the scent of him, a unique mix of aftershave and antiseptic soap.

"Bad dream?"

She nodded, the hair on his chest tickling her nose. "Yes."

He stroked her hair. "Everything's okay now,

sweetheart."

She felt safe in his arms, as if nothing could harm her. "I know."

"Do you think you could go back to sleep?"

She gripped his arm, suddenly afraid. "Not yet. Don't go."

"I'm not going anywhere."

Propping a couple of pillows behind them, he pulled her with him to lean against the headboard. Gently, he tucked the sheet around her and simply held her, his chin resting on the top of her head. Julia felt she could have stayed like that with him forever.

She thought about the way he'd made love to her, like she was something special, like he couldn't get enough of her. When was the last time a man had felt that way about her?

She couldn't get enough of him, either. She loved the feel of his smooth skin over powerful muscles, loved the strength of his body. Last night he'd pushed her to the very edge of every border, every boundary she possessed, and then pushed beyond. Their lovemaking had been fierce and wild, and so intense it had been almost unbearable at times. But it was the most amazing sex she'd ever experienced.

Despite the power of his body and the ferocity of their lovemaking, he could be tender and gentle, and so kind.

She wanted that power, that intensity, focused on her once more. She wanted to forget about Edie's illness. She ran her hand down his chest, past his taut abdomen, to his penis. It sprang to life at her touch. He grabbed her wrist, preventing her from touching him again.

"That's not a good idea."

"Really?" She kissed his beard-stubbled chin. "I thought it was a totally excellent idea."

"I only had one condom in my wallet, sweetheart."'

Her mouth stilled. "Oh."

She leaned back against the headboard and looked up at him. They'd left the bedside lamp burning when they fell asleep, and it threw a soft light across his face, outlining the strong chin and the chiseled cheekbones. His dark hair fell rakishly across his forehead and, along with the stubble, gave him the look of a pirate. A very sexy, well-built pirate.

She wanted him. They just had to be a little creative.

She ran her fingers over the hard muscles of his chest, then leaned in to kiss her way down his body. When she reached his lower abdomen, she heard his sharp intake of breath and felt his hand grip her shoulder.

"Julia, no birth control, remember?" His voice sounded strained, his breathing erratic.

She looked up into his face. "I know. I just thought maybe we could try something…different." She stroked him once more, the need inside her overwhelming her, and spurring her on. She barely recognized herself. All she knew was that she needed him. "I'll make it good for you, I promise. Just don't go. Please don't go."

"Julia." His voice was strangled, the look on his face a mixture of apprehension and desire. "I told you, I'm not going anywhere."

That was all she needed to hear. She bent over him, taking the tip of his penis into her mouth and teasing it with her tongue. Alex moaned and lifted his hips, providing all the incentive she needed to know he liked what she was doing. She took him fully into her mouth, sliding her tongue, her lips up and down from tip to hilt, her teeth raking gently over his shaft. Alex made inarticulate sounds in his throat. Then suddenly his body stiffened and he shouted his release. Julia lapped it up.

His breathing had barely returned to normal before Julia felt his hands around her waist, and suddenly found herself on her back with Alex on top of her. He took her left breast into his mouth, suckling and teasing it with his tongue, at the same time inserting two fingers inside her. She gasped at the sensation. Dear God, it felt so good, *so right.* She threw back her head and arched her back, teetering on the edge.

But then he suddenly abandoned his attention to her breasts and withdrew his fingers, leaving her whimpering with need. He kissed and licked his way down her stomach, to her inner thighs, urging her to open wider for him. The first touch of his tongue to her clit almost rocketed her off the bed. It was the most amazing sensation she'd ever felt, and she wanted more. She thrust her hips towards him, bucking wildly, desperate to be closer to him. He stayed with her, his wicked tongue overloading her system with pleasure, until she felt her climax building low in her belly. It suddenly burst free, overwhelming her with wave after wave of bliss and joy and contentment.

Alex held her, and she fell asleep once more, this time into a blessedly dreamless sleep.

Chapter Twelve

Julia woke slowly, the light creeping in between the slats of the window blinds telling her morning had arrived. She groaned and checked the clock on her bedside table: Six a.m.

The events of the previous evening and night flooded back. *Edie. Cancer. Alex.*

Alex. Oh, God.

She couldn't believe what she'd done, how wanton she'd been. What on earth had come over her?

Fear and anxiety swamped her. She'd used sex to try to forget about Edie's illness, her mother's precarious health, even the stress of her work. But it hadn't worked. Nothing could make her forget that her best friend was facing a possible death sentence.

She turned her face into the pillow to muffle her sobs. The worst was that she'd used Alex to assuage her fears and guilt. *Oh, God.* What must he think of her?

Wiping the tears from her face, she sat up quickly and looked around her room. He was gone; the room empty. Had he gone home? Then she heard the water running across the hall in the bathroom and realized he was in the shower.

Grabbing her robe from the chair where she'd tossed it last night, she quickly pulled it on and securely tied the belt, doubling the knot just to be safe. She remembered the things they'd done to each other during the night, and a flush spread over her body, heating her from the inside out. The sex had been amazing, spectacular, mind-blowing. By far the best she'd ever had.

And they could never do it again.

Maybe it was already too late. What she felt for Alex was already too deep, too strong. It was stupid to feel this way about him, considering the way they'd met and the short time they'd known each other. But he'd been the first person, the only person, she'd turned to after getting the news of Edie's illness. She trusted him. Needed him.

The thought terrified her. She couldn't let herself need him. She couldn't let herself need anyone again.

Losing Russ had been humiliating and gut-wrenchingly difficult. She'd been forced to come to terms with the knowledge that he hadn't loved her enough to want to stay with her in Lobster Cove. In the end, she'd discovered that everything about their life together had been a lie.

None of this was Alex's fault. But she had to put a stop to their fledgling relationship now, while she was still able to do it.

He opened the bedroom door and quietly closed it behind him, a towel wrapped around his waist and his hair wet from his shower. When he turned and saw her, his face lit up in a smile, as if she was the one person in the world he most wanted to see.

She sent up a little prayer to Heaven. *God, please give me strength.*

"Hey, you're awake." He stepped close and reached out his hand to touch her face. She moved, evading his touch.

He let his hand drop to his side, his eyes narrowing. "What's going on, Julia?"

"Nothing. Last night was wonderful, and I appreciate that you…that you…comforted me. But I need to be realistic. We…this relationship…isn't going anywhere, so I think it best if we say goodbye this morning and go our separate ways."

"How do you know this relationship isn't going anywhere? You haven't given it a chance."

"What would be the point, Alex? You'll be back in San Diego in a few months, and I'll still be here."

He edged closer, reaching out to caress her arm. "Baby, that's over six months from now. Why couldn't we see each other until then?"

Moving away from his touch, she wrapped her arms around herself and paced her small room. "People would find out we were having an affair. It would be all right for you, but I've still got to live here after you leave." She gave a laugh that came out more bitter than she had intended. "I'm supposed to be an example of upstanding citizenship to my students. How much moral authority do you think it would give me if everyone in town knew I'd been screwing the good doctor's brains out?"

He flinched at her choice of words. "It's not like that, and you know it."

She lifted her chin. "Isn't it?"

"Not for me," he said softly, "and I don't believe it is for you, either. Why are you doing this?"

She couldn't look at him. "Like I said, I think it's better if we don't see each other…this way again. I have my reputation in this town to think of, not to mention my daughter's feelings."

"For Christ's sake, Julia, this is the twenty-first century, not the nineteenth. Nobody gives a damn if we're sleeping together."

"I care!" she said, her voice louder than she'd intended. She deliberately lowered it, not wanting to wake Ava. "My reputation is all I've got."

For a moment he stared at her, confusion and frustration etched on his face. Then he grabbed his clothes from the floor and headed to the door. With one hand on the doorknob, he paused, not looking at her.

"You can't deny that there's something strong between us. I'm not sure what's going on with you, Julia, but I never thought you were too much of a coward to find out what we could have together. Call me if you change your mind."

She heard him go into the bathroom to dress. Sitting on the edge of her bed, her hands clasped in her lap, she listened for him to leave the house. At last she heard him go down the stairs and close the back door of her house. She got up from the bed and moved to the window to watch him leave her yard through the back gate. She watched him walk down the back alley until he was out of sight.

Sinking into the chair next to the window, she dropped her head into her hands and cried. She cried for her mother, for Edie, and for the life she could never have with Alex.

****

The day dragged on and on for Julia. She was tired from lack of sleep and worn out with worry over Edie and her parents. And then there was Alex. Had she been wrong in sending him away?

No. It was the only thing she could do. They had no

future, and to carry on an affair would leave her open to criticism and attack by people like Ralph Sykes and her former father-in-law. She was a single parent. She needed her job.

But as much as she tried to justify her decision, her heart still cried over and over that she was wrong. So damn wrong.

She closed the lid of her laptop and rested her forehead on top of it. Her world was spinning wildly. Everything was going wrong, and she couldn't keep up anymore. She wanted to get off this crazy merry-go-round and catch her breath before she spiraled completely out of control.

The cordless phone on her desk rang, startling her out of her melancholy. She saw her former in-laws' number on the screen and contemplated letting the call go to voice mail, but that was just putting off the inevitable. She either dealt with Wyatt now or later. It might as well be now. Steeling herself, she punched the talk button.

"Hello?"

"Hi, Julia. Lily here. How are you?"

She sagged with relief at the sound of Lily's voice, and belatedly realized she couldn't have dealt with any problems from Wyatt today.

"I…I'm—"

To her surprise and distress, she burst into tears. Putting a hand over her mouth, she tried to stop, but she simply couldn't. Through the window she saw Ava playing outside in her sandbox, and she was grateful her daughter wasn't nearby to witness her breakdown.

"Oh, honey," Lily said. "I heard about Edie. I'm so sorry. I know she's a good friend of yours."

"Yes." She managed the word through her tears. Lily and Edie's mother were friends, so it was no surprise she'd heard the news. Edie's mother must be worried sick. She should call her, see if there was anything she could do for her…

The tears fell harder.

"Julia, would it be all right if I came over and visited with you and Ava today?" she asked gently. "Have you had lunch?"

Her stomach rebelled at the thought of food, but Ava needed to eat. It was past lunchtime. What kind of mother lets her child go hungry? "No, we haven't."

"I can be over in a couple of minutes and make lunch for the two of you. Would that be okay?"

Julia hesitated a moment, torn between the desire to maintain her privacy and her need to have someone look after her today and tell her everything was going to be all right.

Need won.

"I guess that would be fine."

"I'll be right there."

Julia punched the Off button and set the phone on her desk. She reached for a tissue and blew her nose and wiped her eyes, trying to get herself under control. She didn't want to frighten Ava, and she couldn't let Lily think she was a basket case, unable to care for her daughter. With that thought in mind, she closed her eyes and concentrated on taking deep, even breaths until the tears stopped.

By the time Lily knocked on her door a few moments later, she felt almost back in control of her emotions. She even managed a smile for Lily.

"I'm sorry about that phone call. It's been a…a

difficult couple of days."

To her surprise, Lily enveloped her in an embrace. "I know, Julia. I know."

She held tightly to Lily, surprised at how much she needed support today. Finally, her mother-in-law held her at arm's length and took a good look at her.

"You look like a girl who could use a bowl of chicken noodle soup."

That made her laugh. "Oh, yeah? Maybe that's true, but I don't think I've got any in my pantry."

Lily picked up a bag she'd dropped by the door when she entered the house. "You're in luck. I just made some. I brought over enough for lunch."

"Ava needs something to eat, but honestly, I'm not sure I could keep anything down right now."

Lily nodded, her face full of empathy. "We'll see how you're feeling in a few minutes when the soup's ready. If not, you can fake it for Ava's sake. Where is she, by the way?"

"In the back yard, in her sandbox. She's probably filthy."

"I'll bring her in and get her cleaned up, and then we'll have lunch. Would that be okay?"

She managed a genuine smile. "Yes. Thank you."

Lily rubbed her arm. "Good. Why don't you rest for a few minutes?"

"Okay."

She pulled Julia into a hug once more. "It's going to be all right."

Julia let herself take comfort in her mother-in-law's embrace, grateful to her for being here. She'd needed someone to look after her today. At one time, she would have sought solace from her own mother, but she was afraid those days were over.

She fought back more tears at that thought and pulled away from Lily.

"I think I could use a cup of tea. Would you like some?"

"Sure."

Julia forced a smile. "I'll put the kettle on."

Lily patted her arm once more, then went out the back door to retrieve Ava. Julia padded into the kitchen in her bare feet, glad for the small task. She needed to keep busy, to keep her mind engaged in chores and activities so it didn't have time to dwell on all the scary things going on in her life.

The kettle boiled, and she took it off the heat. Pouring a little of the boiling water into her teapot, she swirled it around to warm the pot. Then she dumped the water into the sink and threw a couple of teabags into the pot. Adding hot water from the kettle, she watched as the bags released their brown coloring. The fragrant scent of orange pekoe filled her nose.

You can blame my grandmother. She's Mexican-American, but she has an obsession with all things English. She's a big fan of afternoon tea.

Julia bent her head, pushing back tears again. Could she not even make tea anymore without it reminding her of Alex?

She heard Lily and Ava enter the back door, and she struggled to pull herself together. Somehow she managed to present a smiling face for her daughter.

"Mommy! Grandma Lily is here!"

"I know, sweetheart. Isn't that a nice surprise? She's going to have lunch with us."

Ava threw her arms around Lily's waist. "I'm so

glad you came."

A wave of guilt rushed over Julia. She hadn't exactly welcomed Lily into her home the last three years.

"Let's go upstairs and get you cleaned up, Sweet Pea," Lily said with a smile.

"That's what Dr. Alex calls me, too! Dr. Alex is my friend, isn't he, Mommy?"

Julia didn't have a clue how to respond to that. Luckily, Lily took Ava's hand, distracting her.

"My goodness, look at those dirty hands! You can't sit down at the table with those. Let's get you upstairs to the bathroom so you can wash up."

"Okay, Grandma."

Before leaving the room, Lily flashed a curious look at her. Had she somehow heard about her and Alex? Her stomach knotted at the thought.

While they were upstairs in the bathroom, Julia busied herself by pouring tea, emptying the dishwasher, and setting the kitchen table. A few minutes later they returned, Ava chattering happily to her grandmother. Lily set about making lunch.

"No, you sit down. I want you to relax," Lily said when Julia tried to help her. She steered her to the kitchen table and made her sit down with her cup of tea.

To her surprise, she was able to eat her soup when Lily put a bowl in front of her. Her stomach had called a truce, recognizing that she needed nourishment, even if Julia hadn't. She pushed the bowl away when she'd finished.

"Thank you, Lily, that was delicious. It was very kind of you to make us lunch."

"It's my pleasure. It's lovely to look after my

girls."

Julia blinked and looked away, feeling guilty once more.

She couldn't bear it. She simply couldn't bear it.

The doorbell rang, and Ava ran to the front door. One of her little friends from down the street walked into the kitchen with her.

"Can I play with Amber? She wants me to come over to her house."

"Ava, Grandma Lily came here to see you today. You can play with Amber some other time."

"That's okay, Julia. I'll come visit again soon. Come give Grandma a kiss before you go, Sweet Pea."

Ava hugged Lily and then, grabbing her friend Amber's hand, headed to the door.

"I want you home by three o'clock," Julia called. "Tell Amber's mom."

"Okay, Mommy." The door closed with a loud bang.

"I'm sorry about that, Lily. She could have played with her friend some other time."

"That's all right." Lily sipped her tea. "Like I said, I'll be back to see her sometime soon. If it's okay with you."

"Of course it is. Lily, I'm sorry I haven't made much of an effort for Ava to spend time with you and Wyatt."

"I understand. Wyatt hasn't exactly made you feel welcome in our home the last three years."

She swallowed. "It's been a difficult situation."

"Yes, it has. It can't be easy for you, raising Ava alone and dealing with a sometimes very stressful job. I remember how it was when Wyatt was principal of the school. I should have supported you more. I'm sorry."

Julia shook her head, on the edge of tears once more. "You have nothing to apologize for."

"Neither do you. Let's just say from now on we'll make a bigger effort to spend more time together and to support each other." She took Julia's hand in hers. "How does that sound to you?"

"It sounds good." She managed a genuine smile. "Thank you."

"Good." Lily squeezed her hand before letting it go. "Louise told me that Edie will be having surgery in a couple of days."

A trickle of anxiety rippled through Julia's body at the thought of her friend going under the knife. "Yes, that's what Edie told me, too, but I don't know any of the details."

"She said Aaron's taking it hard."

"Poor Aaron. He must feel so helpless."

"Men like to fix things, to make things better. But there's nothing he can do to fix this."

"He can be there for Edie. I know that just having him with her will mean the world to her."

Lily frowned. "He'll be with her during her surgery, but Louise said he can't afford to take any more time away from work, especially with all the medical expenses they're going to have."

"I hadn't thought of that." She sat up a little straighter. Aaron was an electrician and owned his own one-man business—one-man except for Edie, who did his books and kept him organized. Being self-employed meant that if he didn't work, he didn't get paid. "Does he have medical insurance?"

"No. Louise is also concerned about Edie's chemo

and radiation treatments. She's not going to be able to drive herself back and forth to Bar Harbor. They've warned her the treatments could cause nausea and fatigue. Even though it's not very far, it would be best if she didn't drive herself."

"No, of course not. I could drive her."

"The treatments won't start until she's healed from the surgery. You might be back at school by then. Louise and her husband are going to take some time off work, but they only have so many vacation days."

"Aaron's folks work too, don't they? Doesn't Aaron's dad have a heart condition?"

"I believe he does, but he still works at the hardware store."

"Who's going to look after the kids while Aaron's at work and Edie's in treatment? How are Edie's parents going to take her to her treatments and look after the kids at the same time? What happens when the grandparents run out of vacation time?"

Lily shook her head. "I don't know."

"We should do something."

"Like what?"

"I don't know. Maybe I can call around and see if I can find other people who may be willing to help with the driving, when the time comes."

"That sounds like a great idea. I could call my friends. Some of them are retired and have the time to help."

"That would be awesome."

"Some of my friends like to cook. I'm sure the Cosgroves would appreciate good food they don't have to cook themselves."

"Yes." Julia stood up and walked to a kitchen

drawer where she kept a pad of paper and some pens. She started to write down ideas. It felt good to do something positive, to help someone else instead of wallowing in her troubles.

"Your mother is a wonderful baker. Wyatt buys her pies every year at the church bake sale. We could ask her to make something."

Julia's pen stilled, her thoughts screeching to a halt. "I don't think that's a good idea."

"Oh? Why not?"

She took her seat at the table once more. "My mother isn't well."

She found herself telling Lily everything, from Alex's suspicions over Ava's broken arm to his finding her mother wandering in her nightclothes in the middle of the night.

"Alex suspects she has the beginnings of Alzheimer's disease, but my dad is in denial. I got him to take her to see Dr. Willson for some initial testing. He's supposed to take her to a neurologist in Bangor, but he's been putting it off."

"Oh, Julia. I'm so sorry." She covered Julia's hands with her own, compassion in her blue eyes. "It must be so difficult for you. And then Edie's illness on top of it."

She swallowed. "It's been a rough few weeks."

"It's a lot for you to handle on your own. I wish you had felt you could come to me. Just to talk, if nothing else."

"Please don't say anything about my mother, Lily. My dad would be very upset if he thought people were talking about her. Please, don't say anything to Wyatt about it."

"If that's what you want, I won't say anything."

"Thank you."

Lily patted Julia's hand before pouring herself more tea. "I've never met Alex Campbell, though I've heard he's a very good doctor. My friend Pat went to see him about her arthritis. She found him very helpful, and very sympathetic."

Julia took a sip of her tea, averting her gaze. "Yes."

"It sounds like Ava likes him."

"Yes. He's very good with children."

Lily cocked her head to one side. "Do you like him?"

Julia put a neutral expression on her face and answered cautiously. "Sure, he's a nice guy. We play ball together on Aaron's team."

"That's good. You should go out. After all, it's been three years since your divorce."

"We're not…there's nothing…we just play ball on the same team."

She couldn't talk about her feelings for Alex, especially not to Russ's mother. And she certainly couldn't tell her about last night.

"That's too bad. It sounds like he's a very special person."

Julia looked away. *Very special.*

Lily drank the last of her tea and got up from the table. "I should be going. I'll start calling some of my friends today and see which of them can help."

"That would be wonderful. I'll do the same, and maybe we can put together a list and make some plans."

"Okay. We'll keep in touch." She leaned over and kissed Julia's cheek. "Don't worry, dear. Edie's going to be just fine. We'll have the whole town pulling for her by the time we're done."

Julia smiled and rose to her feet. "Yeah, we will."

"And you're not alone." She took Julia's hand. "Whenever you need to talk, I hope you'll come to me. I know we've been on opposite sides of the fence in the past, but I hope those days are over."

"So do I, but I'm not sure Wyatt feels that way. I know how much he dislikes me."

"He doesn't really dislike you, honey. It doesn't help that Ralph Sykes fills his head with nonsense about you."

"It doesn't surprise me that Ralph is spreading rumors about me, but I hate that he's upsetting Wyatt."

Lily sighed. "He's still hurting over Russ. Our son has cut us from his life as if we don't exist. It's painful for both of us, but my husband is taking it particularly hard."

This was news to Julia. She hadn't known her ex-husband had chosen to ignore his parents the same way he pretended his daughter didn't exist. "I'm so sorry."

"It hurts, a lot, but what can we do? We've reached out to him, but he wants little to do with us. We can only hope his attitude changes in the future."

"I hope so, too." Did Wyatt blame her because Russ had abandoned them? She wondered what sorts of things Ralph was whispering in his ear. Was her job in jeopardy?

She walked Lily to the front door. "I hope you'll come by again soon."

"I'd love to. What if I come over Saturday afternoon? I can spend some time with Ava, and we can go over our lists, maybe do some brainstorming."

"Saturday would be great. I'll see you then."

"Goodbye, dear."

She stood in the doorway and watched as Lily walked to her car, gave one last wave, and drove away. Julia went back into the house and closed the door, determined to do something to help her friend.

For the next hour she phoned everyone she could think of, asking them to help Edie and her family. Almost everyone volunteered to do something. Several mentioned throwing a fundraiser to collect money for the family. It was a good idea. She imagined the cost of Edie's treatment, along with transportation costs, hotel rooms, prescription drugs, and whatever else they were going to need, would be substantial. She'd talk to Lily on Saturday, and see what she thought of the idea.

She shook her head and smiled to herself. She hadn't expected so much support from her former mother-in-law, but it had felt good to unburden herself about some of her problems. She'd been surprised at Lily's positive reaction to Alex and the possibility of them dating, but she was sure Wyatt wouldn't share her open-minded attitude.

It didn't matter what they thought. Nothing more could ever come from her relationship with Alex.

The thought caused her infinite sadness.

Chapter Thirteen

Alex sewed five neat stitches in Aaron's left thumb, then wrapped the hand in gauze. His friend vibrated with anxiety.

"How could I be so stupid," Aaron said for what must have been the tenth time. He ran his uninjured hand over his tired face. "I've drilled a thousand holes through two-by-fours and strung a million miles of electrical wire, and today I manage to skewer my own thumb with my drill. How the hell am I supposed to work with my hand wrapped up like a God-damn mummy?"

"You're probably going to have to take a few days off. The stitches need to be in for about five days, but you've got to keep it clean or else you're going to get an infection."

"I can't afford to take a few days off!" Aaron shouted. He closed his eyes and wiped his hand over his face once more. "Sorry, Alex. This isn't your fault. I shouldn't be yelling at you."

"Don't worry about it. You're entitled to do a little yelling. Edie's surgery is the day after tomorrow, isn't it?"

"Yeah. We're leaving for Bangor tomorrow morning. They're going to do some preliminary blood work and some other tests, and then her surgery is scheduled for early the next morning. I've got to spend three nights in a hotel and pay for meals and gas, on top of the cost of Edie's surgery." He lifted his bandaged hand. "And then I go and do this. I need to work! How stupid can I be?"

"Don't beat yourself up. You're under a lot of stress. Have you been sleeping?"

Aaron sighed. "Not a lot. Neither of us has."

Alex nodded. "It's understandable. But remember, Dr. Collins is very highly thought of. He's going to take good care of Edie."

"I know. He has to. If he doesn't, I don't know what the kids and I would do…" He looked away, his voice trailing off.

"Don't even go there. Edie's going to be fine." He prayed he was telling the truth. "Listen, I've got a little extra money put aside. It's not much, but you're welcome to it."

Aaron looked up at him in surprise. "I appreciate that, Alex, more than I can tell you, but I can't take your money. Isn't the whole reason you're in Lobster Cove so you can pay off your student debt?"

He waved away Aaron's concern. "Some things are more important. I'm serious, Aaron. The money's yours if you want it."

He saw him swallow and press his right thumb and forefinger against his eyes before he turned away. When he'd composed himself once more, he looked up at Alex and nodded. "Thank you."

"You're welcome. I'll get the cash to you as soon as I can. But right now I want you to get the hell out of my ER and go home to your wife. And for God's sake, look after yourself. You're going to be useless to Edie if you don't. You can start by getting some sleep.

Doctor's orders."

Aaron hopped off the examining table. "Yeah, you're right. Thanks, Buddy. For everything."

Alex clapped him on the back. "Let me know how things go with Edie's surgery."

"I will."

He left the room, and Alex sat at the desk to complete his notes in Aaron's medical file. On top of all the worry about Edie's illness, Aaron had to deal with the stress of paying for her health care. The costs of the surgery and the ongoing treatments would be steep. The few hundred dollars that he could give would be a drop in the bucket. He hoped Edie and Aaron had some money stashed away. Or maybe their families could help.

He set down his pen and stared out the window. Despite all his years of medical training, he felt absolutely powerless to help. He closed Aaron's file and sighed. This was what happened when he let himself get involved in his patients' lives.

When he returned to work in San Diego, the anonymity of the big city meant he wouldn't know his patients outside of the ER. He could remain completely detached and uninvolved when treating them.

A tug-of-war began in his head. Was that what he really wanted? To never know who his patients were? The people of Lobster Cove meant something to him, and he fought for the health of each one of them. He was dealing with a variety of illnesses and conditions, some of which challenged all his training.

Alex's cell phone sounded, a text message alerting him that he was needed elsewhere. He didn't know all the answers, but he had a few months left on his contract in Lobster Cove to try to figure it out.

****

At first Alex thought Julia wasn't going to show up for their game, but five minutes before they were scheduled to begin, he saw her and Ava hurrying toward the ball diamond. Ava waved at him and continued on to the playground. Without a word, Julia put on her cleats and ran to her position at shortstop. He ran toward her, taking a detour on his way to the pitcher's mound.

"Everything all right?" he asked.

She didn't quite look him in the eyes. "Yeah. Fine. Just lost track of time. Sorry."

"It's okay." He wanted to say more, to ask her if she really was as fine as she claimed, but this was neither the time nor the place. He jogged over to the pitcher's mound.

An hour later the game was over. They were beaten badly by the Cranberry Island team, the mercy rule being invoked when their team was down by seven runs after the fifth inning. By now, everyone knew about Edie's illness, and an aura of worry and unease had settled over the team. Softball was the last thing on their minds.

Tracy sat next to Alex on the bench and removed her cleats. "Have you heard anything from Aaron yet? How did Edie's surgery go?"

"I got a text from him this afternoon. He said everything went well with the lumpectomy. They're going to keep Edie in the hospital overnight, and likely send her home tomorrow."

"I wish I could be with her," she said.

"I know, but she's getting great care, and Aaron's

with her. She'll be okay."

Julia sat on the other side of Tracy. "Are you talking about Edie? How's she doing?"

Alex repeated his news for her. She looked tired, her face strained.

"I'm glad she's okay. Trace, Lily Stewart and I are talking to people about what we can do to help Edie and Aaron, like babysitting, rides into Bangor and Bar Harbor for Edie's treatments, things like that. Can you give us a hand?"

"Of course." She paused, and Alex saw the way Tracy's brow wrinkled in concern. "You and Lily are working together?"

"Yeah, we are, amazingly enough. She's been very supportive."

"Lily is Ava's paternal grandmother," Tracy said for his benefit.

"I see. Is there anything I can do?"

"I don't know yet, but if there is, we'll let you know," Julia said, bending forward to tie her sneakers. She still hadn't looked at him directly. It was almost as if she was afraid to.

"I'd better get going. I'll call you tomorrow, Jules," Tracy said.

"Okay. Talk to you then."

Ava ran across the ball diamond toward them, stopping to give Tracy a hug on the way.

"Dr. Alex!"

She threw her arms around his neck, and he caught her and placed her on his knee.

"I guess I don't have to ask how your arm's doing. You almost knocked me over with it!"

She giggled. "Are you coming over to our house

tonight?"

Julia answered before he had a chance. "Not tonight, sweetie."

"Why not?"

"Because Dr. Alex has other plans."

He lifted an eyebrow at that, and she had the good grace to blush. But he wasn't going to contradict her.

"I'll see you at the next game, Ava."

"But I don't get to talk to you when you're playing ball. I'm too far away. I like when you come over to our house and we make you a sandwich."

He didn't know what to say. He glanced at Julia for help, and she laid her hand on Ava's knee.

"Honey, Alex can't come over to our house all the time. Sometimes he has to work and sometimes he has to do other stuff, and see other friends."

Ava put one arm around his neck and rested her head against his shoulder "Please come over to our house. I love you."

Alex felt like he'd been blindsided by a Mack truck. He hugged Ava close, unable to speak. When he looked over at Julia, she was struggling for composure.

"I know you care for Alex," she said, trying to smile. "He's our friend, honey, but he's got his own life. He can't come to our house all the time."

"I know," she said in a tiny voice.

"We should go home now," Julia said. "Say goodbye to Alex."

"Bye, Dr. Alex." She sounded as morose as he felt.

"Bye, Ava."

She slid off his knee and took Julia's outstretched hand. As they walked away, Ava turned to wave at him, but Julia continued to walk, refusing to look back.

She was determined to forget about their night together, to stomp out any tender feelings between them. Hell, maybe she was right. They wanted different things in life, wanted to live in different parts of the country. The chances of her changing her mind about him were remote. They were over before they even started.

But as he watched her walk away from him, his heart told him not to give up. She was worth fighting for.

****

"Hey, Nona. I'm glad I caught you."

"Alejandro, good to hear from you! How's the weather up there? Is it cold?"

Alex chuckled. Another discussion of the weather. His grandmother was nothing if not predictable. "Actually, it's hot and very humid. It is July, Nona. Southern California isn't the only place that gets hot in July."

"I'm glad to hear it. I was afraid your blood was going to freeze up there. So aside from the weather, how are you, Alejandro?"

He hesitated, not sure how to answer that. A few days ago he would have told her he was great, but now… When he closed his eyes he saw Julia walking away without a backward glance, and Ava holding her hand, looking at him with a forlorn expression in her eyes, her "I love you" ringing in his ears.

"Alejandro? What's going on?"

"I…I met someone, but it didn't work out."

He found himself telling her all about Julia, how they'd met, how strong she was, how special she was, how adamant she was about staying in Lobster Cove.

He told her about Ava and the bond they'd developed so quickly.

When he finished, Nona was silent, which was totally unlike her.

"Nona? Are you still there?"

"Yes, yes, I'm here. I've never heard you talk about a woman like this before. And I've definitely never heard you speak of a child this way. Are you sure she no longer wants to see you?"

"She doesn't think there's any point, since I'll be leaving in February. She's afraid of Ava becoming even more attached to me than she already is. She doesn't want her to get hurt."

"I suspect it's already too late to avoid hurt feelings, Alejandro, especially yours. I'm worried about you."

"I'm fine, Nona." *Or at least I will be. Someday.*

"What are you going to do?"

"I don't know if there's anything I can do. Julia is determined to shut me out. Maybe she's right. I couldn't bear to hurt her or Ava."

"You're a good boy, Alejandro, always thinking of other people. Maybe it's time to think about what you want."

"What do you mean?"

"You have to do what makes *you* happy. You have to be with the people who make you happy."

He wasn't sure how he was supposed to do that when Julia didn't want him. Even if he decided to stay in Lobster Cove, there was no guarantee of a future together.

"Thanks, Nona. I'll think about what you said. I've got to run now. I'll talk to you again soon, okay?"

"You'd better. But Alejandro, talk to your mother. She needs to hear from you."

He groaned. "We'll just get into a fight again."

"Talk to her," she said firmly. "Soon. Understand?"

"Yes, Nona."

"Good. *Te quiero.*"

"I love you, too, Nona. Talk to you soon."

He rang off and stared at his cell phone for a few minutes. What did Nona mean about his mother needing to hear from him? Was something going on with her?

He punched in his mother's number before he could change his mind. She answered after a couple of rings.

"Alex? Is everything all right?"

"Yeah, fine. What about you?"

She sighed. "Not bad under the circumstances. Getting better."

Alex sat up straighter. "What do you mean? What's going on?"

"I thought Nona would have told you. Tom and I have split."

"Oh!" That was a surprise. He stood and started to pace. "What happened? When did you split?"

"I think it's been coming for a long time. We haven't really been happy for years. Maybe we never were. Anyway, Tom came home one day a few weeks ago and said he'd met someone else. He wanted a divorce."

"The bastard dumped you?"

"It was a relief, really. Like I said, we haven't been happy for a long time."

"I'm sorry, Mom."

He wished he could offer more, but he didn't know what else to say. He'd never been in her position. Over the years he'd had many girlfriends, some he'd liked more than others, but his heart had never been truly broken when a relationship ended. There'd been no one he'd considered spending the rest of his life with. Julia's face immediately came to mind, and a shiver of unease passed through him. He had a feeling she'd be his first real broken heart. When he left, he knew a part of his heart would stay here in Lobster Cove with her.

"I appreciate that, Alex. I'm so glad you called."

He felt immediately guilty. "I'm sorry I've been so lousy about keeping in touch with you."

"I know I nag you sometimes."

"Sometimes?" Alex couldn't resist teasing her a little.

She chuckled. "Okay, a lot of the time. But I only do it because I love you and I want the best for you."

"I know, Mom, but you've got to understand that I'm a grown man and very capable of making my own decisions about my work and where I live. I'm really happy with what I'm doing right now."

"Yes, but you could make a lot more money in a another specialty—"

"Mom, I really don't want to argue with you about it."

She sighed again. "I don't want to argue with you, either. I miss you, Alex. I can hardly wait till you get home."

Another wave of guilt swamped him. Even when he'd lived in San Diego he hadn't visited her as often as he should have. Part of it was his schedule, and part was his dislike of his stepfather. But another part was that his meetings with his mother always turned into a tug-of-war.

"It won't be long," he said evasively. "Are you going to stay in the house in La Jolla?"

"No. It's on the market. We have to split all our joint property."

"Have you thought about where you're going to live after you sell?"

She sighed. "I've looked at a couple of places, but real estate in La Jolla is so expensive."

"Chula Vista isn't as expensive, and you'd be closer to your family there."

"I suppose." She sounded less than enthusiastic. Her voice cracked. "The hardest thing is starting over again. I'm not sure I have the energy."

Alex ached for her. "You're going to be okay. I know you are. Listen, you could come out here for a visit. Maybe a change of scenery would do you good. I've got plenty of space."

"I appreciate the invitation, I really do, but I've got so much to do right now with selling the house and finding a new place. But I'll think about it."

"Good." He looked at his watch. "It's getting late, Mom, and I have an early start tomorrow. I'll talk to you soon."

"Goodnight, Alex. Thanks for calling."

"Goodnight, Mom."

He set the phone on the kitchen table. He and his mother had always had their issues, but he loved her. He wished he could go to her right now and give her a big hug. For the first time since he'd moved to Maine, he felt the huge distance between them, both literally and figuratively, and wished it wasn't so far.

****

Julia, Ava, and Tracy arrived at the Cosgrove house with several bags of groceries and a bouquet of lilies, Edie's favorite. Natalie let them into the house and led them to the living room, where Edie was lying on the couch in front of the TV. Ava took Natalie's hand and they ran upstairs together. The baby screamed in her playpen, and Michael played with Legos that were spread all across the living room floor. Blankets and pillows were strewn across the dining room table and chairs where the kids had built a fort. Julia knew Edie had to be feeling rough for her house to be in this state of chaos. She normally ran a tight ship and hated mess and disorganization of any kind.

Julia set her bags on the floor and picked up the crying baby, who settled as soon as she was released from the playpen. She stooped to kiss Edie's forehead. "How are you, sweetie?"

"Good. A little sore, but mostly tired."

"That's to be expected after general anesthesia and a procedure like yours," Tracy said.

"Yes, so I've been told." Edie pointed to the bags in Tracy's hands. "What have you got there?"

"Groceries. Mostly stuff you can put together easily to make a meal tonight."

"You guys didn't have to do that."

"You'd better get used to it," Julia said. "Starting tomorrow, we've got an army of people organized to look after you and the kids. We're going to make sure you get plenty of rest."

"What?"

"We don't want you to worry about anything,"

Tracy said. She lifted one of the bags she carried. “Julia, I’ll take care of the food if you look after the baby.”

“Okay.” Julia sniffed Abigail. “I think I’d better change this little one. She doesn’t smell so good.”

Edie tried to get to her feet. “You don’t have to do that.”

“You stay right there. It’s not like I haven’t changed a poopy diaper before. I’ll be right back.”

Julia took little Abigail upstairs to her room. Despite what she’d said to Edie, she was out of practice when it came to changing the diaper of a squirming baby, and it took her a little longer then she’d expected to complete the task. But she finally got a clean diaper on her, along with a clean set of clothes.

When she and Abigail returned to the living room, she saw that Tracy had placed the lilies in a vase on a side table. Julia put the baby back in her playpen, though Abigail let her displeasure be known with a loud screech. Julia was afraid if she let her out, she’d grab one of the Legos lying on the floor and stick it in her mouth.

“C’mon, Mike. Let’s pick these up.” In a few minutes they had the Legos back in their plastic containers.

“Where’s Aaron?” Tracy asked when she came back into the room.

Edie sighed, closing her eyes briefly. “He’s working. With the medical bills starting to pile up, he’s worried about money.”

“How can he manage, with his hand bandaged and his thumb full of stitches?”

“His thumb full of stitches?” Julia asked. “What

happened?"

Edie told her how he'd injured himself. "He was overtired from not sleeping, and his mind just wasn't on his work. I'm afraid he's pushing himself so hard he's going to hurt himself even worse."

"It was just a momentary slip," Tracy said. "Aaron will be fine. You need to concentrate on looking after yourself."

Edie's chin quivered. "How can I do that when my husband is worrying himself to death about money and my kids are picking up on how scared we both are?" She glanced at her son, clearly worried she'd said too much.

"You're not in this alone, Edie. We're going to get you through it." Julia made a quick decision. "Is your mother coming over to look after the kids today?"

"Yes," Edie said with a sniff. "My parents are both coming over when they get off work."

"Good. I'll tell you what. We were going to stay here, but I think it would be better if Tracy and I took the kids for the afternoon. I'll call your mom and tell her to pick them up at my house after work. I want you to relax and sleep while the house is quiet."

"I can't let you do that, Julia."

"Oh, yeah? And how are you going to stop me?" She gave her friend a smile. "Just take care of yourself, okay?"

Tears streamed down Edie's face. "Okay. I love you guys."

"We love you too, sweetheart. And like I said, there will be someone around tomorrow to look after you and the kids, and we're going to keep on looking after you until you don't need us anymore. You and

Aaron aren't alone."

Julia bent to kiss Edie's forehead once more. She couldn't do anything about the cancer, but she was going make damn sure her friends got everything they needed to get safely through this ordeal.

****

The following Saturday afternoon, Lily arrived with a binder filled with names and phone numbers of people who had volunteered to help the Cosgroves.

"You've been busy," Julia said with a laugh.

"You bet! I'm glad to help Edie and her family. It feels good to do something positive for someone else instead of worrying about my own problems."

"I know exactly what you mean." Concentrating on Edie took her mind off her parents' problems, at least temporarily.

She wished she could say the same about Alex. Not an hour went by that she didn't think of him, wonder what he was doing, who he was with. Every night she remembered what it had been like between them. She remembered his scorching kisses, the gentle touch of his hands, the feel of his body against hers. She remembered what it had been like to have him inside her, thrusting, pushing, stretching—

Enough. With an effort she pushed thoughts of Alex away.

"Grandma!" Ava ran toward them, a look of pure joy on her face. "You're here! Can you play with me today?"

Lily bent to give Ava a hug. "Your mom and I have some business to do, but I think there'll be some time for us to play."

"Can we go to the playground at the school?"

Lily looked to her for confirmation, and Julia smiled. "I think you and Grandma will have time to do that, honey. Why don't you play by yourself for a while so we can finish our work?"

"Okay. Can I bring my dolls down here?"

Julia knew she just wanted to be close to them. "Sure, but what do you have to do when you're done playing with your toys?"

"Put them back in my room."

"Good girl. Go ahead."

She ran up the stairs. Lily smiled at Julia. "She's a sweet child, a joy to be around. You've done such a good job with her."

Julia was surprised at her praise. "Thank you. I'm very proud of Ava."

"You should be. And you should be proud of yourself, too. You've raised her by yourself these last three years. I know that couldn't have been easy."

"No, not always. It was tough sometimes, but my mom and dad helped me a lot." And now Lily had stepped in to give her a hand. Perhaps it was time to trust her a little more. "Ava's a little older now. Maybe she could have a sleepover at your house sometime soon."

Lily's chin quivered, and for a moment Julia thought she was going to cry. Instead she reached across the table and squeezed her hand. "You can't imagine how happy I am to hear you say that. I know Wyatt will be thrilled, too."

"I'm doing this for Ava. She deserves to know her family."

"Yes, she does." Lily wiped a tear from the corner of her eye. "Well. Let's get to work, shall we?"

For the next hour they made schedules for their volunteers and made lists of things to do and people they still wanted to contact, while Ava had a tea party with Snowball the cat and her dolls in a corner of the kitchen. Julia phoned Tracy at the hospital at the time she'd told her she'd be on her break, in order to get her thoughts about holding a fundraiser. She was all for the idea, so the three of them did some brainstorming over the phone. They decided they'd have a dance, with admission fees going to the Cosgrove family. They also made plans for a live auction sale during the dance. A few big ticket items, hopefully donated for the cause, would go up for bids. Smaller donated items could go into a silent auction, where people bought tickets for the chance to win the prize.

"It looks like the two of you have the volunteer situation under control. Edie told me people have been arriving at her house like clockwork to offer food and babysitting services," Tracy said.

"All we need to do now is get lots of donations for the fundraiser," Julia said.

"Not to mention booking a venue and a disc jockey and convincing them to give us their services for free," Lily added.

"I'll see if the school board will waive the usual rental fee for the high school gym," Julia said, writing a note to remind herself. "It's big enough to hold a lot of people. Hopefully we'll fill it up."

"Sounds good, Jules. I've got to get back to work," Tracy said, "but I'm off tomorrow. I'll phone around and see if I can scrape together some donations."

"Thanks, Tracy. I'll talk to you tomorrow."

"Bye."

The doorbell rang and Ava ran to the front door to see who was there. A minute later Julia heard her say, "Hi, Chloe!"

"Oh, shoot!" she whispered to Lily. "I forgot I asked Chloe to come over to watch Ava this afternoon. I was going to going to go over to the school today and do some work to get ready for the fall term."

"You've had a lot on your mind," Lily said sympathetically.

"I know, but I still feel bad. I'd better go talk to her."

She went into the living room where Ava was busy showing Chloe her Barbie doll's newest outfit.

"Hi, Chloe," Julia said. "I should have called you, but I forgot. I won't be working at the school today after all. I'm so sorry to make you come over for nothing. But of course I'll pay you for your time."

To her surprise, the teenager appeared distressed by her news, almost on the verge of tears. She turned her head, her long, blonde hair partially hiding her face.

"No, that's okay. I'll just…I'll just go, I guess."

Julia put her hand on her arm as she turned to leave. "Wait a minute, will you, Chloe? Ava, can you go see Grandma in the kitchen? I'm going to walk Chloe out."

"Okay. Bye, Chloe. See you later." She skipped into the kitchen.

Julia grabbed her purse from the front hall closet and pulled out some bills. "Let's go for a little walk."

She held the door open and, avoiding her gaze, Chloe stepped through. They walked in silence to the street. Julia stopped and turned to Chloe, putting the bills in her hand.

"Is there something wrong, honey?"

With her eyes downcast, Chloe shook her head. "No."

"You know, if there's ever something, anything, you need to talk about, if you need a friend, I'm here. Believe me, I know how much it helps to talk to someone when you have a problem. Whatever you say will stay between us. Okay?"

She looked up then, and Julia saw the pain in her green eyes. "Okay."

Julia patted her thin shoulder and attempted a smile. Something was going on with her, but if she didn't want to talk, she couldn't make her. "Good. I'll talk to you soon. I'm working on raising money for some friends with medical expenses, and I'll probably need you to help look after Ava."

"Okay. Bye."

"Bye, Chloe."

She watched her walk down the sidewalk for a few minutes before sighing and going back into the house. Chloe was not the kind of kid who was equipped to deal well with adversity. She was fragile and, even at sixteen, almost childlike. Julia wished she could take her under her wing and protect her from a harsh, uncaring world.

Wouldn't Ralph Sykes love that?

Chapter Fourteen

Tracy Novak waved Alex over to the table where she sat with a group of nurses in the hospital's small cafeteria. When he reached their table, he set his tray at the empty spot beside Tracy.

"Alex, I was just telling everyone about the fundraiser we're trying to organize for Edie and Aaron."

"A fundraiser?"

"Yeah, something to help offset some of Edie's medical expenses. Julia's trying to put together a dance and an auction where people can bid on prizes. We're trying to come up with some donations, things people can get excited to bid on."

Julia. How like her to try to help her friends. "Is there anything I can do?"

"Maybe you can make a cash donation. I'm taking up a collection here at the hospital so we can buy some prizes for the fundraiser."

Alex reached into his back pocket and pulled out his wallet. He took out two twenties. "This is all the cash I have right now. I'll talk to you again after I have a chance to go to the bank."

"Thanks, Alex. Much appreciated."

Some of the other nurses made donations, as well. Brenda, a tall blonde woman who worked in the family medicine clinic attached to the hospital, handed over a five-dollar bill.

"I've known Edie since we were kids. Julia said she planned to have a bake sale to go along with the fundraiser, so I'm going to do some baking when I'm off later this week."

"I'll make a poster and let everyone on the second floor know you're collecting money, Tracy," Gloria said.

"I could send out a mass e-mail." Alex knew Connie worked in the administration office. "I'm sure my boss won't mind, but I'll clear it with him first. That way everyone who works at the hospital will hear about the fundraiser and the need for donations."

"My mother-in-law volunteered to help with cleaning at Edie's house. She and Aaron's mom are good friends," Denise said. "I'm taking over a casserole tomorrow."

Alex was astounded by their generosity. "It's good of all of you to help the Cosgroves out."

Gloria shrugged. "It's what you do in a small town. When someone's in trouble, you help them out."

"I know that if I ever got sick and needed help like Edie does now, my community would be there for me," Connie said.

"We're pretty tight here," Tracy said. "Lobster Cove is a very special place."

Alex was beginning to see she was right.

****

Alex used his scissors to carefully remove the stitches in Aaron's thumb. After flushing the affected area with a saline solution, he applied an antibiotic cream and wrapped his hand with clean gauze.

"How does that feel?"

Aaron flexed his hand. “Better. I couldn’t bend my thumb before, because of the stitches.”

“Would it do any good to tell you to stay off work until it healed?”

Aaron grinned. “Probably not.”

“At least humor me and promise you’ll keep the wound clean.”

“I’ll try.”

That was probably the best he was going to get. “Good. So aside from the thumb, how are you doing, really?”

Aaron hung his head for a moment before looking up at Alex with a rueful smile. “Better than the last time I saw you. I’m hanging in there.”

“I’m glad to hear it. Tracy told me about the fundraiser. You have a lot of friends in town.”

He laughed softly. “I’ve lived in Lobster Cove all my life, and I knew it was a great community, but I had no idea how great, until Edie got sick. People have been there for us every step of the way. From the day we came home from the hospital after her surgery, someone has been over every day to look after the kids so Edie can rest. Someone else cleaned the house. Every evening another person shows up with a new casserole or a dessert. And now this fundraiser is coming up. It’s been remarkable, and very humbling.”

It *was* remarkable. Alex had never heard of anything like it.

“What I’m really thankful for is that Julia has already arranged for people to drive Edie into Bar Harbor for her radiation treatments when they start next week. Like I told you before, I can’t afford to take time off work. Our parents all work, too, and they were prepared to take some time off, but this takes the pressure off all of us. We know someone we trust will be driving Edie and looking after her."

"Julia arranged for drivers?"

Aaron smiled. "Yeah, Julia's our master organizer. She had lots of help, from what I understand, but if you want to get something done, give the job to Julia. If you want to get the job done in a hurry, tell her it can't be done."

Alex laughed at that. She was really something, his Julia.

His Julia.

"She's an amazing woman."

Aaron gave him a curious look. "Yeah, she is pretty amazing. Some men find that intimidating. Like Russ, her ex-husband. He never appreciated her."

He couldn't help himself from asking, "You knew him? What was he like?"

"Sure, I knew him. We all grew up together, Edie, me, Julia, Tracy, Russ. Julia and Russ started dating in the tenth grade. They seemed like the perfect match. Both were smart, and they both wanted to be teachers. But when I think back now, there were cracks in their relationship even back then. Julia had always been a sports nut, an athlete. You've seen her play ball."

"Yeah." When she committed herself to something, no matter what it was—a ball game, an issue at her school, a fundraiser—she gave it everything she had. It was one of the things he admired most about her.

"Russ wasn't much of an athlete, so he made fun of her love of playing ball and other sports. It was subtle, but when they came back to Lobster Cove after living in Thailand, she didn't play ball the summer after Ava was born. She said it was too soon after the birth, but then she didn't play the next summer, either. She didn't start playing ball again until Russ left.

"I think he was jealous of her. Back in high school, if she got a higher mark than he did, he'd get upset. I remember him going back to our chemistry teacher and arguing with him about the mark he got on an exam. The teacher finally caved in and gave him two extra marks on a problem, which just so happened to give him a higher mark than Julia."

"He sounds like an insecure ass."

"I guess he was, but we didn't realize it back then. He was funny, and we all had a good time together. Julia adored him." Aaron frowned. "I didn't realize how bad things were between them until Julia was offered the job as principal of the school and, essentially, became Russ's boss. That's when he started insisting on going back to Thailand."

It sounded like he couldn't handle his wife having a better job than he did, so he found a way to take it away from her. "But Julia didn't want to go?"

He shrugged. "As far as I knew, she was planning to. I'm not sure what happened to change her mind."

"Any man who'd let a woman like Julia slip through his fingers is a moronic jerk."

Aaron lifted his eyebrows and grinned. "Are you talking about Russ or yourself? Sounds like the words of a man who has a serious addiction to a cute, blonde, ball-playing teacher."

He hadn't meant to let his feelings show. "Just shut up and try not to mangle your other hand."

"Aye, aye, Doc," Aaron said with a grin and a crisp salute. As he hopped off the table, his demeanor sobered. "Look, I get that you like Julia. She's a terrific girl. But you're only here temporarily. I wouldn't want her to get hurt, you know?"

"I wouldn't want her to get hurt either."

Aaron stared at him with solemn hazel eyes. Finally he nodded. "Good. Are we done here?"

"We're done. Remember, if you or Edie have any questions, if you need any medical advice or you just want to talk, you have my number. Call any time."

"We will, thanks. The same goes for you, you know. Well, not the medial advice, but the talking part. That's what friends are for, right?"

It had been a while since he'd had a close male friend, probably not since his early college days. The last few years he'd maintained a laser focus on his studies and his career, to the detriment of his personal relationships. He was touched by Aaron's offer.

"Yeah. That's what friends are for."

****

Two weeks later, Alex walked up the sidewalk to the Lobster Cove High School. Even the outside of the school had been decorated for the fundraiser. Twinkling lights outlined the main door of the school, which opened to a corridor leading to the gymnasium. The place was already packed with people of all ages: adults, kids, even the elderly. Everyone in Lobster Cove, and beyond, wanted to support the Cosgrove family. Alex was surprised to see players he knew from the opposing ball teams in Bar Harbor, Cranberry Island, and Tremont. It said a lot about Aaron and Edie that so many people cared about what happened to them.

It said a lot about the community, too.

Inside the gym, a deejay had people on the dance floor doing an energetic jive. Little kids on the edges of the floor tried their best to imitate the older dancers. Tables had been set up along the perimeter of the gym, except for one section in the far corner where silent auction prizes were being displayed. Money quickly changed hands as people bought tickets on the prizes. Alex knew that every dollar raised would go to Edie's substantial medical expenses. He bought fifty dollars' worth of tickets and dropped his entries into the paper bags taped next to the prizes.

Next to the silent auction tables, some older ladies manned a table loaded with baked goods for sale. The offerings were impressive—fresh breads, pies, cookies and at least twenty different kinds of cakes. Before he left, he'd pick up a couple dozen cookies to take to the emergency room for the people who couldn't make it here tonight.

"Alex!"

He turned at the sound of his name and saw Edie and Aaron heading toward him. Edie embraced him.

"I'm so glad you could make it!" she said with a beaming smile.

"I wouldn't miss it. This is quite the production you've got going on here."

"It's great, but we can't take any credit. We didn't do a damn thing," Aaron said.

Edie's eyes were misty with tears. "Our friends did all this for us. It's wonderful, isn't it?"

He put his arm around her shoulder. "You have great friends. You're very lucky."

"Yes, we are."

"How do you feel?"

"I actually feel very well, very rested. I haven't had to lift a finger since my surgery, with so many people looking after us. I've gotten quite spoiled."

Alex squeezed her shoulders. "You deserve to be spoiled. I understand your radiation starts next week. Are you okay with that?"

"I say bring it on! The sooner I get rid of all those nasty little cancer cells, the better."

Her attitude was remarkable. "Go get 'em, Tiger."

She stood on her tiptoes to kiss his cheek. "Thank you, Alex."

"For what? All I did was send you on for further testing. You're the one who found the lump."

"You took the lump seriously. At the cancer clinic in Bangor, I met a woman not much older than me whose breast cancer had spread to her lungs. She went to her GP about the lump she found in her breast, and he told her it was nothing, that someone as young as she was didn't need to worry about cancer. By the time she sought a second opinion, it was too late. Her cancer was incurable. So, thank you, Alex."

He swallowed hard. "You're welcome."

He didn't know what else to say. All he knew was that he was profoundly grateful he'd investigated Edie's lump when he did.

Aaron shook his hand. "We should probably say hello to more folks. Thanks for coming, Alex. We'll talk soon."

They walked off and were soon mobbed by more well-wishers. Alex smiled to himself. If anybody deserved to be looked after like this, it was Edie and Aaron.

He spent the next hour mingling. People he didn't

know made a point of introducing themselves and of introducing him to others. There were people he knew from the hospital, a couple of fellow doctors, and many nurses and technicians. Maggie from Maggie's Diner was there, along with her business partner Jill. Jill introduced her friend Marge, though he already knew Marge since she'd been cutting his hair at her hairdressing shop since he moved to Mount Desert Island. Beth, Julia's secretary at the high school, was there with her kids and her husband Marty. Tracy's brother Logan introduced himself, as did her parents, Opal and Leo Novak. He hoped there wasn't a quiz after the party, because he wasn't sure he'd remember everyone's name.

"Dr. Alex!"

A familiar child's voice drew his attention. Ava ran toward him at full throttle. She threw herself at him with her arms wide, and he picked her up and hugged her close.

"I knew you'd be here," she said in his ear. She smelled of shampoo and soap and sunshine. A tender emotion squeezed his heart. He knew Julia didn't want him getting close to Ava only to break her heart in a few months when he left, but it was getting harder and harder not to fall in love with this child.

"Where's your mom, Sweet Pea?" The endearment came out of his mouth before he remembered he wasn't supposed to call her that.

"She's busy, so I'm here with my Grandma and Grandpa."

Alex was surprised to hear that Paul Dawson had brought Dora here, until he saw an older couple coming up to him, and he realized she was talking about a different set of grandparents. The man held out his hand.

"I'm Wyatt Stewart, Ava's grandfather, and this is my wife Lily."

Alex shook hands with them, balancing Ava on his left arm. "Alex Campbell. Good to meet you."

Lily Stewart arranged Ava's dress and straightened the barrettes holding back her blonde curls. "You certainly like Dr. Campbell, don't you, Sweet Pea?"

Ava turned to Alex. "See? Grandma calls me that, too."

"That's because you're so pretty, like a Sweet Pea. And you smell kinda good, too, at least sometimes."

Ava giggled and put her arm around his neck. He saw her grandparents exchange a look and wondered what it meant.

"I understand you'll be leaving Lobster Cove next February when your contract is up," Wyatt said.

At least he didn't beat around the bush. "Yes, that's my plan."

"Ava's welfare and happiness is very important to us," he said.

"I'm sure it is. It's important to me, too."

Wyatt smiled, though there was no warmth in the gesture. "I'm glad to hear you say that. I would hate for us to have any misunderstandings."

"Wyatt." Lily Stewart's voice held a note of warning for her husband. She placed her hand on his arm, her smile strained. "Let's just concentrate on having fun with our granddaughter tonight. Please?"

He sighed and placed his hand over hers. "Yes, you're right." He looked up at Alex. "I hear good things about your medical skills, Dr. Campbell. You're a welcome addition to the community. It would be a shame if you left Lobster Cove just when we're getting to know you."

He didn't know how to respond. Luckily, Julia stepped up to the mike on the stage at that moment, preventing him from having to speak.

"Can I have your attention, everyone? Our big auction extravaganza is about to begin!"

Whoops of excitement filled the gymnasium. Ava whispered in his ear, "Doesn't Mommy look pretty tonight? I helped her pick out her dress."

"You did a great job, Sweet Pea. Your mommy is very pretty."

The word "pretty" hardly expressed how Julia looked tonight. *Gorgeous, sexy, delicious*, sprang immediately to mind. Her pale blonde hair gleamed under the stage lights. She wore a sleeveless blue and white print dress that hugged her curves and ended several inches above her knees to show off shapely, toned legs. High-heeled sandals accentuated her well-formed calves. For a petite woman, she had legs that went on for miles.

"Our auctioneer tonight is Jacob Wright from Wright Country Auctions in Bar Harbor. Mr. Wright is donating his services tonight, so I want you to put your hands together and give him a warm Lobster Cove welcome and a big thank you."

The crowd complied with generous applause. "There's still time to purchase an auction paddle for a nominal fee at the ticket booth. Remember, you've got to have a paddle in order to bid on the fantastic goods and services we've gotten together."

Alex wasn't sure if he was going to bid on

anything, but he set Ava on her feet and stood in line at the ticket booth to purchase a paddle, number two hundred twenty-one. He wondered if it was his lucky number.

By the time he got back to his spot next to Ava and the Stewarts, volunteers were carrying, or wheeling, the auction items onto the stage. Ava tugged at his pant leg.

"I can't see, Dr. Alex."

He picked her up once more, settling her in his left arm. "No problem, Shorty. I wouldn't want you to miss any of the action."

She grinned at him before draping one arm across the back of his shoulders, and idly stroking the hair at the nape of his neck.

The lights in the gym went on, signaling that the bidding was about to begin. First on the block was a fifty-inch flat-screen TV. Julia described the television's make and model. "This TV was donated by Addison's Furniture and Appliances in Bar Harbor. A big thanks to Merv Addison. And now, I'm turning the mic over to Jacob Wright. Take it away, Jacob."

"Thanks, Julia." Jacob walked to the edge of the stage and addressed the crowd. "Okay, everyone! We all know we're here to support one of our island families, so let's all be generous. What do you say we put this fundraiser in motion? Let's start the bidding on the TV at five hundred dollars."

Paddles shot up all over the gymnasium. In his auctioneer's patois, Jacob Wright acknowledged each outstretched arm, until finally there was only one hand left raised. "Sold for two thousand five hundred dollars to paddle number seventy-five!"

Alex was reasonably sure twenty-five hundred was

above the retail price for the television, and he was also sure everyone in the room realized that. But he knew the person who purchased the TV was okay with paying a little more if it meant Edie could afford her treatments.

A long list of electronics went up for auction: another television, DVD players, laptops, tablets, MP3 players, and e-readers. The crowd bid enthusiastically. Alex stuck his paddle in the air for several of the prizes but was outbid every time.

Next up were services donated by local businesses. Marge the hairdresser donated two prizes: a year's worth of haircuts, and a year's worth of cuts and colors. Maggie's Diner offered three separate prizes: a catered sit-down dinner for up to twenty people, a cocktail party with hors d'oeuvres for fifty, and a meal a month for two for a year in the diner. The vet clinic donated a free spay or neuter for a dog or cat, as well as a year's supply of pet food. A dentist in Bar Harbor offered free teeth cleaning for a family of four. Many other local businesses on the island donated their services. Paddles rose furiously. The Stewarts bid on both the haircuts and the diner meals. They were successful in their bid for the meals. Lily Stewart raised her arms in triumph at the auctioneer's, "You bought it!"

"Yay, we did it!"

"Yay, Grandma!" Ava cheered with a pump of her tiny arm. Alex tightened his hold on her as she squirmed.

"Now it's time for the last two auction items to go up for bid," the auctioneer said. "These are the items marked as surprise entries on your list of auction prizes, and we've kept them top secret to this point. So without further ado, let me bring out your first surprise auction prize!"

He swept his hand toward the back curtain, and, after some rustling and shaking, the curtain opened and Tracy Novak stepped through. A murmur of surprise and lots of claps and cheers rippled through the crowd. She stood next to Mr. Wright and spoke into the microphone, talking directly to Edie, who stood with Aaron in front of the stage.

"You're the only person in the world I'd do this for, with the possible exception of Julia. I love you, Edie." She threw her a kiss.

"Tell the folks about your prize, Tracy," Mr. Wright said.

She took a deep breath that was clearly audible over the sound system. "I am offering a dinner and movie date with me as my prize. The location of said dinner and movie is the winner's choice. I'm really hoping someone bids on my prize, aside from my relatives. And it goes without saying, but I'm going to say it anyway: Please, no bids from married men. Or women."

Everyone laughed. Alex knew Tracy well enough to realize putting herself up for display like this was not easy for her. Though very confident and competent in her work, she was actually quite shy. But tonight, her desire to help her friend had trumped her usual reserve.

Perhaps he could boost her confidence a little while helping Edie and Aaron.

"What do think, Sweet Pea? Should we bid on Tracy?"

Her eyes lit up. "Yes! Can I hold the paddle?"

"Sure. I'll tell you when to stick your hand up."

Lily Stewart grinned at him. “Tracy doesn’t give herself enough credit. You’re going to have to do some serious bidding if you want to win a date with her.”

“We’re ready, aren’t we, Ava?”

“Yes!”

Lily was right. Six other men bid on Tracy in rapid-fire succession, moving the price of her prize to five hundred dollars in a matter of minutes. Finally it came down to him and one other man.

“One thousand dollars!” the man shouted from the floor.

“That’s Rob Perkins,” Wyatt whispered to his wife.

“Fascinating,” Lily replied. “I had no idea the school superintendent was interested in Tracy.”

“Neither did I. But now the whole town knows,” Wyatt replied with a grin.

It looked like Tracy needn’t have worried that no one would bid for her. Alex whispered in Ava’s ear. “Put the paddle down, Sweet Pea.”

She obediently complied. A minute later the auctioneer pointed at Perkins and cried, “You bought her! Come and get her!”

The gymnasium erupted in spontaneous applause, apparently approving the purchase. Perkins weaved through the crowd and bounded up the stairs to the stage. Tracy stuck out her hand to shake his, and he took it, then leaned in and gave her a brief hug. Hoots rose from the crowd. As they left the stage, he took her hand again to help her down the stairs. Alex noticed the shy smile she gave him, and he realized Tracy approved of the purchase, as well.

When the crowd settled down, the auctioneer began speaking again. “We’ve come to our second top secret prize, the last auction item of the evening. I'll turn the floor over to my co-host, the lovely and talented Julia Stewart."

Julia took the mic from Jacob Wright, and for the first time this evening, Alex sensed her nervousness. She took a step toward the front of the stage.

"Like Tracy said, I wouldn't do this for anyone but you, Edie. I'm not even sure I'd do it for Tracy anymore, since she was the one who talked me into this. In any event, my prize is an all-expense paid date with me. The winner has the choice of a round of golf at the beautiful Mount Desert Island Golf and Country Club, a day of sailing, or hiking in Acadia National Park. Our day of adventure will be followed by a lovely meal at Maggie's Diner, and Maggie has promised to whip up something special that she doesn't normally serve on the menu, so that should be a real treat. I guess that's about it."

She handed the mic back to Mr. Wright. "Before we start the bidding, I just want to say that both these ladies have worked tirelessly the last few weeks to put this event together. Not only are we raising money to help Edie through her treatments, we're having a lot of fun doing it. So please show your appreciation for Tracy Novak and Julia Stewart."

The crowd burst into applause once more. Julia raised her hand in acknowledgement, looking somewhat embarrassed by the praise. Pride for her swelled in Alex's chest. He knew from Tracy that because of her schedule at the hospital, Julia had done the bulk of the planning. She'd had help from a lot of different people, including Lily Stewart, but she'd been the one to put it all together.

The auctioneer began the bidding. "Can I have two hundred dollars to start? And remember, no married men or women need apply."

Dozens of hands shot up. "Can I have three, four, five, gimme six, now gimme seven."

Lily leaned close. "Why don't you bid, Dr. Campbell?"

He hesitated, not wanting to embarrass Julia. She'd been pretty clear about not wanting to be with him again. It still hurt.

"I don't think Julia would want me to."

"I think you'd be surprised. Trust me."

Something in Lily Stewart's smile made him lift Ava's arm into the air. She waved the paddle with enthusiasm, squirming with excitement in his arms. He wasn't even sure where the bidding was at.

"We've got nine hundred. A thousand anyone? Going once, going twice, sold to the good doctor for nine hundred dollars! You bought her! Come and get her!"

Alex's heart thumped painfully. As he set Ava on the floor, his gaze collided with Wyatt Stewart's. Pain flashed across the older man's face, and he wondered at its cause.

"Grandpa, Dr. Alex won Mommy!"

"I know, sweetheart."

People within earshot chuckled at Ava's statement. Mr. Stewart smiled for his granddaughter, laying a gentle hand on her head. But there was no happiness in his face. Would he have objected to anyone dating his son's former wife, or just him?

Ava pushed at Alex's leg. "Go get her! Quick!"

"All right, all right."

He headed through the crowd, accepting good-natured congratulations and slaps on the back. His feet felt heavy and leaden. Would Julia be angry with him? He decided he wouldn't push her to go on the date. He'd leave the decision to her. If she was interested in seeing him, she had to make the first move.

He climbed the stairs to the stage and accepted Julia's outstretched hand. Her smile felt strained, like he was the last person in the room she'd wanted to win the bid. His heart fell. As he gave her a brief one-armed hug, he whispered in her ear.

"I'm sorry."

But he couldn't stop himself from breathing in her scent or squeezing her hand. She blinked at him when he stepped back, confusion flashing in her eyes before being replaced by a bland smile.

Edie and Aaron stepped on the stage, and Edie wrapped her arms around Julia. Aaron shook his hand, his face full of emotion. Alex clapped him on the back in a gesture of support.

Edie let Julia out of her embrace, but held tight to her hand. The auctioneer passed her the microphone. A hush fell over the crowd as she took a couple of minutes to compose herself before speaking.

"I want to thank everyone for coming out tonight. I can't tell you how much your support means to Aaron and me. You've turned one of the darkest times of our lives into one of the brightest."

The crowd cheered. When they quieted, she spoke again. "Lobster Cove is a very special community. We look after each other here. We care for each other. There's no place else in the world I'd rather live, no place else in the world I'd rather raise my children.

From the bottom of my heart, thank you."

Another cheer rose from the crowd. "I especially want to thank everyone who made this night possible, especially my two best friends, Tracy Novak and Julia Stewart. I can't express how thankful I am for you two. I love you both."

She hugged Julia once more. Tears rolled down Julia's face as she clung to Edie, and Alex knew she was hanging on to her composure by a thread. He fought the urge to go to her and pull her into his arms. She wouldn't thank him for showing his feelings in front of the entire population of her hometown.

He stepped off the stage as inconspicuously as he could, and made his way to the table manned by Jill from the diner and several other volunteers who were collecting the proceeds of the auction. Writing a check for his purchase, and adding an extra hundred dollars to make an even thousand, he handed it to Jill.

"Thank you very much for your contribution, Dr. Campbell," she said with a smile.

"Please, call me Alex. I spend so much time in your diner I feel we should be on a first-name basis."

"All right. Alex it is." She wrote a receipt and handed it to him. "You made a very fine purchase."

"Yeah."

He couldn't help turning his attention back to the stage. Edie and Aaron had stepped down, leaving Julia alone to handle the master of ceremonies duties. Her voice sounded shaky, as if she was still struggling with her emotions.

"I invite you to take a look at the silent auction prizes we've assembled. There's something there for everyone. We'll be picking the winners in an hour, so there's still time to get your tickets. And the ladies at the bake sale booth tell me they still have some items for sale. Everything has to go, so please go see them. I'm going to turn over the mic to our deejay now. Let's get this party started!"

Alex closed his eyes. He had to get out of here. He couldn't listen to Julia's voice anymore, couldn't watch her, and still pretend there wasn't something between them. He couldn't hide his feelings any longer.

He was in love with her.

"Dr. Campbell? Alex? Are you okay?"

Jill stared at him with a concerned look on her face. She probably thought he was crazy. Maybe he was. He couldn't be in love with Julia. He was leaving in six months.

He made himself smile. "Yeah I'm fine. Just a little tired."

"Go home and get some rest. We can't have our favorite doctor keel over from lack of sleep. We need you!"

"No rest for the wicked, I'm afraid. I'm heading to the hospital to work a partial shift so Dr. Willson can take in some of the festivities here."

"That was good of you."

Alex shrugged. "He would have done the same for me."

"True, but you look like a guy who needs some pampering. Come into the diner this week, and I'll fix you up with some home cooking. *Gratis*."

"Thanks, Jill, I appreciate that. I'll see you soon. Good night."

"Good night, Doc."

After saying good night to Edie and Aaron, Alex

bought two dozen cookies and some brownies to take to the staff at the hospital. Then he looked for the Stewarts so he could say goodnight to Ava. He spotted them not far from the stage, talking with Julia. She looked up when he approached, her expression guarded.

"I have to take off for work now," he said, shaking Wyatt's and Lily's hands. "It was nice meeting you."

"Good to meet you, too," Wyatt said. Alex wondered if he meant it.

Ava tugged at his pant leg. "Good night, Dr. Alex. When will I see you again?"

He laid his hand on her head, and stroked her soft curls. "There's still a couple of games left in our ball season. I guess I'll see you there."

"But I don't get to talk to you there. When are you coming to our house again?"

Alex glanced at Julia. She blinked and looked away. He picked up Ava and gave her a hug. "I'm not sure, Sweet Pea, but I'll be thinking about you."

She hugged his neck. "I'll be thinking about you, too."

He squeezed his eyes closed and did his best to compose himself before setting her down. He turned to Julia.

"You did a great job tonight. Congratulations."

"Thank you, but I had a lot of help from people like Lily." She gave him an uncertain smile. "Thanks for bidding on my prize. I guess I'll see you on our date. What would you like to do?"

Visions of making love to her danced through his head. He pushed them away, desperately trying to keep his expression neutral.

"I'll leave that up to you. I should get going. Good

night."

"Good night."

He left the gymnasium as quickly as he could manage, but he couldn't outrun his thoughts. He was in serious trouble. He was in love with a woman he couldn't have. A woman who didn't want him.

Chapter Fifteen

Julia followed Alex's progress as he left the gym, his movements easy to trace since he was taller than most people in the room. His dark hair gleamed under the harsh gymnasium lights, and she remembered how soft it was, how thick, how like silk it had felt as it slid between her fingers…

"Julia? Are you all right?"

She blinked and turned her attention to Lily. Forcing a smile, she said, "Yes, of course. I'm sorry, what were you saying?"

"I was just saying that we're going to head home with Ava after the silent auction winners are announced. In the meantime, I'm going to convince Wyatt to dance with me and Ava."

"Oh, yes, Grandpa! Can we dance?"

Wyatt chuckled. "Okay, but I'm warning you, I'm not a very good dancer. I might step on your toes."

"That's okay, Grandpa. I don't mind."

Wyatt laid a gentle hand on her head. "You are the sweetest little girl."

"That's why Dr. Alex and Grandma call me Sweet Pea," she said with a grin.

"I guess it is." He took Ava's small hand in his. "I'm going to show Ava how to trip the light fantastic. Do you care to join us, Lily?"

"I'll be there in a minute, dear."

Wyatt glanced at Julia before giving a brisk nod and heading off with Ava, who skipped along beside him.

"It's nice to see them together," Julia said.

"It is. Wyatt adores her. He doesn't want to lose her again."

"I won't let that happen."

"No, I'm sure you won't. At least not intentionally. But what if an opportunity comes up for you to move away? Perhaps a job opportunity, or maybe something more…personal."

"That's not going to happen. My life, and Ava's life, is here. We're not going anywhere."

"Dr. Campbell will be leaving in just a few months."

Julia looked away. She didn't need to be reminded that time was slipping away. Her calendar told her Alex's departure was getting closer every day.

Lily touched her arm. "Wyatt and I talked this over. You have a right to live your own life. We can't expect you to stay in Lobster Cove forever simply because we want you to. You have a right to be happy, and so does Ava. She needs a father."

"She needs her family," Julia managed around the lump in her throat. "I could never leave my parents. They need me."

"I just don't want you to lose out on a chance for happiness."

Julia couldn't help glancing toward the exit of the gymnasium. Alex was gone. She closed her eyes briefly and took a deep breath. Lily needn't have worried about her leaving Lobster Cove to follow him to San Diego. It wasn't like he wanted her to.

She'd been shocked when she realized Alex had bid on and won the date with her. She'd also been secretly thrilled. But then he'd whispered "I'm sorry" in her ear, and had been totally indifferent about getting together. Was he sorry he'd bid on her? He'd probably only done it as a way to make a donation to Edie and Aaron.

It was time to push aside any lingering feelings for him. But it was so hard to do.

"Ava adores Dr. Campbell, and from what I can see, the feeling is mutual."

"I've tried to keep them apart, but I haven't succeeded very well. She's going to be so upset when he leaves."

"Perhaps there's still time to convince him to stay."

Julia stared at Lily. Was that possible? Could she convince him to stay? What if he stayed, then decided later that Lobster Cove wasn't what he wanted? That *she* wasn't what he wanted?

"I don't think so."

Lily sighed and patted her arm. "We'll bring Ava home right after lunch tomorrow. Would that be okay?"

"Yes, that would be fine." Julia was relieved their discussion about Alex was over.

Lily kissed Julia's cheek. "All right. We'll see you then. You've done a remarkable job tonight."

"I couldn't have done it without you. Thank you, for everything. You have no idea how much your support means to me."

Lily cupped her cheek with her hand, her smile fond. "You're a dear girl. Enjoy the rest of the evening. We'll see you tomorrow."

Julia watched with a smile as Lily rejoined Wyatt

and Ava. Wyatt held Ava in one arm and twirled both of them in a slow waltz.

How could she take Ava away from her grandparents? They needed each other.

It was a moot point. It wasn't like Alex was begging her to leave with him.

****

By the time he got home from the hospital, it was past three in the morning. Just before midnight a man had arrived at the ER having a heart attack, and it had taken over an hour to stabilize him. At the same time, ambulances brought in three victims from a house fire. He and one of the other doctors, who'd arrived at midnight, had had their hands full for a couple of hours. He was exhausted, mentally and physically. All he wanted was to crawl into his bed and sleep for a week.

He pulled into the carport and cut the engine. Just as he was about to open the door, a small figure walked in front of the car, startling him. Dora Dawson. At least this time she was fully dressed. But the confused expression on her face spoke of her illness. She looked like a lost, scared child.

Alex got out of the car and went to her. "Hi, Dora. You must be cold." He took off his jacket and placed it around her shoulders.

"Is Polly home?"

"No, Dora, Polly's not here. I'll take you home, okay?" He held out his hand.

After a moment of hesitation, she took it, her grip surprisingly strong. "Okay."

He walked her across the lawn to her house, knocking on the front door when they reached it. There was no response, and the house remained dark. He knocked again, banging harder this time, and pushing the doorbell simultaneously. Dora stood beside him, shivering in the dark. What would he do if Paul didn't answer the door? There was no way he was going to wake Julia in the middle of the night and upset her with this. He began to worry about Paul's health. Had something happened to him? He tried the knob, but the door was locked.

Just when he thought he'd have to call the police again, a light came on over the front door. Paul unlocked the door and opened it. He took one look at Alex and then at Dora, and began to cry.

Dora stepped inside and patted his back. "Why are you crying? Everything's all right."

He tried to pull himself together. "Yes, everything's all right. You're home now."

"Of course I am." She walked into the house as if nothing had happened.

"Can I come inside, Paul?" Alex asked.

"Yes, come in, please." Paul stepped aside before pulling a tissue from his pocket to wipe his eyes. "Can you wait downstairs? I'm going to get Dora into bed."

"Sure. How about I make us some tea? I think I could use some right now."

"Help yourself. The kettle's on the stove, and the teabags are in the cupboard next to the fridge."

Paul coaxed Dora upstairs while Alex went to the kitchen and filled the kettle with water. While he waited for it to boil, he found teabags and a couple of mugs, then slid into one of the kitchen chairs, his whole body aching in fatigue. He'd just close his eyes for one moment…

The whistling of the kettle roused him. He pushed

himself out of his chair and poured hot water into the cups. A moment later, Paul entered the kitchen. He looked as exhausted as Alex felt.

Paul lowered himself carefully into a chair at the table, and Alex placed the cup in front of him before sitting down with his own mug. Paul's fingers wrapped around the warm mug, and for a few moments he silently stared into the amber depths. At last he sighed and looked up. Alex saw tiredness and resignation in the older man's eyes.

"I thought I could care for Dora myself, but I know now it's not possible," he said. "She wanders, especially at night, and it's getting worse. I try to stay awake at night to keep her safe, but I can't watch her every minute. She's gotten away on me a few times. But I guess you already knew that."

"Yeah. Why didn't you ask for help? Why did you try to keep her illness a secret, even from Julia?"

Paul's face crumbled. "Because I didn't want to believe it. I couldn't bear the thought that I was losing the woman I loved."

He turned away, tears streaming down his cheeks, his shoulders shaking with his sobs. Alex found a box of tissues on top of the fridge and set them on the table in front of Paul. He took one and blew his nose, taking deep breaths to pull himself together. Alex could only imagine what he was going through with Dora's illness. But he had a pretty good idea what it was like to know the woman he loved was slipping away from him.

Julia was nearly gone, and he didn't know how to get her back.

Paul drank a few sips of tea before beginning to speak. "At first, it was easy to dismiss Dora's memory loss as just getting older. We even joked about it. But as her behavior started to get more unusual, it became harder to ignore or pass off as just a senior moment."

He paused to drink more tea. "She started repeating herself, over and over, asking the same questions until I thought I'd lose my mind. But then there were periods when she seemed like the old Dora, and I thought I'd only imagined she had any problems at all. Those moments are gone now. This disease crept up on us so slowly we almost didn't realize anything was wrong until it all fell apart."

"I suspect Dora has Alzheimer's disease, but we need to do some tests before we can make that diagnosis. Dr. Willson said you've been stalling about taking her to see the neurologist in Bangor."

"I really didn't want to know, so I put it off. Guess I can't do that anymore, can I?"

"No. We need to know what's going on with Dora. It's not in her best interests to hide the truth, and it certainly isn't in yours. What happens if you get too sick to look after her?"

He hung his head. "Yes, I know."

"This situation isn't good for Julia, either. She's worried about both of you, but she feels powerless to help you. You haven't let her help." Alex paused before asking his next question. He didn't want to upset Paul further, but he had to know. "Did Dora have anything to do with Ava's broken arm?"

"She never touched Ava," he said fiercely. He looked away. "But Ava fell because she tripped over a box of detergent Dora had left on the basement stairs."

"Why was she even in the basement? I got the impression Julia didn't want her using the stairs."

"No, she didn't. Everything seemed fine that day, so I went downtown to get some groceries. I wasn't gone more than an hour, but when I got back, Ava was screaming downstairs, and Dora was barricading the basement door with anything she could lift or push in front of it. When she heard Ava crying, she got scared. She didn't recognize her and thought someone was trying to break into the house. I had to push away all the things in front of the door to get to Ava."

"Ava told us she'd gone down the stairs to find her teddy bear. Is that what happened?"

"Yes. Apparently Dora became confused when she was down there doing laundry, and Ava was trying to help. Dora couldn't remember how to turn on the machines, or how to fold the clothes, something she'd done for years." Tears streamed down his face once more. "I told Ava she couldn't tell anyone that Grandma locked her in the basement, because they'd take her away and we wouldn't see her anymore. God help me, I know I shouldn't have scared her like that, but I was afraid of what would happen if anyone found out."

"You have to tell Julia what happened to Ava. She needs to know."

He nodded and reached for another tissue. "Yes."

"But we'll worry about that tomorrow. Right now you need to get some sleep."

"I can't. What if Dora wakes up and wanders outside again?"

"I'll stay here and make sure she doesn't go anywhere."

"You'd do that?"

"Yes." He'd do just about anything for Julia and

Ava. "Why don't you go upstairs and get some rest? Everything will be all right."

Paul pushed back the chair and slowly got to his feet. "Thank you, Dr. Campbell."

"Please, call me Alex."

"Okay. Alex. Thank you."

"Good night."

"Good night."

With a sigh, Paul shuffled out of the kitchen. Alex heard him slowly climb the stairs and close the door to his bedroom. Hopefully, he'd be able to relax enough to get some much needed sleep.

Unfortunately, Alex wouldn't be able to do the same. He washed and dried the empty mugs and put them back in the cupboard. Then he turned on the TV in the living room and tried to stay awake enough to follow what was going on. His eyes wouldn't stay open on their own, his head too heavy to hold up…

The sound of the front door closing startled him awake. Cursing himself for falling asleep, he scrambled out of the lounger and ran to the door. He caught a flash of white as Dora hurried across the lawn to his house. For some reason, the house drew her like a magnet, but at least he knew where she was headed. He raced barefoot across the lawn, the grass cool and soft against his feet.

He found her on his front step, once more banging on the door.

"Dora, there's no one home here. Come with me, and I'll take you back to your house."

She cowered away from him, as if she'd never seen him before. "No. I'm not going with you."

He stood at the bottom of the steps and held out his

hand. “Please, Dora. I’ll take you back to Paul.”

“Paul?” A glint of recognition lit her eyes.

“Yes. He’s looking for you.” Alex took one step closer. “He wants you to come home.”

Slowly, she extended her hand. As soon as she was within reach, he grasped her hand and helped her down the stairs. Keeping a secure arm around her shoulders, he walked her back to her house.

Fortunately, the incident hadn’t woken Paul. Alex took Dora into the kitchen and fed her a snack of cheese and crackers and milk. When she was finished, he brought her into the living room.

“Would you like to lie down on the sofa and have a sleep?” he asked.

She didn’t answer. Instead she sat in a recliner on the opposite side of the room from the one he’d previously occupied and picked up a ball of yarn from a basket on the floor. Alex lowered himself into his recliner and watched, curious to see what she would do.

Carefully, she unraveled the yarn until a pile of pale blue wool covered her lap and spilled onto the floor. Then just as carefully, she began rolling the yarn into a tight ball once more. Before the sun came up around seven a.m., she had unrolled and rolled the yarn four times.

Paul came downstairs around seven-thirty, looking more rested then he had the previous evening. “How did it go last night?”

“She didn’t sleep much.” Alex told him how she’d slipped out of the house. “You might have to get some sort of alarm system to warn you when she leaves. Or you might have to get some overnight help. But eventually, you’re going to have to consider long-term care."

Paul turned away, watching as Dora unraveled the ball of wool once more. His throat worked. "I'd like to look after her as long as I can."

"I understand. I want you to call the neurologist in Bangor on Monday and take the first available appointment. Once we get a diagnosis and we know what we're dealing with, I'll get you in touch with the hospital social worker, and we'll see what arrangements we can make for Dora so she can stay at home as long as possible and still be safe."

Paul clasped his hand. "Thank you for understanding, Alex. Thank you for everything."

"You're welcome. Talk to Julia today. Tell her what's going on. She needs to know."

"I will. I promise."

Alex headed for the door, anxious to get to his bed. He was exhausted, but he had to be at the ER by three, so he wouldn't have the luxury of a long sleep. He had no doubt he'd be asleep before his head hit the pillow.

But he was surprised to find himself awake and staring at the ceiling an hour later. He couldn't stop thinking about Julia. How would she react to this news about her mother?

****

Her dad sounded tired when he called the morning after the fundraiser for Edie and Aaron. Something else in his voice, apprehension maybe, worry perhaps, set alarm bells ringing in her head.

"What's going on, Dad? Are you okay? Is Mom okay?"

He let out a long sigh before speaking. "Actually, I want to talk to you about your mother. There's something you need to know."

He told her about her mother's slow decline over the months, even years, and how he'd been in denial. She was shocked to learn what had really happened the day Ava broke her arm.

"She was wandering again last night. Alex Campbell brought her home and stayed with her all night so I could sleep. It was the first good sleep I've had in a very long time."

Alex. How like him to do something so selfless. She wanted to cry at the loss of everything that might have been between them.

"So what happens now?"

"On Monday morning, I'm going to make an appointment for your mother with the neurologist in Bangor. I guess he'll confirm what we already suspect, that your mother has Alzheimer's."

"I want to come with you," Julia said. School was starting again next week, but she'd take the day off. This was too important.

"I was hoping you'd say that."

"In the meantime, you need to sleep. Maybe the social worker has some ideas about what we can do to help with Mom's wandering. I can stay overnight with you for a while, at least until school starts."

"What about Ava?"

"We can either put her to bed at your house, or she can stay with the Stewarts."

"Alex mentioned hiring someone to look after her at night, or perhaps installing an alarm."

Her mind whirled with the perils of what lay ahead. The mother she knew and loved was drifting away. She wondered if Dora realized what was happening to her.

Or had she already passed that point?

She wanted to weep at the injustice, to rail against the disease. But that wasn't what her father needed her to do right now.

"I'll be over tonight, Dad. See you then."

"All right, honey. I love you. I'm sorry I didn't tell you sooner. I didn't want to believe it was true, you know?"

"Yeah, I know." She put a hand over her mouth, holding back a sob. "I love you too, Dad. Bye."

Her tears began to fall in earnest as soon as she put the phone back on its cradle. In that moment, she desperately wished she could go to Alex. He'd know what to do, and what to say, to take away some of the pain. She could take comfort in his strong arms.

But she wasn't with him. He was leaving soon, and she couldn't lean on him.

First Russ, then Alex, and now her mother. Would everyone she cared for leave her?

Chapter Sixteen

Julia leaned back in her office chair and stretched her arms above her head in an effort to work out the kinks. Two weeks had passed since her father had told her the truth about her mother's condition, and the fall school term had begun. The previous week she'd driven her parents into Bangor for her mother's appointment with the neurologist Dr. Willson had recommended. He'd confirmed what everyone suspected: Dora was suffering from Alzheimer's disease. Her disease had already passed the mild cognitive impairment stage and was entering a more serious phase.

It had been a hectic and exhausting couple of weeks. In addition to doing her work at the school during the day, she'd spent every night at her parents' house, watching over her mother and making sure she didn't leave the house, since they hadn't yet found someone to stay overnight with her parents.

In the interim, she was coping. By doing some research on the Internet she'd discovered ways to keep her mother safe. She had new locks installed on both the front and back doors of her parents' house. These old-fashioned sliding locks were placed at the top of the door where her mother couldn't easily reach them. Julia also placed bells on the doors that chimed whenever they were opened, alerting her or her father that Dora had escaped. She and her father also began doing simple things that seemed to make a difference. They made sure to take Dora for a walk each evening, which helped her to sleep. They also limited her intake of fluids before bedtime and made sure she went to the bathroom before they put her to bed. Julia had read that sometimes an Alzheimer's patient might wake during the night and simply be looking for a bathroom. In their confusion, they could open an outside door and be locked out of the house.

Pulling double duty meant she didn't get a lot of sleep, and she didn't spend a lot of time with Ava, either. Lily had stepped in to help, and Ava had stayed with the Stewarts several times, both overnight and during the day. Julia wasn't sure what she would have done without them.

Her father had made arrangements for a new alarm system to be installed in the house. Dora would be fitted with a bracelet that automatically locked the doors when she came near them. That way she couldn't leave the house unescorted. The idea of the new alarm system was a relief to Julia. It meant she and Ava would soon be able to sleep in their own beds, and hopefully she could get a full night's sleep again. But the alarm company wouldn't be able to install the system for another week or two, so until then, she'd cope as well as she could.

The new alarm system would allow her father to look after her mother at home a little longer, but they all knew she'd eventually need more care than he could give her.

Julia glanced out the window of her office as she rotated her stiff shoulder and massaged the back of her neck. How she wished she could go for a run. It was a glorious fall day, sunny, bright, and warm, perfect for being outside. But she knew the only outdoor exercise she'd have time for would be her evening walk with her parents.

The phone rang, jolting her back to the present. "Julia Stewart speaking."

"Hi Julia. Rob Perkins here. How are you?"

"I was fine, but now I'm not so sure. I have a feeling you have bad news for me."

She heard him sigh. "I'm afraid I do. I just learned that Ralph Sykes has convinced the school board to call a public meeting about the daycare. He's hoping the public will bring pressure on the board to cancel the program."

Julia bowed her head. This was the last thing she needed. "When's the meeting?"

"At the end of October. I put it off as long as I could. Hopefully by then the community will have a chance to see what the program is really about before they make any judgments about it."

She wondered what such a meeting might mean for her job. Was it in jeopardy? "That gives me a little time to prepare."

"I want you to be ready for heavy opposition. I've heard through the grapevine that Sykes has political aspirations. My guess is that he's using this fight as a springboard for election to the state legislature. He likes to portray himself as a champion of wholesome family values."

"As opposed to me, the whore of Babylon."

Rob laughed. "Well, I wouldn't have put it quite like that, but yeah, that's how he wants to draw the lines. Listen, is there any way you can talk to Wyatt

Stewart, feel him out on which way he's leaning? He supported the daycare initially, but I'm not sure what he's going to do this time around. You can talk to him. He is your father-in-law, after all."

"Ex-father-in-law. That's a big distinction in Wyatt's book." Their relationship had improved over the summer, ever since she'd allowed Ava to spend more time with the Stewarts, but she was still unclear how he felt about her. "I don't want my daughter in the middle of a scuffle between us. I think it's best if I leave our personal relationship out of the equation."

"I guess I understand, but it really would be a shame if the daycare got axed. It's a worthwhile program."

"You don't have to convince me. We've got the children of five students in the daycare right now. That means five young women are going to finish their education."

"I know, but I think we've got an uphill climb ahead of us in convincing people like Ralph Sykes."

Julia sighed. "Looks like I have a fight to get ready for. Maybe I'll start lifting weights or take up kick boxing."

Rob laughed again. "That's the spirit. I'll talk to you soon."

"Bye."

Julia had no sooner put down the phone when there was a knock at her door. She called "Come in," and Ralph Sykes stood in her doorway.

Speak of the devil.

"Ralph. What can I do for you?"

"Do you have a moment?"

"Sure. Come in."

He closed the door as he entered her office. “I just wanted to let you know, as a courtesy, that a public meeting to discuss the future of the daycare has been called.”

“Yes, I just heard. Superintendent Perkins called me. But thanks for telling me personally.”

“You’re welcome. I wanted to give you the opportunity to remove the daycare yourself and avoid the public embarrassment of a meeting.”

Her eyebrows rose at that statement. “I’m not afraid to defend the daycare in public. In fact, I welcome a discussion. Perhaps you’re uncertain of your support?”

His expression hardened, his lips compressing in a thin line. “Absolutely not. A lot of people support my position, including Wyatt Stewart.”

“Really? I understand Wyatt voted for the daycare at the initial school board meeting.”

“Well, perhaps,” Ralph sputtered, “but that doesn’t mean he still does.”

“I guess we’ll find out at the public meeting, won’t we?” She reached into her desk and plucked a file from her bottom drawer. “Actually, I’m glad you dropped by, because there was something I wanted to discuss with you.”

“What is that?” he asked warily.

“I’ve been doing some investigation, and I’ve discovered that on standardized math tests your students have some of the lowest scores in the state. I’ve also talked to a number of parents who’ve been unhappy with the grades their children have been getting. Their kids are not understanding the concepts. Many have had to hire outside tutors to help.”

"A lot of students find math and calculus difficult."

"That's true," Julia conceded with a dip of her head. "They're difficult subjects. But even some of our best and brightest students have trouble with your math classes. Why do you think that is, Ralph?"

"How should I know?"

"But that's precisely my point. You should know, and you should care. I'm recommending that you take a remedial course in teaching math."

"That's ridiculous! I've been teaching math for twenty years, and I've never had a principal question my skills!"

"I believe that you did care at one time, Ralph, but you've become so focused on your political views that you've lost sight of actually teaching. If you spent as much time helping your students as you do trying to establish your political career, we'd all be better off."

"How did you know about that?"

"It's a small island, Ralph. Everybody knows." She sat back in her chair and folded her arms. "I need teachers who are fully engaged in their jobs. I think you need to decide which career path you want to take."

"I don't have to listen to this."

He stormed out of the office, not bothering to shut her door. Julia sighed. She didn't deliberately go looking for confrontations, but they seemed to find her pretty easily.

She gritted her teeth. If Ralph Sykes wanted a fight, he damn well was going to get one. Her students were worth fighting for.

But with all the blows she'd taken lately, she hoped she had enough stamina left to go the distance.

****

Over lunch, Alex took a break from the clinic and walked along the pier. The wind blowing in from the ocean was cool, though the sun was shining. Maybe the wind could blow the cobwebs from his brain. All morning the only thing he could think about was Julia. She was constantly in his thoughts. He wondered what she was doing, how she was feeling. Was Ava okay?

Finding an unoccupied bench, he ate the sandwich he'd picked up at the Love Caters All truck in the hospital parking lot and watched as waves crashed against the shore. The power and magnificence of the ocean soothed him, and he felt himself gradually relax. Even with its sometimes crazy weather, the beauty of this place had wormed its way into his heart. There was no place on earth like Lobster Cove.

Especially since the love of his life was here.

His cell phone rang, and he saw his mother's phone number on call display. He clicked the Talk button.

"Mom, hi. How's everything?"

"It's good. I'm at work right now, but I wanted to share my news with you. The house in La Jolla sold, and I got a new place. I bought a condo."

"That's great. Where is it?"

"It's part way between the university and Nona's house. I have a little farther to commute to work, but I'm closer to my family. I think it's the best of both worlds, and I love the place. It's small, but it's really cute, and the best thing is, it's all mine." She sounded excited and happy.

"I'm really glad for you, Mom. You deserve it."

"Thanks, honey. I'll send you an email with the new address." She paused. "You sound…I don't know, a little blue. Are you okay?"

"Mom, I'm..."

He was going to say he was fine, to deny his feelings, but in reality he was anything but fine. And for the first time in a very long time, he didn't want to shut his mother out of his life.

"Mom, I met someone here, and I love her very much."

Alex told her about Julia, and Ava, and Paul and Dora Dawson. "So she's on one coast and I'm going to be on the other, and never the twain shall meet. I understand why she wants to stay here, why she needs to stay here. I don't know what to do."

"Do you really love her, Alex? And you really love her little girl?"

"Yes, I love them." He bent his head and squeezed his eyes shut. "I can't imagine not being with them. These last few days, not seeing Julia, or not being able to touch her when I do see her, it's been painful. When I leave here...I don't know what I'm going to do, Mom."

"I loved your dad like that," she whispered. "When he died, part of me died too, the best part of me. I don't want you to go through that."

He'd never heard his mother talk about his father that way. "I'm sorry, Mom."

"I know it was a long time ago, but sometimes it feels like yesterday. Mostly, now, I can remember the good times we had together, and the love we shared, and it doesn't hurt so much. But there are times, like the anniversary of his death, when I miss him so much."

"I wish I remembered more about him."

"You were so young. The night he died, he'd just worked a double shift in the emergency room. He'd worked several nights in a row before that, and he was so tired. But they were short-handed, so they asked him to stay. When he phoned me to tell me he wouldn't be home until after midnight, I begged him not to stay. He was wearing himself out."

"He had the accident that night, and you think it was because he was overtired."

"There's no doubt. The police told me he must have fallen asleep. He drove straight into a retaining wall." He heard her take a shaky breath. "All the fights we had about your work, all the times I nagged at you, I just couldn't bear the thought of you working so hard like your father. I want you to have a wonderful life with a family and friends and the time and energy to enjoy them. I want so much more for you than your father and I were able to have."

"Why did you never tell me this before, Mom?"

"I don't know. I wanted to, but for so many years we haven't been close. We seemed to fight every time we talked. I didn't feel like you wanted to hear what I had to say. Talking about your father was too painful to have it dismissed like it was nothing."

"I'm sorry I made you feel that way."

"It's my fault. I didn't talk to you about your father when you were growing up. It was too painful. But he was always in my heart. He still is."

Alex blinked back tears. "I'm so sorry, Mom."

She gave a hiccupping laugh, as if holding back tears of her own. "I guess we had to be three thousand miles apart to get closer."

"I guess that's true."

"Alex, if Julia is truly the one for you, don't let her slip away. Love like that is so precious and so rare. I didn't realize that until it was too late."

"I understand." He took a deep breath, blew it out. "I've got to get back to the clinic. They're going to wonder what happened to me."

"I should go, too. My coffee break was over a half hour ago. You'll call soon and let me know what's happening?"

"I will." *For better or for worse.*

"*Te quiero, Alejandro.*"

He smiled. His mother hadn't spoken Spanish to him since he was a little boy.

"*Te quiero, Mama.*"

****

After finishing at the clinic for the day, Alex drove to Tracy Novak's house, hoping she could provide him with some news. He hadn't heard anything about Julia or her parents since the night he found Dora in his carport again, and he was worried about them, especially Julia.

He knocked on her door and heard a dog barking. A very large, annoyed dog, by the sound of it. A minute later Tracy opened the door, holding a German Shepherd by its collar.

"Alex, hi! I didn't expect to see you. What brings you to my door?"

The dog made a low growling sound deep in its chest, its eyes fixed on him. "Well, I was going to pump you for information, but now I'm not so sure. Your dog looks like it would be happy to use me as a chew toy."

"Oh, sorry about that. Cookie tends to be overprotective."

"Cookie? That's the beast's name?"

Tracy laughed and pulled the dog inside. "Come on

in. She's really a sweetheart once you get to know her."

"I'll take your word for it." He stepped into the house and closed the door. Following her into the kitchen, Alex took note of the neat little house with its gleaming hardwood floors, comfortably worn furniture, and colorful braided rugs. The house was unpretentious and down to earth, just like Tracy.

The orderliness of the house ended at the kitchen table, which was strewn with paper, notepads and binders. Tracy pushed all the papers to one side of the table, then let go of the dog's collar.

"Cookie, lie down. Stay."

The dog immediately dropped to the floor next to the table, her head on her paws. But her eyes remained alert and focused on him. Alex decided to stay a cautious distance away.

Tracy filled a kettle. "I was about to have another cup of tea. Would you like some?"

"Sure."

She pointed to one of the kitchen chairs. "Have a seat. And don't worry about Cookie. She hardly ever rips out anyone's throat. She usually goes for the groin."

"Very funny." He sat down, resisting the urge to put a protective hand over his crotch.

"Seriously, Alex, she won't hurt you. Would you like some cookies? They're chocolate chip. I just made them."

"Thanks."

Placing a plate of chocolate chip cookies between them, Tracy took a seat. "So what's this about wanting to pump me for information?"

Now that he was here in Tracy's kitchen, he found

it difficult to ask his question. He averted his eyes. "It's just that I haven't heard anything about the Dawsons, and I wondered how they were doing. That's all."

Tracy took her time answering. She got up from her chair when the kettle began to whistle, and proceeded to make a pot of tea. After bringing the teapot and two mugs to the table, she sat down once more.

"Paul finally took Dora to the neurologist in Bangor, and she was officially diagnosed as having Alzheimer's."

Alex sighed. "I guess we all knew that was coming."

"I didn't," she said. "I had no idea Dora's health had deteriorated so badly. Julia hadn't said a word to me, not until she asked me to take over the scheduling."

"The scheduling?"

"Someone's got to coordinate all the volunteers who are helping Edie and Aaron. I just make sure we have drivers and babysitters when we need them, and that six people don't show up on Edie's doorstep with casseroles at the same time."

"I can't believe how many people have stepped up to help them."

"It's what we do here. The best news is that we tallied up the net proceeds from the fundraiser, and it looks like we should have enough to cover most of Edie's treatments."

"That's very good news. I'm sure it's a huge relief to Edie and Aaron. Now she can just focus on getting better."

"Yes. Hopefully the surgery and radiation will have zapped all the cancer cells, and she won't have a recurrence." She frowned as she lifted her mug to her lips. "I'm glad Edie's situation is working out. I don't have the energy to worry about more than one friend at a time."

That got his attention. Was she worrying about Julia? "What do you mean?"

She waved her hand toward the papers and binders on her table. "Julia tends to take on a lot of responsibility. She only gave up coordinating Edie's volunteer schedule because school is back in session and she's staying every night at her parents' house to watch her mother. She just doesn't have time. Or the energy, I imagine, though she'd never admit it."

"Wait a minute." Alex sat up straighter, his voice rising. "Are you telling me Julia is working at the school all day and then staying up all night to make sure her mother doesn't wander?"

Cookie lifted her head and stared at Alex, probably detecting his anxiety. Tracy reached down and scratched the dog's ears, and Cookie settled again.

"She couldn't let her father stay up night after night. She was concerned about his heart."

"How can she maintain a pace like that? She's going to make herself ill."

"I know. I'm worried about her, too. But she promised me it's only for a few more days, until her dad gets the new alarm system installed." She told him about the alarm system and the locks Julia had put in place until the new system was ready. "She told me they're managing Dora's Alzheimer's much better now. She doesn't wander as much, so she's able to get some sleep. I offered to stay with her mom and dad on my days off, but she wouldn't let me."

Alex ran his hand through his hair. “Why does she have to be so damn stubborn? Why can’t she accept some help? She’s the first person to help someone in trouble, but she won’t let anyone give her a hand when she needs it.”

“She’s proud, Alex. And she feels like she has to be the one to take care of her parents. They’re her responsibility.”

“She feels responsible for everyone.” Julia was the most infuriatingly wonderful person he knew. “What about Ava? How is this affecting her?”

“Ava’s been staying with the Stewarts the last couple of weeks. Julia said the only time she gets to spend with her is on weekends and after school when she walks her to Wyatt and Lily’s house.”

“Damn.” He settled back into his chair. Picking up his mug, he sipped some of the tea, hoping it would calm him. “I’ll go over there right away. I’ll make her go home and get some rest.”

“Slow down, Alex. If you go in with guns blazing, you’ll only get Julia’s back up.”

Tracy passed him the plate of cookies, and he took one. The chocolate melted in his mouth and reminded him he hadn’t eaten dinner yet. He knew she was right. Telling Julia what she should do was a sure way of making sure she did just the opposite. “What do you suggest?”

She sighed. “Leave it alone. Let Julia handle it.”

“I can’t do that, Tracy.”

He scrubbed a hand over his face, feeling irritated and frustrated and a little out of control. Being in love with a woman who didn’t feel the same way tended to have that effect on him.

Tracy leaned over to scratch Cookie's ears once more. The dog continued to stare at him with a watchful expression. "I know it's not what you want to hear, but maybe it would be best if you didn't see Julia anymore. You've only got, what, five months left on your contract."

"Four and half." The last day of his contract was February fifteenth.

"Julia comes off as this dynamo, this strong person who can handle anything, and in many ways she is. But she's been hurt before, and her heart is still bruised. I wouldn't want her heart to break again."

"He really hurt her, didn't he? Her ex-husband Russ, I mean."

"Yeah, he did. The louse."

He averted his eyes as he asked his next question. "Is she still in love with him?"

"No. Absolutely not. It's totally over between them." Tracy's adamant reply gave him hope.

"Do you really think I have the power to break her heart?"

"Yes."

Alex looked away again. It was the last thing he wanted to do.

"How do you do it, Tracy? You know practically everyone on the island. How do you work in the same community you live in, the same community you grew up in? How do you maintain any kind of professional objectivity? How can you treat people you know and care about?"

"I think it makes me a better nurse. I *do* care about all my patients. They're not faceless numbers to me. They're people I know, my friends or my friends' families. That makes me work harder for them. Because I want the best for them."

"You're probably the best nurse I've ever worked with. Maybe now I know why."

"And you're an amazing doctor. We need you here."

Alex looked away, not sure what to say to that. He could no longer imagine leaving Julia. And Lobster Cove had proven what a special and caring community it was. But was it the place he wanted to live and work for the rest of his life? Would the work here challenge him enough? Would the smallness of the community prove to be too confining, too stifling, after a while?

"I have another question for you. How do you live in a town as small as this and not let the gossip drive you crazy? I swear my own mother doesn't know as much about me as most of the people in this town do."

Tracy laughed, and Cookie turned her head to look at her, her ears twitching.

"I can't help you there. When it comes to a small town, you have to be prepared to take the good with the bad. The good is that people are there for you when you need them, and the bad is that they're in your business when all you want is privacy. You've got to measure both sides and decide whether the good outweighs the bad."

She was right. He was the only one who could make a decision about what would work in his life.

"How did you get to be so wise?"

"Probably comes from babysitting big city doctors."

"Smart ass."

She laughed, then sobered. "So what are you going

to do about Julia?"

"I have to go to her folks' place tonight, convince her to get some sleep. I can't let her try to handle everything with her parents on her own."

"I understand. What about later, when your contract's up? What are you going to do about Julia then?"

He didn't have an answer.

Chapter Seventeen

Julia blinked in surprise when she unlocked the door at her parents' house and saw Alex on the back stoop. Her heart made a flip inside her chest when he smiled at her.

"Hi. What are you doing here?"

He held up his medical bag. "I thought I'd make a house call. I was concerned about your dad not getting enough sleep. I want to make sure his blood pressure is under control."

"Oh." It was probably a good idea to have her dad's blood pressure checked. He'd been under a lot of stress. Still, a part of her was disappointed that he wasn't here for her. "Come in."

She stepped aside to let him in, then closed the door, setting off the little bell she'd installed over the frame. Pulling over a chair, she stood on it to reach the slide bolt lock at the top of the door. After fastening the lock, she climbed off the chair and saw Alex was watching her.

"Does that help with your mother's wandering at night?" he asked.

"It seems to. When the door doesn't open right away, she gives up. She hasn't gotten out of the house since the last time you found her at your house."

"That's good. You're doing a great job of looking after her, Julia."

His praise gave her an inordinate amount of pleasure.

"Thank you."

She found herself momentarily mesmerized by the look in his dark eyes. She saw kindness, empathy, even respect there. It made her want to bury her face against his chest and take comfort from him. Forever.

Instead she averted her eyes and took a deep breath. "Mom and Dad are in the living room. Why don't you come with me?"

She was acutely aware of him as she led the way to the living room, of his large presence, the heat from his body, the scent of his aftershave. It was almost painful. Would she always be so acutely attuned to him?

Her father smiled with genuine pleasure when he saw Alex.

"Dr. Campbell! It's good to see you."

Alex took a seat on the sofa, close to her father's armchair. "I'm glad to see you looking so well."

"It's thanks to Julia for letting me get my sleep."

"Good." He glanced up at her with a smile that made her breath hitch and then opened his medical bag. "I brought over a portable blood pressure cuff. I'd like to take your blood pressure, if it's all right with you."

"Yeah, of course. If it wasn't for you bringing Dora home those times… Well, there's not much I wouldn't do for you, Dr. Campbell."

"It's Alex, remember?"

"Right. Alex."

Julia swallowed around the lump in her throat as she watched Alex wrap the cuff around her father's upper arm and squeeze the bulb, then press his stethoscope against the inside crook of her father's arm and listen intently. Julia held her breath, letting it out in a rush when Alex released the cuff.

"Not bad. One thirty over eighty." He caught Julia's eye. "Maybe I should take your blood pressure. It sounds like you're the one who hasn't gotten much sleep lately."

"I'm fine."

Her father frowned. "He's right, Julia. You've been up half the night watching over your mother, and then you get up early and go to work. You can't keep up that pace forever."

"It's not like I don't sleep at all. I catch a few winks on the couch." She didn't bother to mention how fitful her sleep had been. "Besides, it's not forever, just till we get the new alarm system installed. That'll happen any day now."

"In the meantime, why don't you humor me and let Alex take your blood pressure?"

Julia wanted to argue with him, but it seemed easier to just give in. She walked to the couch and sat next to Alex, sticking out her right arm.

"Fine. Do it and get it over with."

Alex affixed the cuff to her arm without a word, though a little smile played around his mouth. He squeezed the bulb, and pressure built against her arm until it was almost unbearable. At last he released the pressure and listened with his stethoscope to her blood swooshing through her veins, his gaze fixed on hers.

He pulled the stethoscope from his ears. "It's perfect. One ten over eighty."

"I told you I was fine."

She tried to get up, but he grasped her hand and held on. "I was thinking," he said. "I could stay here tonight and give you a chance to sleep a full night."

She was touched by his offer, but she couldn't accept. "That's kind of you, Alex, but don't you have your own job to go to in the morning?"

"Actually I'm working in the ER tomorrow. I don't start till four, so I have all day to sleep. What do you say?"

It was tempting. She was tired, and she knew the lack of sleep was starting to take a toll. Her mind wandered at work, and she felt foggy and a little disoriented sometimes. With the town meeting deciding the fate of her daycare coming up, she couldn't afford to be anything less than sharp.

"I'll make you a deal. What if you take the early shift and wake me up at two am? Then you can go home and sleep as long as you need to. That way we both get a decent amount of rest."

He looked like he wanted to argue, but at last he nodded. "All right. I can do that."

Julia got to her feet. "In that case, I think I'll go to bed right now. I know it's only eight o'clock, but two am is going to come very early. Goodnight, Dad."

"Good night, dear. Sleep well."

She hugged her mother and kissed her cheek. "Good night, Mom."

Dora didn't make eye contact. "Good night."

She walked toward the stairs, and Alex followed. Turning, she stared into his eyes, reluctant to leave him.

"Don't forget to wake me at two."

"I won't." He took her by the shoulders and pulled her in for a brief hug, then kissed her forehead. "Sleep well."

Releasing her, he gave her a slight push toward the

stairs. With one last look back at him, she climbed the stairs and entered the bedroom that had been her childhood refuge until she'd gone away to college. As she undressed, she studied the trophies and ribbons she'd won in sports and academics as a child and teenager. Her parents had kept all of them, proudly displaying the awards on some shelves and a bulletin board. Julia couldn't help thinking how uncomplicated life had been back then, though she hadn't appreciated it at the time. She'd only had herself to worry about, and her parents had taken care of all her needs and wants, looking after her with loving care.

Now it was her turn to do the same for them, perhaps with a little help from her friends. Like Alex.

She crawled into bed and pulled the blankets over herself, falling asleep almost as soon as her head hit the pillow.

****

"Wake up, sweetheart. It's time to get out of bed."

Julia felt soft lips against her forehead, and smelled a familiar aftershave. She smiled, her eyes still closed, her mind still drifting somewhere between sleep and wakefulness.

"Alex."

"Good morning, baby."

He kissed again, this time on her lips. She wanted to stay in this room with Alex for the rest of the night, lying in his arms and feeling warm and safe. But something niggled at her sleep-deprived brain, something he said… "Morning?"

She struggled to open her eyes. Alex sat on the edge of her bed, smiling down at her, a full night's growth of beard on his chin. It just made him look sexier.

"It's seven a.m. You were sleeping so peacefully, I hated to wake you, but I know you have to get ready for school."

Julia pushed herself to a sitting position, then rubbed the sleep from her eyes. "You were supposed to wake me at two."

He gave a negligent shrug. "So sue me. You needed to sleep."

"My mom—"

"She's fine. She and your dad are in the kitchen having breakfast."

"Did she get up during the night?"

"Once. I woke up when she wandered into the living room. I helped her to the bathroom and put her back to bed, and she slept until a few minutes ago."

"You must be so tired."

"I slept, on and off, on the sofa, like you have the last couple of weeks."

She knew from experience his sleep couldn't have been very restful, with one eye open to watch for her mother. The lumpy old sofa didn't help, either.

"I don't know what to say to you, except 'thank you.' Now go home and get some sleep."

He grinned, reaching out his hand to caress her face. His thumb idly rubbed the tender skin beneath her eye. Julia stared into his eyes. She'd give anything to be able to wake up with Alex every morning, to love him every day.

Finally, he dropped his hand. "I should go and let you get ready for school."

"Thanks again, Alex. Sleep well."

He rose to his feet but didn't leave the room. For a

moment they stared at each other. Julia knew the longing in his eyes must also be reflected in hers. At last he turned and left her room, closing the door softly behind him.

Julia bent her head, squeezing her eyes shut to hold back the tears. Alex was the most caring, loving man she'd ever known. Losing him would be the hardest thing she'd ever faced.

****

Alex punched his grandmother's familiar number into his cell phone, feeling a little guilty that he hadn't called her in a while. He smiled when he heard her voice.

"Hello? Alejandro?"

"Hi, Nona. How are you?"

"I'm very well, especially now that I'm hearing from you. How are things way up north? Are you keeping warm?"

Alex laughed, but found himself feeling defensive. "It's not like Lobster Cove is on the Arctic Circle, Nona. I'm still keeping warm. It'll be a couple of months yet before the weather turns really cold."

"That's good. I'd like to visit you, but I don't think I could handle the cold weather."

"Maybe you could come up next summer."

"But aren't you moving back to San Diego in February?"

He'd almost forgotten. His pang of regret at the thought of leaving Lobster Cove was unexpected. "Right. Yes, in February."

His grandmother was silent for a moment before she spoke again. "You *are* still coming back to San Diego, aren't you?"

The question caught him off guard. “Yeah, sure.”

“You don’t sound happy about it. What’s going on?”

“Nothing. I just…I like it here. Nona, do you remember when I was a kid and Mom and I moved in with you?”

“Yes, of course. I loved having you with us.”

“I loved it, too, and I think I’ve finally figured out what made it such a happy time for me, even though my dad had just died and my mother was away working so much. I was in a community. I had you and Tato, but I also had all my cousins and aunts and uncles, and people in the neighborhood. I knew that if I got in trouble, you would all be there to help me. But then when Mom married Tom and we moved to La Jolla, I lost that. I thought it was just you and Tato I missed, and it was, but it was everyone else too, the whole neighborhood. Coming here to Lobster Cove and seeing what a tight-knit community is like reminded me of the old neighborhood and what’s been missing in my life.”

“You’re not coming home, are you?”

“I don’t know,” he said honestly. “I miss home, and I miss you, but I’m beginning to wonder if San Diego is really where I’m meant to be. For the first time, I’m starting to think Lobster Cove could be home.”

“And Julia is there, too. Are you thinking your home could be with her? Is she the reason you’re having a change of heart about coming home?”

He wasn’t sure how to answer that question. “Julia and I… It’s complicated, Nona.”

“So uncomplicate it! Do you love her?”

He sighed. “Yes.”

"Then don't let her go. You know how much I want you to come home, and whether you realize it or not, your mother does, too. But if living in Maine is what will make you truly happy, than that's what you have to do."

She made it sound so simple.

****

Ava ran ahead and shuffled through the gold and orange leaves covering the sidewalk. The brisk autumn wind caught the dry leaves and sent them gracefully gliding through the air as Julia and Ava walked home from her parents' house. They'd stopped on their way home from school to see how Paul and Dora were doing, much as they'd done most afternoons since school had started nearly five weeks ago. Despite Dora's progressing journey into Alzheimer's, they were doing okay. Home care checked in on them a couple of times a week, as did many of their long-time friends. Now that everyone knew about Dora's condition, they stopped by often to visit and make sure Paul wasn't overwhelmed. Sometimes some of Dora's old friends would spend the afternoon caring for her so Paul could have respite. Having friends helped to make a difficult situation more bearable.

They reached home and made their way to the back door. As they went around the rear of the house, Julia was surprised to see Chloe Sykes sitting on her back steps.

"Chloe! I haven't seen you in ages!" Ava ran to give her a hug around her waist. Chloe bent over her, wrapping her arms around her small body.

"Hi, Chloe," Julia said. "I didn't make a babysitting appointment I forgot about again, did I?"

"No, I just thought I'd drop by. To see Ava," she added hastily.

Julia knew there was more to the visit than a desire to see her six-year-old, but she'd likely have to wait for Chloe to tell her what was going on in her own good time.

"We're glad to see you. We were just going to have a snack of cookies and milk. Would you care to join us?"

Relief passed over the teenager's face. Had she thought she wouldn't let her into the house? Julia wondered what Ralph had been saying to Chloe about her.

She pushed aside the thought. It didn't matter what Ralph said. Chloe was always welcome in her house, and at the moment it looked like she needed a friend. She unlocked the back door and they went inside.

After instructing the girls to go upstairs to wash their hands, Julia set out glasses of milk and a plate of homemade oatmeal cookies Lily had brought over. She didn't know what she would have done without Lily the last couple of months. She'd stayed with Ava when she needed a babysitter on short notice. She'd cooked for them and looked after them. Like a mother would. Lily would never replace her own mother, but her help and support had been very important to both her and Ava, and Julia loved her for it.

Ava chattered happily to Chloe as they ate their cookies, telling her about school and her friends. Chloe listened politely, interjecting a question occasionally, but Julia could feel the tension emanating from her. She was like a watch spring wound too hard and ready to explode.

When the cookies and milk were finished, Julia turned to her daughter. “Honey, I’d like to speak to Chloe alone for a minute. Could you please go upstairs to your room? But wash off the milk moustache first, okay?”

“How come you want to talk to Chloe alone?”

“That’s none of your business. Go.”

Ava frowned and slid off her chair. “Okay. Bye, Chloe.”

Julia waited until she heard Ava’s bedroom door close before she spoke. “I got the feeling you wanted to talk to me in private about something.”

Chloe stared at her hands in her lap. “My dad said I’m not supposed to babysit Ava anymore. He doesn’t think you’re a good person because you want to teach us about sex.”

Did he think she planned to give a primer on the Kama Sutra to her students? She wasn’t really surprised at Ralph’s command to his daughter or his deliberate misinterpretation of her objectives.

“Actually, I want to teach my students to make good choices about sex, including abstaining. I’m sorry to hear you won’t be babysitting Ava any longer. She’ll be disappointed.”

“I’ll miss her, too,” Chloe whispered.

Julia reached out and clasped one of her cold hands. “What did you want to talk to me about?”

Chloe lifted her head, her face full of anguish. “I think I might be pregnant.” Her face dissolved in tears, as if speaking her secret out loud opened the floodgates to allow a torrent of emotion to escape. “My dad will hate me when he finds out. What am I going to do?”

“Have you gone to a doctor to be sure?”

She shook her head morosely. “I can’t. My parents will find out.”

“Chloe, if you really are pregnant, your parents will have to find out. You can’t keep this from them.” She squeezed her hand. “Can you tell me what happened?”

“I went to a party in July,” she said, swiping at her tears with her free hand. “I didn’t want to go, but my friend Emily likes Kevin Graham, and he was going to be at the party, and she didn’t want to go alone, so she made me come along. There was a boy there from Bar Harbor. He was cute, and he kept giving me beer. Then he took me away from the bonfire on the beach, and we were alone. We were kissing, and then he…touched me.”

Julia went cold inside. “Did he force you? Did you tell him no?”

She shook her head. “I didn’t say no. I wanted to know…what it was like. I’ve heard the popular girls talking about sex, and they make it sound so wonderful, but it wasn’t like that. It hurt.”

Julia gathered her into her arms and let her cry. *Good lord, what do I do now?* Ralph Sykes wouldn’t thank her for giving him this news.

When Chloe’s tears abated, she handed her a tissue. “The first thing we have to do is to confirm whether or not you’re pregnant. I think you should see a doctor.”

“Not our regular doctor. He’d tell my dad for sure.”

“I can call Dr. Campbell. Maybe he can see you right away. Is that okay?”

She nodded her head and wiped fresh tears from her eyes. “Yes.”

"Won't your parents worry that you haven't come home after school?"

"They think I'm at Emily's house. I told them I'd be home late."

She didn't like deceiving Ralph and his wife, but Chloe hadn't given her much choice. Julia made herself smile. "Okay, then. I'll phone Dr. Campbell."

She dialed the number for the family clinic and Susan Buttersworth, Alex's nurse, answered the phone. "Dr. Campbell's office."

"Hi, Susan. Julia Stewart here. I was wondering, would it be possible to speak to him for a minute?"

"Can I tell him what it's regarding?"

She knew Susan wasn't being nosy; it was her job to ask. Even so, a blush heated her face. "It's a…a personal matter."

"All right. He's with a patient at the moment. Can you hold?"

"Yes, I'll hold."

She paced the kitchen with the cordless phone. The wait felt interminable, even though she realized only a couple of minutes had passed. Chloe watched as she paced, making her even more nervous.

"Julia? What's going on? Is everything okay?"

She relaxed immediately at the sound of his voice. The concern she heard warmed her heart.

"Yes, everything's fine, but I need some help. One of my students thinks she may be pregnant. I know it's short notice, but do you think you could see her right away?"

"Absolutely." He spoke without hesitation. "I'm just seeing my last couple of patients of the day, and I'll wait here for you."

"Thanks, Alex. I appreciate your help." She paused, wanting to say so much more. But with Chloe hanging on her every word, it wasn't the time.

She wondered if the time would ever be right for them.

"You're a fantastic teacher, and a wonderful, loving person, you know that, don't you? Not every teacher would go the extra mile for her students like you do."

Oh, Alex. "I… Thank you. That's very kind of you to say. We'll be there soon." She hit the Off button and set the phone down with shaking hands. Pushing thoughts of Alex from her mind, she forced herself to think of practicalities.

"I'll call Ava's grandmother and see if she can watch her for a while."

Chloe nodded. "Thank you for helping me. I know I'm being a bother."

Julia squeezed her hand. "Chloe, honey, you could never be a bother."

She dialed the Stewarts' number and was grateful when Lily answered rather than Wyatt. Julia was deliberately vague when explaining her need for a babysitter.

"I have to run some errands, and I was hoping you could watch Ava. It shouldn't take more than an hour." She looked at Chloe's pale face. "Or two."

"Sure, I can stay with Ava. Do you want me to come over?"

"No, that's fine. I'll drop her off at your house. Thanks, Lily."

"No problem. Is everything okay, Julia?"

"Yes, of course. I'll see you in a few minutes."

She bundled both girls into the car and headed to the Stewarts' house. Lily opened the door as she and Ava came up the walk.

"Is that Chloe Sykes in your car?" she asked.

"Chloe had milk and cookies with us," Ava said.

"She babysits Ava sometimes," Julia added, hoping her simple explanation would satisfy Lily's curiosity. She nodded, even though she obviously had more questions.

"I'll see you in an hour or so. Ava can have dinner with us."

"That would be great. Thank you."

She hurried back to the car. Chloe was silent during the drive to the clinic. Fortunately, since it was now after five-thirty, most of the staff and nearly all the patients were gone. She wouldn't want word to get back to Ralph that Chloe had been seen with her at the doctor's office.

Alex met them at the door of the clinic. He smiled and shook Chloe's hand. "I'm Alex Campbell. I understand you're one of Mrs. Stewart's students."

She gave a brief nod. "I'm Chloe Sykes."

"Nice to meet you, Chloe. Why don't we go to my office?"

Chloe seemed to relax slightly. He put her at ease much the same way he'd done with Ava when she'd broken her arm. Children instinctively trusted Alex to make everything better. Of course, if Chloe really was pregnant, even Alex wouldn't be able to make everything better.

They followed him to his office and sat in the chairs in front of his desk. Rather than sitting behind his desk, Alex pulled his chair next to Chloe's.

"Mrs. Stewart told me you think you may be pregnant. Did you have unprotected sex recently?"

"Unprotected?"

"That means you had sex without using any form of birth control," he explained patiently. "Did your boyfriend use a condom?"

"No, I don't think so. I don't know." She sniffed, on the verge of tears again. "He's not my boyfriend."

Alex glanced at Julia in alarm, and she shook her head to his unspoken question, *Was it rape?* "I see. When was your last period?"

"At the end of June, just before…you know."

"Okay. What we're going to do is a simple urine test to see whether you really are pregnant, and I'm also going to draw some blood and have it tested. We'll get the results on the blood test later, but the urine test results are immediate. We'll know right away. Neither one will take very long to do. Are you ready?"

"Okay." Chloe looked like a frightened child. A baby having a baby. Julia squeezed her hand and offered her a smile.

They went into an examination room, where Alex drew a vial of blood from Chloe's arm. When he'd labeled the vial for the lab, he handed her a small plastic container with a lid.

"I need you to fill this container with urine. Okay?"

"Okay."

"Good girl. There's a washroom around the corner. After you're done, put the lid on the container, wash your hands, and bring it back here."

"Okay," she repeated.

Once she left the room, Julia got to her feet, too agitated to sit any longer. "She's so naïve. She doesn't even know if the boy was using a condom." She told him what Chloe had told her about the boy. "I don't know what Ralph will do when he finds out she's pregnant."

"Do you think he could be violent toward her?"

"No, I don't believe so. But he's certainly not going to be happy. He could make Chloe's life very uncomfortable."

"If she is pregnant, and her last period was in June, she's about twenty weeks pregnant."

Julia nodded. She knew what he was saying. It was likely too late to terminate the pregnancy, if that's what Chloe wanted.

"She'll be showing soon. Do you think she'll stay at your school?"

"I don't know. Whatever she decides to do, it's not going to be easy for her."

"No, probably not. But you're not her parent, Julia. You can't shield her from the world."

"I know, I just… Sometimes it's hard for me not to get involved."

Alex moved close, brushing back the hair from her forehead. "You have such a good heart, always trying to look after everyone."

The tenderness she saw in his eyes caused hot tears to prickle at the corners of her eyes. She wanted to feel his strong arms around her. She longed to kiss him, touch his skin, the consequences be damned.

The doorknob rattled, Alex stepped away from her, and the moment was over. Chloe entered the room carrying the container of urine. He pulled on a pair of latex gloves and took it from her.

"The test will only take a minute." He pulled a kit

from a cupboard and took out some paper strips. "We simply dip the litmus paper in the urine. The paper reacts to a hormone in the urine that is only present when a woman is pregnant. If you're pregnant, the paper will turn a different color. If there is no pregnancy, the strip will remain its original beige color."

Julia found herself holding her breath as Alex dipped one of the strips of paper into the urine. It immediately turned dark blue. Alex turned to Chloe, sympathy in his dark eyes.

"You're pregnant, Chloe. The blood test will confirm it in a couple of days, but I'm confident this test is accurate."

She started to sob, and Julia gathered her in her arms, letting her cry out all her fears. As she rubbed her back and whispered reassuring words, Chloe's tears slowly abated. She accepted a tissue from Alex and blew her nose.

"What do I do now?" she asked.

"You have to tell your parents, the sooner the better," Julia answered.

"I can't tell them myself." Chloe grasped her hand. "Can you be there with me when I tell them? Please?"

The last thing she wanted to do was to confront Ralph Sykes with news of his daughter's pregnancy. The meeting was sure to be unpleasant, and Ralph would likely find a way to blame her. But she couldn't let Chloe go through this alone.

"All right. I'll call your parents tomorrow and ask them to meet us in my office after school."

Alex put his hand on the girl's shoulder. "I can be there too, if you think it will help."

"Would you? Maybe my dad would listen to you."

"I'll be there. But I want you to promise me that as soon as your parents are told, you'll start getting prenatal care. I want you to make an appointment to see me or one of the other doctors right away."

"I will, I promise. But you'll be there?"

"Yes."

Alex's offer took Julia by surprise. Despite the rollercoaster of their relationship, he'd been nothing but supportive to her and her parents, and now Chloe. On more than one occasion she'd allowed him to get close only to push him away. She wouldn't blame him for hating her for the way she'd ended things last time. Most men would have had enough by now, but Alex stood steadfastly beside her.

Her chest ached with longing, and she had to look away. If only…

She stopped herself from going down that road. It only led to heartache.

Chapter Eighteen

Julia dreaded the meeting with Ralph Sykes and his wife all day, her stomach tensing nervously whenever she thought about it. But she'd made the appointment, and for Chloe's sake she had to go through with it.

Chloe was the first to arrive at her office when school was over for the day. She took the seat closest to the window and drew up her knees, resting her cheek against them and staring out the window. It was as if she was folding in on herself, trying to become as small as possible. Maybe she was trying to disappear. Julia didn't blame her. She wouldn't mind disappearing herself.

Then Ralph and his wife Cynthia arrived. She didn't know Cynthia well, but she'd always appeared to be a timid woman, easily overshadowed by Ralph's more forceful and acerbic personality.

Julia stalled a little, hoping Alex would arrive soon.

"Can I get anyone coffee or water?"

Ralph waved his hand. "We don't want anything. Let's just get to the point, Mrs. Stewart. Why did you call us here today? What has Chloe done that warrants a trip to the principal's office?"

"Chloe is a sweet, wonderful girl. She's a good, hard-working student, and on a personal note, I know she's a kind person because of the way she treats my daughter."

"Thank you—"

Ralph cut off his wife. "Then what are we doing here?"

Julia took a deep breath. "Chloe wants to tell you something—"

A knock sounded on the office door and she sighed in relief.

"Come in."

Alex stepped inside. "Sorry I'm late."

"You're just in time. Dr. Campbell, these are Chloe's parents, Ralph and Cynthia Sykes. Ralph, Cynthia, Dr. Alex Campbell."

"Why is Dr. Campbell here? What does he have to do with a school matter?"

Julia turned her attention to Chloe, who looked like she wanted to be anywhere but here. "Chloe, your parents are here, and they want to know what's going on. Can you tell them?"

She shook her head, and tears began to run down her cheeks. Alex moved to stand behind her, his hands on her small, thin shoulders. Julia smiled reassuringly for her. "Okay, honey."

She took a deep breath and faced Ralph and Cynthia. "Chloe came to me yesterday and told me she thought she was pregnant."

"What?" Ralph burst from his seat and turned furious eyes on Chloe. "Is this true?"

"Yes," Chloe said between sobs. She was crying in earnest now.

"I took her to see Dr. Campbell so we could either confirm the pregnancy or rule it out, and he confirmed it."

Ralph began to pace her small office. "I can't believe this. I tried to teach the girl good moral values, and this is how she repays me. I'm ashamed of you, Chloe."

Cynthia gasped. "How can you say that, Ralph? She's our daughter, our only child."

"It's the truth! How can I hold up my head in this town when I have a pregnant teenage daughter? No one's going to take my candidacy for the state legislature seriously now."

"Is that your only concern right now?" Alex said. "You need to think about what's right for Chloe and her baby. This isn't about you."

Ralph turned on him, eyes blazing. "Just because you're sleeping with the principal, don't think you have any right to tell me what to do for my own family."

Julia rose to her feet, fury making her deadly calm. "I suggest you keep your comments and your prejudices to yourself, and begin thinking about your daughter. She's scared, and she needs you."

"This is great for you, isn't it? I can just imagine how you'll use my pregnant daughter against me at the public meeting."

"I would never use Chloe like that!"

"If you hadn't brought that daycare with all those bastard children to this school, maybe she wouldn't have gotten crazy ideas about having sex! This is all your fault!"

Alex straightened to his full height and stepped in front of Ralph. He towered over the older man, his eyes full of an emotion she'd never seen in them before. Julia shivered, afraid they were going to come to blows right there in her office.

Before she could say anything, Cynthia got to her feet and pushed herself between them. “Ralph, that’s enough! For once in your life, think of someone besides yourself! Chloe needs us, but obviously she felt too afraid to come to us for help. And no wonder, the way you’re acting.” She turned to Julia. “Thank you for your concern for Chloe. I’ll make sure she’s well cared for.”

“I’d be happy to look after Chloe’s prenatal care if you want,” Alex said. “Just make an appointment with my nurse at the clinic.”

Cynthia nodded her head. “Thank you. I’ll do that.” She held out her hand. “Come on, Chloe. Let’s go home.”

“Cynthia—” Ralph sputtered.

She gave him a withering look. “We’ll finish this conversation at home.”

Chloe took her mother’s hand and left with her. Ralph stared after them for a few moments in stunned surprise, obviously not used to his wife speaking out. With one last glare in Julia’s direction, he left her office, slamming the door behind him.

Julia blew out the breath she’d been holding and sank into her chair. “Gee, that went well.”

Alex chuckled and slid into the chair Chloe had just vacated. “If that’s a sample of a typical workday for you, I’m glad I don’t have your job.”

“There are days when diffusing bombs or driving trucks filled with dynamite sound like nice, safe occupations.”

Alex laughed out loud. “Poor old Ralph didn’t know what hit him. First you stood up to him, and then his wife delivered the knockout punch.”

“You had me worried for a second,” Julia said. “I

thought you might actually hit him."

The smile left his face. "Believe me, I thought about it. The things he said about his own daughter…" He shook his head, his jaw clenched. "But when he started ragging on you, I nearly lost it."

She knew it would have been professionally damaging to both of them if he'd actually struck Ralph, no matter how much he'd deserved it. But she felt a perverse spark of pleasure knowing he'd been willing to defend her.

Alex checked his watch and rose to his feet. "I've got to get back to the clinic. My patients are probably wondering what happened to me."

"Thanks for coming. I know it meant a lot to Chloe to have you here. It meant a lot to me, too."

He stopped with his hand on the doorknob, his expression intense. "I'd do anything for you. I hope you know that. You mean everything to me, Julia."

Her chest grew tight, and she could hardly breathe. "Don't say that, Alex. Please."

He stepped toward her. "Why don't you want me to tell you how much you mean to me?"

"Because you'll be leaving soon."

A part of her wished she could simply run away and follow Alex wherever he wanted to go. But she couldn't. Her life was here, and so were her responsibilities.

He took her hands and squeezed tight. "Then I'll stay. I love you, Julia. I don't want to lose you."

She shook her head, trying not to cry. "I know you mean that, at least for now. But if you stay just to make me happy, you'll soon grow to resent me. You'll want to pursue better opportunities, and I'll just hold you back."

"No, that's not going to happen. I love you."

She couldn't hold back the tears any longer. "I wish things could be different, but I can't go through that again."

"I'm not your ex-husband, Julia," he said fiercely. "I'm not going to abandon you and Ava."

"Is Lobster Cove really the place you want to live and work for the rest of your life? Do you honestly want to live in a town this small forever?"

He hesitated, uncertainty evident on his face, and Julia pulled her hands away from his, her heart breaking.

"That's what I thought. It's not your fault. We just need different things." She took a deep breath and looked away. "Thank you for helping Chloe."

"Julia, don't do this. Don't push me away. I need you."

She couldn't breathe. What could she possibly say to that?

"Alex—"

"I'm not going to give up on you, on us."

He pulled her in for a brief hug, and Julia closed her eyes and inhaled, trying to memorize his scent and the way she fit perfectly against his body. Then he pushed away and slipped out of the room, the door closing softly behind him.

A flood of longing washed over her. If only…

She shook her head. Wishing and hoping only brought disappointment and heartache. She'd wished for Russ to be happy with her in Lobster Cove, but it hadn't made any difference. In the end he'd left her.

She couldn't let herself forget that.

****

The following Saturday, Wyatt and Lily arrived shortly after lunch to collect Ava. Lily had asked if they could take her to the annual Harvest of the Sea Festival, and even though Julia would have liked to spend the day with Ava herself, she'd agreed. She couldn't deny Lily the only thing she'd asked of her. Ava would attend some of the festivities with the Stewarts and then spend the night with them. There was no guarantee how long they'd be in Ava's life. Her mother's illness had driven home that point very clearly.

After the Stewarts left with Ava, she puttered around the house, straightening things and throwing a load of laundry into the machine. For a while she tackled some paperwork she'd brought home with her from school, but she had to abandon it when she found her mind wandering. The house was cold and quiet without Ava. She knew it was ridiculous to feel this way; Ava had been away before for an afternoon. Yet today Julia felt alone. And lonely.

She'd been lonely for a long time, she realized. Even when she was still married.

Especially when she was still married.

Was she missing Ava, or was it Alex she needed?

She'd been restless ever since Alex told her he loved her, needed her. Maybe he was telling the truth. Maybe he could learn to be happy in Lobster Cove.

But she didn't really believe it. He was a big-city boy. He'd soon grow tired of small town life. And he'd soon grow tired of her. She had to let him move on.

She got to her feet. It was time to stop being ridiculous. She had to move on too, and get on with her life. With careful strokes she applied her makeup and then dressed in her best jeans. She'd go to the festival for a while, even though her heart wasn't really in it. At least she'd be out with people instead of brooding at home alone. She grabbed her jacket and her house keys and walked downtown.

Most of the festival events were taking place downtown in the community center. All the Lobster Cove stores were decorated with brightly colored banners and flags for the Harvest of the Sea festival, many of them featuring the cartoon depiction of Lionel the Lobster, the festival's mascot. Some shops had bright red stuffed Lionel toys in various sizes displayed in their front windows. It was pretty kitschy, but fun.

She'd no sooner arrived at the community center when her secretary, Beth, approached her, looping her arm through hers.

"Boss! I'm glad to see you! Can you help us out? We need another person to judge the pie contest."

"Beth, I hate doing stuff like that. It's like picking the prettiest baby; you always end up hurting someone's feelings."

"Please, please, please, Julia. It'll be fun. I promise. Everyone who helps to judge the contest gets a free ticket to the dance tonight. How about it?"

She wasn't planning to stay for the dance, but she couldn't say no to Beth's request. She was a wonderful secretary, always going above and beyond for her, and for the kids.

"Okay, fine. But I'm doing this for you. You owe me."

Beth did a little happy dance. "Thanks, Boss. I promise you that every morning next week you'll have a latte from Julie's Coffee Shop on your desk by nine a.m."

Julia laughed. "I'm going to hold you to it."

Beth led her to the judging area, where her fellow judges—Jill, from Maggie's Diner, and Bob, the local chiropractor—were already waiting. Eight pieces of pie were set in front of her. Julia inwardly groaned. She liked pie as much as the next person, but eight pieces was a bit much.

Fortunately, she wasn't expected to eat every morsel. Jill was a veteran judge, so following her lead, Julia nibbled a little from each pie, sampling the filling and testing the crust for flakiness. The three of them decided unanimously on the blueberry pie.

After that, Beth dragged her around the community center to judge more contests; best dried flower arrangement, best pickled cucumbers, and best artwork in the ten- to twelve-year-old category. She ran into Ava and the Stewarts and spent a little time with them, but didn't want to intrude on her daughter's day with her grandparents. After confirming that they'd bring Ava home at ten Sunday morning before they met friends for brunch, she left Wyatt and Lily in the midway area, where they watched Ava and one of her friends on the mini rollercoaster.

Julia realized part way through the afternoon that her blue mood had lifted and she was having fun. She'd needed this outing, needed to do something to get out of her own head.

She met Edie and Aaron and their kids just before the community supper, which was held outside. Oak Avenue had been blocked off to allow for dozens of picnic tables to be set up on the street next to the community center. Later, the tables would be pushed to the sides to allow for dancing. The band was already setting up on one end of the street. Thankfully, the night was warm for early October. There wouldn't be many more nights like this before winter settled in.

The thought of winter almost doused the happy mood she'd worked so hard to attain. Winter meant cold winds and mountains of snow. And it meant the coming of February and Alex's departure. She forcefully pushed the thought from her mind, not wanting to let it spoil her evening.

Together with Aaron and Edie and their kids, she ate her supper of fresh boiled lobster, corn on the cob, baked potato with all the fixings, and coleslaw. Julia passed on the homemade pie, having had enough for one day. She helped Natalie and Michael crack their lobsters, and showed them how to dip the succulent pieces in the small bowl of melted butter that sat on a stand and was warmed by a candle. It was a fun if messy meal.

After they finished eating, Julia helped clean up the kids, wiping sticky fingers with wet naps and removing the plastic lobster bibs. A few minutes later, Aaron and Edie said good night and headed home. By then some tables had already been pushed aside, and people were starting to dance. That was Julia's cue to go. The last thing she wanted was to spend the evening as a wallflower on the sidelines. Or worse, to find herself the recipient of pity dances from the husbands and boyfriends of her friends. She put on her jacket and moved toward the exit.

"You're not leaving already, are you? It looks like the party's just getting started."

She turned toward the familiar voice, her heart in

her throat. Alex smiled down at her, his dark eyes warm and full of an emotion she was afraid to name. The last words he'd said to her came immediately to mind: *I'm not going to give up on you, on us.* She clasped her hands together, disconcerted to find they were shaking.

"I'm not really much of a dancer," she said. Her voice sounded husky, as if it came from someone else.

He tucked a piece of her hair behind her ear, his fingers brushing against her sensitive skin and making her shiver. "I don't believe that for a minute. Not someone who plays ball with the grace and athleticism you do."

"It's true. I have two left feet when it comes to dancing."

"Prove it. Dance with me."

He extended his hand. Julia stared at it for a moment, warring with herself. If she danced with him, here in public, the whole town would know. They'd talk about her, about them. Once more she'd be the subject of gossip.

But when she looked into Alex's eyes, she discovered she didn't care. She hoped she wouldn't regret her decision tomorrow.

She took Alex's hand and let him lead her out onto the dance floor. The band was playing a slow waltz. He linked his fingers with hers and drew her hips against his. They moved slowly, swaying seductively to the music, their gazes locked. Julia simply couldn't look away. She was lost in a turbulent sea of desire and longing.

"Where's Ava tonight?"

"With the Stewarts. She's staying the night."

The slow song ended, and the band played an

upbeat tune that had everyone on their feet. They crowded onto the dance floor. Julia and Alex remained in the middle of the street, staring into each other's eyes as people danced around them. Then he lowered his head and whispered in her ear.

"Come home with me, Julia. Please."

He rested his forehead against hers, waiting. Alex was the first man, the only man, she'd wanted since the end of her marriage. Their one night together had been magical. She didn't know what to make of his assertion that he loved her. Her feelings for him were too confused to make sense of them. All she knew was that in this moment, she wanted him, needed him.

"Yes."

Alex leaned back to look into her eyes as if needing to see the confirmation of her words. Then he took her hand, and without another word they left.

Chapter Nineteen

Alex led Julia to his room, not quite believing she'd agreed to come home with him. He was almost afraid that if he let go of her hand, she'd bolt.

But she didn't. As they stood facing each other at the foot of his bed, she brought their linked hands to her mouth, and softly kissed his fingers. Then she placed his hand on her cheek, and covered it with hers as she looked up into his face. Desire burned in her eyes. She wanted him as much as he wanted her.

The knowledge set his blood on fire. He lowered his mouth to hers. The instant he touched her lips, she moaned and pressed herself against him, winding her hands around his neck, sifting her fingers through his hair. Her mouth opened eagerly to his, the tip of her tongue touching his in an innocent caress. He devoured her, thrusting his tongue inside her mouth to taste her sweetness. Their tongues touched, caressed, mated, loved.

Julia began pushing his jacket off his shoulders. "I want to touch you," she said between kisses. "Let me feel you. Please, Alex."

He'd do anything to please her. He tossed his jacket to the floor, then lifted the hem of his T-shirt and pulled it over his head. Julia spread her hands across his abdomen. Her fingers glided over his chest and shoulders, caressing each muscle with loving attention.

Her touch drove him wild with excitement. It was all he could do not to throw her onto the bed and sink himself into her, over and over. Grasping her shoulders, he made himself stand still and endure her tender torture.

She touched the eagle tattoo on his shoulder. “This is so perfect for you. You’re strong and brave like an eagle. And so beautiful. So very beautiful.”

“Julia.” *God, I love this woman.* “I need to see you, too.”

She smiled shyly and removed her jacket, tossing it on a chair in the corner of the room. Then she pulled her T-shirt over her head and stood before him in a lacy white bra. She reached behind her to unfasten the bra. Alex’s breath hitched as it slid slowly down her arms to reveal her lovely, pale breasts.

“Perfect,” he said, touching the impossibly soft skin. He traced the shape, tested the weight of each milk-white breast with his hands.

She inhaled sharply, her eyes drifting shut. “Not perfect. Too small.”

“No, baby. Perfect. I’ll show you.”

Turning her to face the mirror on his dresser, he stood behind her and wrapped his arms around her, his hands cupping her breasts, kneading them with his fingers, his thumb and forefinger gently rolling the hard nipples.

“See how your breasts fill my hands. They’re just the right size, as if they were made for me to touch.”

“Yes,” she breathed. “Only you.”

Her words nearly sent him over the edge. He kissed her shoulder, trailing light kisses to her neck, and she let her head fall back against his chest to allow him better access. She smelled so good, a combination of vanilla and sweet roses. Her scent, the feel of her skin, her soft sighs, intoxicated him with pleasure. He was drunk on Julia. If this was what it was like to love her, he never wanted to be sober again.

Soon it wasn't enough. He needed more of her, his body demanding satisfaction. Reaching for the zipper of her jeans, he pulled it down and unfastened the button. He pushed the jeans down her legs, kissing her shoulder blades, her spine, the small of her back as he slid slowly down her body till he was kneeling behind her. Her muscles shivered under his lips. When he reached her buttocks, he placed his hands on her hips and turned her to face him. Leaning forward, he touched the tip of his tongue to her sex. She moaned and clutched his shoulders. Alex licked and sucked, his tongue finding the sensitive nub that had her shaking and crying his name. A moment later she tensed and then cried out as her release came. She clung to him, bracing herself with her hands on his shoulders, her cheek resting against his head.

When the tremors in her body subsided, he lifted her in his arms and carried her to the bed. She felt insubstantial, as if she weighed nothing. Without a word he laid her carefully on the bed, then stepped back to strip off his remaining clothes. Julia watched him, her chest rising and falling with her accelerated breath. His cock sprang forward, hard and aching, as he freed it from the confines of his clothing. He found a condom in his nightstand and rolled it over his length. Julia reached out her hand.

"Come to me, Alex."

Shaking with need, he positioned himself between her spread legs, his cock nudging the entrance to her body. She lifted her hips to meet him, her hands moving restlessly down his back, kneading, stroking and fondling each muscle from his shoulders to his buttocks. He sank himself into her, shivering as he felt her tight, wet heat surround him. Bracing himself with his hands on either side of her head, he stared into her eyes. He wanted to see her face as he made love to her, wanted to watch her fly apart.

She lifted her hips, urging him on. "Please. I need you," she said. "Please."

He softly kissed her lips. "I need you, too."

He pushed deeply into her, and watched her eyes go wide. Then he withdrew slowly, almost pulling all the way out. She whimpered, her hands clutching at him in protest. He plunged into her again, a little deeper this time, a little harder, then withdrew with excruciating slowness once more. And then again, and again, and again, deeper and harder with each penetration, slower with each withdrawal. Her head fell back as she whispered incoherent words. But she stayed with him, her hips rising to meet his with each thrust, moving to the rhythm of his body.

"Look at me, baby," he commanded.

Her glazed eyes slowly opened. He withdrew once more, and she shivered, on the brink of release. He was on the edge himself, but he hung on, not wanting to let go until he'd brought her to climax.

On the next plunge, she shattered around him. She cried out and held him tightly. Her cries made him go wild. He thrust into her harder, faster, deeper, until he no longer knew where his body stopped and hers began, where his soul ended and hers began. With one last thrust, he cried out and spilled inside her.

They clung to each other, both breathing heavily, their bodies slick with sweat, hearts racing. Alex held her, never wanting to let her go.

After some time, their breathing returned to normal. He slid off her, knowing he must be crushing her. His breath caught in his throat when he saw the shiny trail of tears down her cheeks.

"Julia, baby, did I hurt you? God, I'm sorry." He ran his hand over her face, her shoulder, her hip, searching for injuries.

She cupped his cheek with her hand. "No, of course you didn't hurt me. It's just…" Fresh tears poured from her eyes.

Her tears destroyed him. Nothing could ever feel worse than seeing Julia cry. He couldn't bear the thought of the woman he loved distressed or unhappy, especially if he was the cause. He massaged her shoulder. "What's wrong, *mi querida*? Don't cry, please don't cry."

She made a sound that was part sob, part laugh. "I'm sorry… I don't know why I'm crying. That was so—"

Her breath hitched, momentarily preventing speech. Alex waited on tenterhooks for her to speak, wiping fresh tears from her eyes with his thumb.

"So amazing," she said at last. "I can't believe…" She took a deep breath to get herself under control, her hands moving over his face, and her fingers running through his hair.

"So amazing," she said again. She smiled at him, and at last he saw her joy shining through the tears. "I don't have words to tell you how I feel right now."

She didn't need to say it out loud. He could read it

in her eyes, and in her smile. He could feel it in his heart, because he felt the same way. Something magical, almost sacred, had passed between them. As if they had spoken to each other, soul to soul.

"I know, baby," he whispered. "I know."

He gathered her in his arms, and in a few moments they were both asleep.

****

Julia awoke to the delicious sensation of Alex's mouth on her breast. She reached for him, arching her body to bring him closer. He took each hardened nipple into his mouth, swirling his tongue, gently suckling, licking, biting. His hand drifted down her belly to the apex of her thighs. She opened her legs for him, her body shivering in anticipation of his touch. He parted the folds of her sex, inserting a finger inside her. She threw back her head and moaned in delight, writhing on the bed. God, it felt so good. *He* felt so good.

"You like that, baby?"

"Yes! Yes!"

He inserted a second finger and she was gone. She convulsed around him as wave after wave of pleasure turned her limbs to water.

But Alex wasn't through with her.

He turned her onto her stomach, her knees tucked beneath her. Covering her body from behind, he held himself up on one elbow, his other hand reaching beneath her to once more find her most sensitive spot. With one touch she was wet and wanting him again. Moaning, she pushed her backside against his erection, rubbing him, encouraging him.

Needing him.

He slipped easily inside her, and she gasped, the

sensation so different in this position than she was used to. He completely filled her, and so deep it was almost painful.

He waited a heartbeat, letting her become accustomed to him being inside her this way. And then he began to move.

With his clever fingers stroking her and his penis pushing deep into her, she was overloaded with sensation. But it was good. So incredibly good.

Her climax came from the tips of her toes. It burst out of her in a kaleidoscope of colors, a cacophony of sound, an excess of emotion. She cried out his name.

She heard Alex's hoarse whisper next to her ear. "Yes, baby, yes. Let it come."

A second later, with one final thrust, his own release came, and she realized he'd hung on, waiting for her orgasm.

Waiting to please her before himself.

When the spasms stopped, he rolled off her. Julia turned to face him. She couldn't form any words to tell him how she felt, how *good* she felt. So she simply stroked his face and stared into the dark chocolate depths of his beautiful eyes.

After a long time, Alex kissed her nose. "I need a shower."

"Now?" She rose on her elbows to check the clock on the nightstand. "It's three a.m."

"I feel like I've had a workout," he said, pushing himself to a sitting position. He chuckled. "A couple of workouts. The best workouts of my life."

She laughed, feeling ridiculously happy and joyously free. "I know what you mean. That was…"

She shook her head and laughed again, not able to

describe her feelings. Alex brought her hand to his mouth for a kiss.

"Yeah, I know, *mi cariño*."

He turned on the bedside lamp. Then he slid out of bed, removing the used condom and tossing it into a garbage can. He stood before her in all his gorgeously naked splendor, and, just like that, Julia wanted him again.

"I could wash your back for you," she said, slipping out of the bed to stand in front of him.

A spark of interest lit his eyes. "Oh, yeah?"

"Yeah." She wound her arms around his neck and pressed herself against him. "I give great…back washes."

"I've got to warn you," he said, his hands kneading her ass and bringing her against his penis, which had come alive once more. "My back is really, really dirty. It might need a lot of attention."

"I'm always up for a challenge."

"So am I."

Without warning, he scooped her into his arms and carried her across the hall into the bathroom. She laughed all the way to the shower.

****

Julia woke slowly, stretching her arms over her head and arching her back. She felt deliciously sore, her inner thighs pleasantly aching. Alex had made love to her with such tenderness, such passion, as if his only concern had been her pleasure. Last night was… She hardly knew how to put it into words. "Amazing" barely did justice to the things she and Alex did to each other. "Transformative" came to mind. Had she been truly transformed by last night? She felt light, free, happy, so different from the last three years. So different from…forever.

This won't last, Julia. It never does.

No! She wasn't going to listen, at least not right now when she felt so happy. She was going to enjoy the feeling as long as she could.

She turned on her side and saw that Alex was awake and watching her. She touched his face and smiled into his eyes.

"Good morning."

"Good morning, *cariño*."

"Mmm, I love when you talk Spanish to me. It's very sexy."

He touched her face, a smile lighting his eyes. "Oh, yeah? I'll tell you what I love. I love seeing you first thing in the morning, when your hair's all messed up and your eyes are still sleepy. But the best part is that sexy little smile that tells me you loved making love with me last night."

"I did, very much," she said with a smile.

His hand skimmed down her shoulder to her waist and then to her breast. She was instantly aroused, wanting him all over again. Laughing, she pushed him onto his back and slid on top of him, straddling his thighs. She stroked him, loving the warm, velvety feel of his penis and the fact she could make him hard so easily.

"Last night was wonderful," she said. "Perhaps we could—"

The doorbell rang. Julia froze. The bedside clock proclaimed the time in bold red letters: nearly twenty minutes after ten. Her breath caught in her throat. *No, no, no. It couldn't be. How could she be so stupid?*

"Oh, my God!"

She pushed herself off Alex and slid from the bed, searching frantically on her hands and knees for her discarded clothing. Tears stung her eyes.

"Julia? What's wrong?"

She hastily fastened her bra and pushed her arms through the sleeves of her T-shirt. "I'm sure the Stewarts are at the door. They were supposed to bring Ava home to my place fifteen minutes ago, and when I wasn't there… Oh, god, they'll know we slept together."

Alex pulled on his pants. "So what if they do? I'm sure they didn't expect you to remain celibate for the rest of your life. They're not going to think any less of you."

He didn't understand. His neighbors were probably watching the scene unfolding on his doorstep right now. They'd put two and two together and figure out why the Stewarts were there with Ava on a Sunday morning. News about them would spread all over town. Soon they'd be the object of gossip. Alex would hate that. He wasn't used to his private life being on public display. Why would he want to stay in a town where he had no privacy?

"I've got to go."

She felt cold inside, her stomach threatening to be sick. She grabbed her shoes and ran to the door.

When she opened the door and confirmed that the Stewarts were indeed on the front step with Ava, the look of disgust Wyatt gave her nearly buckled her knees.

Lily looked from her to Wyatt, clearly uncomfortable. "Good morning, Julia. We would have kept Ava with us, but we're meeting our friends for brunch…I tried texting you…" Her voice trailed off.

"I overslept. I'm sorry for the inconvenience."

"Dr. Alex!"

Ava ran past her to get to Alex. He picked her up and hugged her.

"Hi, Sweet Pea. It's good to see you."

With one last look of contempt, Wyatt turned his back and walked toward his car.

"Ava." Julia's voice was sharper then she intended. "It's time to say goodbye."

"Bye, Dr. Alex." She kissed his cheek, and he set her on her feet. "Bye, Grandma."

Lily bent and kissed her. When she straightened, she looked at Julia. "Don't mind Wyatt. He just…" She sighed and shook her head. "He'll come around."

Julia nodded briskly, knowing Wyatt would never change his mind about her. "Thank you for looking after Ava."

"It was our pleasure. I'll talk to you soon. Goodbye, Dr. Campbell."

"Goodbye, Mrs. Stewart."

Lily walked down the front walk. Wyatt had already started the car, anxious to get away. Julia squeezed her eyes shut as a wave of mortification and shame passed over her. She knew she'd done nothing to be ashamed of. She *knew* that. It wasn't as if she were married. But when she saw the look in Wyatt's eyes, she'd felt like the dirt beneath his shoes.

"Julia? Are you okay?"

"Yes, I'm fine." She couldn't look at Alex or she'd start crying. She held out her hand to Ava. "We have to go."

Ava reluctantly grasped her hand and started down the front steps. She turned once more to wave at Alex. "Bye."

"Bye, Sweet Pea."

Julia hurried home as quickly as she could, anxious to avoid the prying eyes of neighbors. She wanted to cry. For a brief moment she'd let herself believe a life with Alex could be possible, but now the rose-colored glasses had been ripped from her eyes. The most wonderful night of her life had turned into the ugliest morning.

Chapter Twenty

When Alex rounded the corner of Julia's house and entered her back yard, he found Ava playing by herself in her sandbox, plastic pails, shovels and toys lined up on the wooden ledge surrounding the box. She jumped out of the sandbox as soon as she saw him, toys and sand scattering as she ran toward him.

"Dr. Alex!"

He knelt and pulled her into his arms, burying his face in her silky hair. *God, I love this child.* He had to talk to Julia, had to find out what was going on with her. The way she'd left that morning, the look on her face, had scared him as much as it had puzzled him. Didn't she understand they had something very special between them? To hell with Wyatt Stewart and the busybody gossips of Lobster Cove. She and Ava meant everything to him. They belonged together as a family.

He set Ava at arm's distance and looked into her face. "Sweet Pea, I need to talk to your mom about some important grownup stuff. Can you give us some privacy and stay out here in the yard to play?"

"Are you mad at my mom?"

He smoothed her hair. "No, baby. I could never be mad at her."

"Mommy was crying. She thought I didn't hear her, but I did."

She looked so sad that Alex wanted to hold her and

tell her everything was going to be all right. But he couldn't promise her anything. He was suddenly afraid he wouldn't be able to convince Julia to let him into her life.

He hugged Ava once more and kissed her hair. She held onto him so tightly he had to gently peel her little arms from around his neck, and he understood that she was as scared as he was.

Alex got to his feet and, with a smile for Ava, made his way to the back door and knocked. Julia answered a moment later. Without a word, she stepped aside to let him in.

He followed her into the kitchen and when she turned to face him, he studied her face. She looked resigned, as if she'd made up her mind. Had she decided they were over? The thought sent a chill up his spine.

"I couldn't go to work this afternoon without knowing you were okay," he said. "You were so upset this morning."

"Yes," she said. "I was. But I'm okay now."

"Are *we* okay, Julia?"

She looked away. "Last night was wonderful, Alex. I don't want you to think I didn't love being with you. But we both know it can't happen again."

"I don't know that at all. You're acting like we've done something wrong, and we haven't. Neither of us is married. There's no reason we can't be together, despite your father-in-law's attitude. Your *ex*-father-in-law."

"You don't understand what it's like living in a small town. I'm the high school principal. I have to maintain a squeaky clean reputation. How am I going to face the school board, of which Wyatt Stewart is chairman, with any kind of professional credibility, when all they'll be thinking about is that I'm having an affair with you?"

"You're not giving the people of Lobster Cove much credit. I think they're much more open-minded than you think. They're not going to condemn you for being in love."

She visibly flinched at that, and began to pace. "I have to face those open-minded people at a public meeting next week. The future of the daycare at my school is at stake, and probably my job, as well."

"I'll come with you. We'll stand together and show the town we're a couple, that we're committed to each other. Then they'll understand that what we have together is more than just an affair."

She shook her head. "If you stood at the podium with me, it would fuel the gossip. You'd just make things worse."

He drew a hand through his hair in frustration. Why was she being so obstinate? "I don't give a damn what anyone thinks about me. Anybody who wants to gossip about me can go right ahead, because I haven't done anything wrong, and people who know me and care about me in this town understand that."

"That's fine for you. You don't have to live in this town. I do."

He threw up his hands in exasperation. "Have you not listened to anything I've said to you? I told you, I want to stay here in Lobster Cove with you."

"You're not going to say that when people start gossiping about you."

"Dammit, Julia, if the gossip bothers you so much, why do you want to stay here? We can go anywhere.

Come with me to San Diego. I'm sure you could get a job there."

He knew it was the wrong thing to say as soon as the words left his mouth. Julia's eyes flared with anger.

"I knew you didn't mean any of it. Why would someone like you want to stay in this place?"

"I meant every word. I want to make a life here in Lobster Cove."

"For how long? Until something better comes along?"

"No! Why are you doing this? Why are you deliberately twisting what I say and trying to pick a fight?"

"Because I know that no matter what you say now, you won't stay in Lobster Cove forever. You'll get a wonderful opportunity somewhere else and you'll want to take it. But this is my home. This is where I want to raise my daughter, and I'm never going to let anyone drag me away again. I'm staying right here."

He stared at her a moment, the pieces of the puzzle beginning to fall into place. "That's what this is about, isn't it? You're afraid what happened with your ex-husband is going to happen again with me. But I've got news for you, sweetheart. I'm not Russ. I'm not so jealous of your career and your success that I'm going to insist you give up your job and move away. I mean what I say. I won't promise to love you and then let you down. I would never, ever, abandon my child. I'm in this thing for the long haul because I love you, so you're just going to have to deal with it."

Her chin began to quiver, and he knew she was close to tears again. "I think you should go."

"Julia—"

"Please, Alex." One tear rolled down her cheek.

He wanted nothing more than to gather her in his arms and hold her. He wanted to dry her tears and tell her everything was going to be okay. But he had to let her work things out on her own, no matter how much it killed him.

"All right, I'll go. I love you, Julia." Maybe if he kept telling her, she'd believe it someday.

He could only pray that day would come soon.

****

As soon as Alex entered the examining room, Melissa Maloney's face lit up with a wide smile.

"There he is! My favorite doctor!"

Alex laughed. "Careful, Melissa. You're going to give me a swelled head."

"I don't care if your head gets to be the size of a pumpkin. If you hadn't figured out what was wrong with me, I don't know what I would have done."

"How are you feeling?"

"Still tired, but not as bad. And look at this." She removed the hat she'd been wearing. A new growth of hair was beginning to fill in the bald spots on her head. Melissa ran her hand through it. "Pretty soon I'll have my crowning glory back."

"You will. Can I see your elbows? How's the rash?"

She pushed up the sleeves of her sweater to reveal the healed skin. "Almost gone."

"Any recurrence of the urinary tract infection?"

"I'm pleased to report I've been peeing without pain."

Alex laughed again. "I'm glad to hear it. We can't cure lupus, but we can control it. You'll have to take medications for the rest of your life. There are lifestyle changes you'll need to make, too, like staying out of the sun, and avoiding stress. They can both trigger symptoms." He handed her some information he'd found online.

"Thank you," she said. "The medications are expensive, but Davy's going to take another job in town this winter to help pay for it. We'll manage."

Alex nodded. He wished there were some way of helping Melissa with her medical expenses the way they'd helped Edie.

"I've got to tell you, Doc, if you hadn't figured out what I had when you did, I don't know what I would have done. I was at the end of my rope." Melissa's usual effervescence disappeared, her face growing very sober. "I'm not too proud to tell you I thought about ending it all, I was in that much anguish. The only thing that kept me going was my kids. I had to live for them, get better for them."

Alex tried not to let his shock show. The thought that she'd nearly killed herself was frightening. Thank God they'd been able to find the cause of her problems.

"I don't want you to try to deal with this on your own. If you ever feel that kind of distress again, you can come to me and we'll figure something out. We'll get you some help. Okay?"

She nodded. "Okay."

"It's possible with this disease to have flare-ups from time to time. I want you to be prepared for that and know it's not uncommon. I found some lupus support groups online. It might be helpful to talk to people who live with the disease. The information is in those papers I just gave you."

"I'll look into it, thank you." She put her hand on his shoulder. "Thank you, Dr. Campbell, for my life back. You've saved me and my family."

Alex didn't know what to say. "You're welcome. I'm really glad you're feeling better."

"Believe me, so am I!"

After he checked her blood pressure and temperature, he sent her to the lab for some routine blood work. He was determined to keep her disease under control, at least as much as it was in his power to do.

He'd never quite realized before what a profound effect he could have on someone's life. Sure, he'd helped save lives in the ER in San Diego. But this seemed different somehow, more personal.

Since he'd been working in the family clinic in Lobster Cove he'd dealt with a host of diseases and conditions, everything from pregnancy to Alzheimer's, cancer to lupus. Every day he had to bring his A-game to work. The work was challenging and stimulating, and used every bit of his training.

It was suddenly very clear. This was what he was meant to do. And Lobster Cove was where he was meant to do it.

****

For the next week, Julia immersed herself in work. She spent hours preparing her speech for the public meeting, compiling statistics on her daycare and on similar daycares in schools across the country. She and Ava spent time with her mother every day after school, as well as on the weekend. Their visits gave her father a short daily respite and gave her the opportunity to monitor her mother and get to know the person she was becoming.

But no matter how hard she worked, no matter how busy she kept herself, she couldn't stop thinking about Alex. He was in her thoughts constantly. She kept going over and over the things he'd said to her.

You're afraid what happened with your ex-husband is going to happen again with me. But I've got news for you, sweetheart. I'm not Russ.

Was that what she'd done? Compared him to Russ? Assumed he would behave in the same selfish ways her ex-husband had? Alex was nothing like Russ.

She'd loved Russ passionately, had since she was fifteen years old. She'd done everything she could to make him happy. But over the years she'd learned that Russ's jokes and good humor sometimes hid petty jealousies and barbed comments, sometimes directed at others, often at her. His last painful comments and his final betrayal had hurt beyond measure. Inside the bedroom, she hadn't understood what it meant to be a generous lover until she'd made love with Alex.

Had Russ damaged her capacity to trust so badly that she couldn't bring herself to believe Alex could want her? That he would want to stay with her?

On the evening of the public meeting, Julia dressed carefully, selecting a conservative gray suit, a buttoned-down white blouse, and modest black heels. She kept her makeup to a minimum and her hair in a simple low ponytail, going for a look she hoped projected professionalism and respectability.

She dropped Ava off at Tracy's house, knowing Lily would be at the public meeting and Chloe wasn't allowed to babysit at her house anymore. Tracy gave her a hug for good luck and wished her well.

She was going to need all the luck she could get.

The high school gym was nearly full. A lot of people had turned out, many who didn't have children in the high school. Some, like Edie and Aaron, were there to support her, but many others had taken Ralph's side. Others, she suspected, were attending simply because they expected a good fireworks display. She'd do her best to give them what they wanted. She wasn't going down without a fight.

The gym stage had been set up with two tables on either side of a podium, with her on one side, Ralph on the other, and the moderator, a member of the school board, in the middle. She was surprised that Wyatt, as chairman of the school board, wasn't acting as moderator. She wondered what it meant.

Soon the lights in the gym were dimmed and it was time to start. The moderator introduced both her and Ralph and briefly stated which side of the issue each was on. As if everyone on the island didn't already know where they stood.

Then the moderator asked her to give her opening remarks. Julia rose on shaking knees and took her place at the podium. She thanked the moderator, and took a moment to look out at the audience. It was up to her to convince them that the daycare was worthwhile. Chloe and the girls who'd returned to school because of the daycare depended on her.

"I want to thank the school board for arranging this meeting, and I want to thank each of you here for coming out tonight. That tells me you understand the importance of education for our children, and the need for all of them to receive a quality education.

"The school board, members of the community,

and many high school staff members and I came up with the idea for the daycare in Lobster Cove High School in response to a need we saw in the community. Teenage girls who'd had babies were dropping out of school and weren't coming back. One of the biggest reasons they weren't coming back was because they lacked childcare. And once a student is out of school for a year or two, they find it very difficult to go back. What chance does a girl without even a high school diploma have in finding a decent job? Do we really want these girls to fall into poverty, and take their children with them?

"We had the space in the high school, and we determined that by also babysitting children from working families in the community we'd be able to fund the daycare using only minimal resources from the high school and the school board. In getting teenage mothers back into the classroom, the daycare is also providing a much-needed service to this community.

"I know many parents here are concerned that having the daycare in the school promotes the idea of teenagers having sex and glamorizes motherhood for teenage girls. Nothing could be further from the truth. As part of our health curriculum, grade nine and ten students have been required since the term began in September to spend time in the daycare helping to look after the young children there. They are learning the real consequences of having sex. There's nothing like changing dirty diapers or having a baby vomit on your shirt to drive home the point that if they have unprotected sex, a baby, a real live baby that needs constant care and attention, could be the result.

"In addition, one of our teenage mothers has come

forward this term to speak to her peers. She tells them about the upset to her family and the sacrifices her parents have had to make because of her pregnancy, her struggle to finish school, and how much harder it's going to be for her to go on to further education. She also tells them about the assumptions many people have made about her character and her intelligence, and how hurtful and damaging those assumptions have been to her. We're not sugar-coating anything.

"In conclusion, I want to ask for your continued assistance in bringing high quality academic education to Lobster Cove. I need your support to teach our students the life skills, the empathy for others, and the practical knowledge they'll need to become healthy, caring, contributing members of our community. Thank you."

There was generous applause for her remarks, and some people, led by Edie and Aaron, stood to clap for her. She resumed her seat and exhaled. The moderator returned to the podium.

"I'd like to now call on Ralph Sykes for his opening remarks."

Julia tensed in anticipation of the slam she was sure Ralph would make against her. He made his way to the podium, but instead of the bluster she'd expected, he was surprisingly subdued.

"I too would like to thank everyone for coming out tonight and showing such support for education in our community. But if you were looking for a spirited debate on the plusses and minuses of the high school daycare, I'm afraid I'm going to disappoint you. I have listened intently to Mrs. Stewart's opening remarks, and I have come to the conclusion that I have misinterpreted her intentions regarding the daycare."

Julia stared at him in astonishment. What was going on? Ralph had adamantly opposed the daycare from its inception. A murmur of surprise rippled through the crowd. Obviously others were wondering the same thing.

"Mrs. Stewart makes a good case for using the daycare as a kind of real-life lab to teach teenagers about the consequences of having sex. As you may know, I'm a proponent for abstinence for teenagers. Unfortunately, that message isn't always heard. I recently discovered that my own teenage daughter will soon be having a baby."

Excited whispers echoed through the gymnasium. Julia was shocked he'd speak of Chloe's pregnancy in such a public way, but perhaps it was for the best. People would find out soon enough. Might as well come clean.

"My wife and daughter and I have decided that she will be keeping the baby and will likely be taking advantage of the daycare in order to continue her schooling, so it would be the height of hypocrisy for me to advocate getting rid of a facility my family will be using. I will be happy to take any questions you may have, and I'm sure Mrs. Stewart will answer questions also."

A few questions were asked, mainly about financing the daycare, the number of children currently enrolled, and expected future enrollment. Julia easily answered them all. With Ralph's capitulation, all the fight had gone out of the room, and debate was essentially over. When there were no more questions from the floor, the moderator called an end to the meeting. Julia sighed in relief.

She made her way off the stage and headed for the exit, wanting nothing more than to pick up Ava and go home. She was stopped by several people who wanted to shake her hand and congratulate her on a job well done. Their praise came as a total surprise.

She met Edie and Aaron near the coat racks. Edie gave her a fierce hug.

"You were wonderful. So poised and confident, and totally in control."

She had to smile at that. "It's a good thing you couldn't see my knees shaking behind the podium. I was terrified."

"Then you hid it well," Aaron said.

"You know what they say," Julia said. "Never let them see you sweat."

"You're definitely a master at hiding your true feelings." Edie took Aaron's arm. "We'd better get going. We told my mom we'd be home early."

"Thank you for coming. I really appreciate your support."

Edie kissed her. "It was the least we could do for you, Jules."

They retrieved their coats and left. Julia was about to do the same when Lily stopped her. Wyatt stood a couple of steps behind her.

"Wonderful job, Julia," Lily said. "I'm so proud of you for standing up to Ralph, and fighting for what you believe in."

Julia embraced her. "Thank you. That means a lot to me, coming from you."

Wyatt stepped forward, a slight smile on his face. He offered his hand in a shake. "You did a good job.

Congratulations."

She didn't know what to say. Wasn't he on Ralph's side? Wyatt was the last person she'd expected congratulations from, especially after the fiasco at Alex's front door. But his expression told her he meant what he said.

"I…thank you."

Lily touched her arm. "We should be going, but we'll see you and Ava very soon."

"Good night, Lily. Wyatt."

"Good night," he said with a nod.

She watched them leave the school, still reeling from Wyatt's unexpected praise and trying to decipher what it meant. She grabbed her coat and started to put it on.

"Here, let me help you."

The sound of Alex's voice just behind her sent a shiver rippling down her back. He held her coat, and she pushed her arms inside, then turned to look at him. His dark eyes were warm as he looked down at her with a fond smile. After the way they'd parted, after the things she'd said, she was surprised by his demeanor.

"I didn't know you were here."

"I wouldn't have missed it," he said, still smiling. "I got here a little late, but I caught the end of your speech. Your passion really shone through. Everyone could feel it."

"I…I believe in the project." When he looked at her like that, with such intensity and emotion shining in his eyes, she could barely breathe.

"You should let yourself express that passion more often. You're the strongest woman I know, with the possible exceptions of my grandmother and my mother."

She was genuinely touched. "Thank you. I know that's high praise, considering what you've told me about them."

"It is. It seems I've been blessed with a lot of strong women in my life."

Someone diverted her attention for a moment to say hello and congratulate her on a speech well said, and when she turned back to Alex his face was more serious.

"I wish you'd believe me when I say I want to stay here in Lobster Cove and make a life with you," he said softly in a voice meant only for her. "I wish you'd believe that I love you."

She stared at him, not able to speak or look away. She wanted to believe him, wanted it with every fiber of her being. But she was afraid. How could she accept the love he offered? What if he changed his mind and left her? She couldn't go through that again. Russ's betrayal had broken her inside, and she wasn't sure the wound was completely healed. Worse, Russ had broken her trust. Would she ever believe in love again?

"I know this isn't the time or the place," he said, glancing away to watch people visiting in the hallway. "I have to go. Any time you want to talk, let me know."

She desperately wanted to kiss him, to feel his arms securely around her, but as he said, this wasn't the time or place. All she could do was nod. He smiled and walked away.

Julia watched Alex until he left the building and was swallowed by the night. She made herself button her coat and put one foot in front of the other to leave the school.

His words rang in her ears. *I wish you'd believe that I love you.* Despite every obstacle she'd thrown between them, Alex still maintained he loved her. He hadn't abandoned her when things got tough. That had to mean something.

But Julia was afraid to hope.

Chapter Twenty-One

Alex looked in baby Abigail's ears while Edie tried to hold the squirming, fussy toddler. He soon discovered the source of the child's distress.

"Looks like she's got an ear infection," he said. "I don't think she needs antibiotics, at least not yet. These things often clear up on their own in a couple of days. Give her some baby-strength painkillers, and some ear drops to help with the pain. Sometimes heat helps. You can put a warm washcloth on her ear." He wrote some instructions on a pad. "Watch her for a day or two, and if her temperature goes up, or if she seems to be in pain, bring her back right away. Otherwise, I want to see her in a couple of weeks for a followup visit. In someone as young as Abigail, we want to make sure fluid isn't building up behind the eardrum and interfering with her hearing. She's learning to talk right now, and good hearing is imperative."

"Thanks, Alex. I really appreciate knowing you're close by if I have a medical question about the kids or myself."

"My pleasure. How have you been feeling?"

"Pretty good, all things considered. My radiation treatments end next week, and they make me really tired, but I've had so much help at home, I've been able to rest and concentrate on getting better."

"I'm still amazed at the way the community came together to help you."

"Julia did an amazing job."

"Yeah. She's an amazing woman."

Edie smiled as she got to her feet, rocking her baby on her hip. Abigail rested her head against her mother's shoulder and watched him solemnly. "Yes, she is. You're in love with her, aren't you?"

There was no point denying it. "Yes."

"So what are you going to do about it?"

"I've done everything I can. I've told her how I feel, and I've told her I want to stay in Lobster Cove, if she'll have me. I don't know what else I can do."

"Are you serious? Are you really considering staying permanently here?"

"Yeah, I am. I like it here, and I like the kind of medicine I practice here. I can really make a difference in people's lives."

"I can attest to that," Edie said with a smile. "Have you actually signed papers, done whatever it is you have to do to stay?"

"No, I haven't." If Julia didn't want him, it would be torture for him to stay in the same small community, to see her but not be with her.

"Maybe you have to take a leap of faith and show her how you feel. Sometimes words aren't enough." She adjusted Abigail on her hip. "Maybe you have to be the first one to make a commitment. I have purely selfish reasons for wanting you to stay, of course. But I honestly think Julia needs to know she can count on you. She didn't have that in her marriage."

Abigail began to fuss again. Edie set her on the examining table and dressed her in her tiny coat and hat. Then she set the baby on her feet and put on her own coat.

"Don't forget to make another appointment in two weeks," Alex said.

"I'll do it on the way out." She picked up Abigail and then turned to Alex with a smile. "I hope everything works out. Julia is like a sister to me. She needs someone strong and confident, someone who's not intimidated by a determined, passionate, capable woman with deeply held opinions. Perhaps someone like you."

His mouth quirked in a grin. "Perhaps."

"I've gotta run. See you, Alex."

"Bye."

Alex stared at the closed door for a minute. Had he been using Julia as an excuse not to speak to the hospital board about staying? He knew with absolute certainty that family medicine was what he wanted to practice, and that Lobster Cove was the caring community he wanted to practice medicine in. He prayed that Julia would be part of his life, but even if she wasn't, this was where he belonged. What was he waiting for?

He took his cell phone from his pocket and checked through his contacts until he found the chairman of the hospital board. He punched in the man's office number, and when a receptionist answered, he said, "I'd like to make an appointment, please."

****

Two weeks after the public meeting, Julia slipped her arm through her mother's, and they walked the two blocks from Dora's house to her own, with Ava skipping along beside them. Dora seemed to enjoy their walks, and the exercise in the crisp November air was good for all of them. Sometimes a glimpse of the wonderful warm woman she'd been shone through, and other times she appeared lost and a little afraid. That was her reality now.

After having tea and cookies at Julia and Ava's house, they walked Dora home. Paul greeted them at the door. She kissed her parents goodbye and took Ava's hand for the walk home. But they didn't stay there long. Lily had asked if Ava could come for dinner and stay overnight, and then go with them to Bangor on Sunday. They'd take her to the children's museum, eat lunch at a restaurant, do some shopping, and be home in time for dinner. So Julia picked up Ava's overnight bag, and they walked the half mile or so to the Stewarts' house. Even though it was cool, it was a beautiful, bright late afternoon, and Julia wanted to be out in the fresh air and sunshine. Soon the weather would turn cold, and outdoor walks wouldn't be nearly as pleasant.

Ava knocked on her grandparents' back door, and Lily opened it a moment later, her smile wide.

"Hello! How are my two favorite girls?"

"Hi, Grandma! I can hardly wait to go to the museum!" She hugged Lily around the waist. Ever since the Stewarts had proposed the trip, Ava had talked about it nonstop. Her excitement made Julia realize how insular they'd become. They rarely left Mount Desert Island. It would be good for Ava to see a little bit of the world.

"Why don't you go inside and help Grandpa set the dining room table, Ava? He's been waiting for you."

"Okay. Bye, Mommy!" She gave Julia a little wave, then slipped off her shoes at the back door and hurried inside. Julia chuckled.

"She's so excited about your trip. It's good of you and Wyatt to take her."

Lily grinned. "I think we're just as excited as she is. Why don't you have dinner with us? I've got plenty."

Julia hesitated. "Thank you, that's a lovely offer, but maybe Wyatt wouldn't be so keen to have me stay."

"Julia." Lily reached for her hand and squeezed. "I'm very sure. In fact, it was Wyatt's idea."

That surprised her. "Really?"

"Yes, really. He's not the enemy, you know. I think you two have more in common than you realize, if you'd just get to know each other a little better. So will you stay?"

How could she turn Lily down? "Of course. Thank you."

She hung her coat in the closet and followed Lily into the dining room.

"Guess who's staying for dinner?"

"Hi, Mommy!"

Wyatt smiled at her. "I'm glad you could join us."

"Thank you for the invitation. It was kind of you to offer."

"It's our pleasure."

Julia turned to Lily, not sure what to make of Wyatt's new attitude. "Is there anything I can help you with in the kitchen?"

"Sure. You can toss the salad."

She and Lily got the food ready while Ava and Wyatt put the finishing touches to the table, including a lovely bouquet of fresh flowers. A few minutes later they were seated.

To Julia's surprise, they had a stress-free meal together. Julia had known Wyatt for years, but she realized now she'd never really *known* him. She'd always thought him rather serious, even dour, but she discovered now that he had a funny side. He and Ava had a running routine of corny knock-knock jokes and silly limericks.

"They do this all the time," Lily said with a roll of her eyes.

"You're funny, Grandpa," Ava said.

"You're pretty silly yourself, Sweet Pea," Wyatt retorted.

"*Everybody* calls me Sweet Pea. Grandma, Grandpa *and* Dr. Alex." She sighed and toyed with the peas on her plate. "I wish Dr. Alex would live with us forever and be my daddy."

The table went silent. Lily stared down at her lap. Julia glanced at Wyatt and saw that he was watching Ava, an expression of utter sadness on his face.

"Ava, honey, you know that Alex is our friend, but he's not planning to stay in Lobster Cove, right? He's not going to be your daddy. We've talked about this."

She lowered her head. "I know, Mommy. I was wishing."

Julia's heart broke for her little girl. She hadn't realized how deep her attachment to Alex had become or how much Ava missed having a father in her life.

Lily mustered a smile and got to her feet. "Do you think you can help me clear the table, Ava? Then we can have cake and ice cream."

Ava beamed, her previous sadness forgotten. "Okay, Grandma."

They cleared away the plates, and Lily brought

dessert and coffee to the table. Julia made small talk with Lily, desperate to lighten the somber mood that had descended over them. Wyatt said little, though he smiled for Ava.

After dinner they all pitched in to clean up, and the work was finished in a short time.

"I think it's time for a bath, Ava," Lily said. "And then off to bed. We have to get up early tomorrow, you know. Why don't you say good night to your mom, and then we'll go upstairs?"

"Okay, Grandma." Ava ran to Julia, who scooped her into her arms and hugged her. Her baby was getting so big.

"Good night, honey. You be a good girl for Grandma and Grandpa tomorrow, okay?"

"I will. I love you, Mommy."

"I love you too, sweetheart."

She let her go, and with a wave Ava followed Lily up the stairs. Julia turned to Wyatt, ready to say good night.

"Julia, I just bought a new CD. It's a reissuing of an Ella Fitzgerald classic," he said. "I know you like jazz."

"Yes, I do, and Ella is always fabulous."

It surprised her that he remembered. Years ago, when she and Russ were first married, Wyatt had asked Russ what he could get her for Christmas, and he had told him about some of her favorite artists. Wyatt had bought her a Miles Davis CD. It was still one of her favorites.

"Good, good. Have a seat in the living room."

Julia sat on the edge of the sofa, wondering why he wanted her to stay. He put on the CD and brought them each a glass of sherry. Ella's honeyed voice filled the room.

"She's wonderful, isn't she?" Julia said.

"Yes. The best." Wyatt took a sip of sherry.

They listened silently as Ella sang of longing and heartbreak. When the track ended, Wyatt put his glass on the coffee table. "I don't want Ava to forget her father."

"I don't want that either."

He turned to look at her, pain in his eyes. "Then why won't you let Russ talk to her? Why are all his letters to her returned unopened?"

Julia stared at him, not comprehending. "What?"

"She was only three when you divorced him. When I ask her about him, she has very little memory of him. Please, Julia, I'm begging you. Let Ava talk to Russ. She deserves to know him."

She shook her head. "I don't understand. What makes you think I won't let her talk to him?"

"He told me." Wyatt sighed. "A few months ago I hired someone to track him down in Thailand. We got a phone number, and I called him. I gave him hell for not phoning his mother, and especially for not keeping in touch with Ava. He said he's tried on numerous occasions to call her, and you've simply hung up on him, right after you tell him to stay out of her life. Any presents or cards he's sent have been returned unopened."

Julia took a ragged breath and closed her eyes. She'd known Russ had often skated around the truth when it suited him, but she'd never believed he'd tell a bald-faced lie like this, especially to his own father. No wonder Wyatt hated her.

"There's never been a phone call from Russ. Or a present, or a card, or a letter, or anything else in the three years he's been gone." She gave an involuntary laugh that came out sounding bitter and angry. "I would have killed for a present for Ava from him. Do you know what it's like on Christmas morning when your child looks under the tree and there's nothing from her father? She wants to know why other kids' dads send them gifts or call them on the phone, even if they don't live with them. I've seriously thought about buying things and pretending they're from him, but how long do I deceive her? Until she's ten? Fifteen? How much am I supposed to lie to my daughter? At what age are you supposed to stop pretending your child's father cares about her?"

She hadn't meant to let the anguish she'd held inside for the last three years bubble to the surface. She rose on unsteady legs. "I'm sorry. I shouldn't have… I should go."

She grabbed her purse and started for the back door. Wyatt rose and followed her. "Wait. Are you saying what Russ told me isn't true?"

Keeping her face averted, she pulled her coat out of the closet and pushed her arms through the sleeves. "Yes."

"Are you saying he lied to me?"

She turned to face him then, lifting her chin slightly and looking him straight in the eye. Even though her hands shook, she would not back down from the truth. "Yes."

Wyatt bowed his head, sorrow etched on his face. "He lied to me. My son lied to me."

He felt his way to a kitchen chair and sat, slumping

forward with his elbows resting on his knees.

"I wanted to believe him. I wanted to put all the blame on you. It was easier that way." He gave a bitter, anguished laugh. "But I think I knew the truth all along."

"I'm sorry, Wyatt."

"It's not your fault." He laughed again, the sound raw and angry. "That's ironic, isn't it? Russ wanted me to believe you were to blame for everything. Tell me something else. Was the divorce your idea?"

"No."

"Another lie. He said you were all for going back to Thailand, but when he went on ahead to find a place for the three of you to live, you changed your mind. You called him and told him you wanted a divorce."

Julia took a few steps toward him. "I never wanted to go back to Thailand. I wanted to raise Ava here. My parents were getting older, and I wanted to be around to look after them. And I'd just gotten the principalship of the high school. But Russ insisted, and I was afraid if I didn't give in, he'd leave me. So we both quit our jobs at the end of June, and he went on ahead to find us a house, and I stayed here to pack our things. Then I got a call. He said I should stay in Maine. He'd met a Thai woman named Kanda, and he was in love with her. Actually he'd met Kanda three years earlier when we were in Thailand together. He told me they'd had an affair then, though I hadn't known it at the time. But I suspected." She'd never told anyone that Russ had cheated on her, not even Edie and Tracy. She'd been too ashamed to talk about it. "He looked her up when he got back, and he decided he wanted to marry her. So he told me not to come, that he wanted a divorce.

Apparently Kanda is everything he wanted in a woman—domestic, pliable, obedient. Everything I'm not."

"He told me he'd married a Thai woman. They have two children together."

The news wasn't unexpected. She waited for the pain that usually swept over her when she let herself think of Russ and the way their marriage had ended, but this time it didn't come. She sighed in relief.

Perhaps it was finally over.

"That's when you asked if you could have your job back. The board was happy to have you."

"Well, not everyone on the board. As I recall, you had some tough questions for me. The past three years have not been easy between the two of us."

He sighed heavily. "I was angry. Russ blamed you and so did I. He said you were more interested in your career than you were in him."

"That's not true either. I loved Russ from the time I was fifteen years old. I know I made mistakes, but I tried very hard to be a good wife. I realize now I wasn't what he needed."

"What kind of a son did I raise?" Wyatt shook his head. "What kind of man ignores his child and lies to his father? What did I do wrong?"

She closed the distance between them and touched his shoulder. "I asked myself that question a thousand times. What did I do to make Russ stop loving me? I finally came to the conclusion that Russ made his own decisions. You're not at fault any more than I am."

He lifted his head and looked into her eyes, the sadness and grief making him look years older. "Ava is going to be the only grandchild we'll be allowed to know. I asked Russ if we could visit him and meet his wife and children, and he said he didn't want us to come to Thailand. He doesn't want his children to know us."

Julia felt a swift stab of pain for him and Lily. As much as Russ had hurt her, she realized now that he had hurt his parents just as much. Perhaps more. The hurt he inflicted on them kept going on and on. At least hers was over now.

"I'm sorry."

He covered her hand with his. "Yes, so am I. But I'm grateful to have Ava in our lives. She's a wonderful child."

Julia smiled. "Yes, I think she's pretty special. I'm glad she has you and Lily."

"How 'bout I give you a lift home? It's dark now, and getting colder."

"Okay. Thanks."

After slipping on her shoes, she followed Wyatt to his car, and they drove the short distance in silence. Wyatt pulled up in front of her house and put the car in neutral, leaving the engine running. He turned to look at her, his tense face illuminated in the light from the dashboard.

"I need to apologize to you."

She shook her head. "It's over now."

"I don't mean just for everything about Russ, though I want you to know I'm deeply sorry about that. I want to apologize for my behavior the morning after the Harvest of the Sea Festival. I was rude to both you and Dr. Campbell, and it was inexcusable."

Julia felt her face heating at the memory of her humiliation that morning. Worse, she remembered the fight she'd picked with Alex. She looked down at her hands clenched in her lap.

"I'd rather just forget about it."

"When we arrived at Dr. Campbell's house and you were there, it hit me that we could lose Ava just as we're getting to know her. For the first time I realized the relationship between the two of you was deeper and more serious than I'd believed. I realized you and Ava could go with him to San Diego when he leaves, and we could lose her forever. So I lashed out at you."

Julia kept her face averted. "I thought you were angry because you found out Alex and I had slept together."

"You've been divorced from my son for three years. I've always known there was a possibility you would remarry and Ava would have a stepfather. I just hoped it would be someone from the island. The prospect of the two of you moving across the country threw me for a loop."

"We won't be going with Alex when he leaves."

"But I thought—"

"It didn't work out. I can't leave here. I can't leave my parents, my friends, my school." She tried to laugh. "It looks like you're stuck with me."

"I'm sorry, Julia. Alex Campbell is a good man."

She couldn't stop the sob that escaped. "Yes, he is."

"He seems to care for you a great deal, and for Ava, as well. Perhaps you could convince him to stay."

"He says he loves me and that he wants to stay with me in Lobster Cove, but…"

"But what?"

"I guess I have a hard time believing he means it."

Wyatt stared out the windshield. “Not every man is like my son. Some of them tell the truth. Don’t compare him to Russ.”

Was she letting the sad end of her marriage ruin her chance for happiness now?

“I hope you can work things out with him, and for a lot of reasons, mostly selfish, I hope you’ll stay in Lobster Cove. The town needs both of you. But if you decide to leave with him, I want you to know I understand, and I wish you well.”

How strange it was to be having this conversation with her ex-father-in-law. They’d probably talked more honestly and emotionally this evening than they had in all the years they’d known each other. But they’d both needed to clear the air and hear the truth.

“Thank you. For everything.”

“Good night, Julia.”

She opened the car door and walked to her front door. Wyatt waited in the idling car. When she opened the door, she waved, and he took off down the street.

The phone rang almost as soon as she walked in. She turned on the kitchen light and found the cordless phone on the counter, the call display telling her someone from the hospital was on the line. Her stomach flipped. *Alex.*

“Hello?”

“Where have you been?” Tracy asked without preamble. “I’ve been calling you all evening. Why aren’t you answering your cell?’

“I’m sorry. Ava and I were at the Stewarts’ house for dinner.” She rummaged in her purse and pulled out her phone. “I forgot to charge my cell. It’s dead. What’s going on?”

"I wanted to make sure you heard the news."

"What news?"

"Alex told the staff at the hospital today that he plans to stay permanently in Lobster Cove. He signed a new contract with the health board. Isn't that great?"

Alex was staying? Julia dropped into a kitchen chair. What did this mean?

"Julia? Are you still there?"

"Yes. Yes, I'm here. You're sure about this, Tracy?"

"Of course I'm sure! Alex told us himself. He said he's come to appreciate the kind of medicine he practices in Lobster Cove, and he loves the community. He likes the way we look after each other. Didn't he tell you?"

Julia covered her mouth with her hand to hold back her sob. When she could talk, she said, "No, I haven't spoken to him in a while."

"Honey, he's going to stay. He *wants* to stay. He's not going to leave you."

This time she couldn't hold back the tears. "Oh, Tracy."

"Don't let him slip away. He's throwing you a lifeline. Maybe you should grab it and hang on."

She was right. "Is Alex at the hospital now?"

"Yes. He's doing his regular shift in the ER. He'll be off at midnight."

"Thanks for letting me know. I love you, Trace."

"I love you too, Jules. Good luck."

"Bye."

"Bye."

Julia carefully set the phone on the counter, her heart racing as if it were trying to beat its way out of her chest. She checked the clock on the stove; it was only eight-thirty. Midnight couldn't come fast enough.

****

By five minutes to twelve, Julia was sitting in her car in front of Alex's house, waiting for him to come home. Fall had turned to winter in the space of a few hours, and the thermometer had dipped below zero. She turned the heater on high and prayed no emergency would keep him late at the hospital. She needed to talk to him, to see his face and the look in his eyes when he told her about his decision to stay. She needed to see that his decision was sincere, that it was what he really wanted. Regardless of what Tracy had told her, Julia needed to know he was staying because he wanted to, and not just to make her happy.

At twenty minutes after midnight, a car drove down the street and turned into Alex's driveway. She turned off the ignition and got out of her car, her stomach tied up in knots. As she took a few steps down the driveway she saw Alex get out of his car.

"Alex!"

He saw her then and hurried toward her, clasping her shoulders when he reached her.

"What are you doing here? You're cold. Let's go inside."

She dug in her heels when he tried to pull her along. "Wait a minute. Is it true? Have you decided to stay in Lobster Cove?"

His face was perfectly calm. "Yes, it's true. I signed a new contract yesterday."

She watched his eyes. "Why did you extend your contract?"

He grinned. "Because there's never a dull moment

as a family physician in Lobster Cove."

"Be serious, Alex."

"I am serious. I deal with a wide variety of diseases and injuries that test all my abilities and skills as a doctor. I don't just treat one body part and move on, never to see that patient again. I treat the whole person, and I can't tell you how satisfying it is to follow a patient's progress and see them getting better. As an added bonus, I still get the rush of working in the emergency room."

"You mean that, don't you?"

He kissed the end of her nose. "Of course I mean it. Lobster Cove has become my home in the last few months. This community cares about its members, and I want to be part of that." He wrapped her in his arms and brought her close. "And then there's this cute little blonde shortstop that I'm crazy about. There's no way I'm ever leaving her."

A tear rolled down her cheek. "You really mean it."

He brushed away the tear with his thumb. "Of course I do. There's nowhere else I want to be. I love Lobster Cove, and I love you."

"I love you, too."

He rested his forehead against hers. There was a hitch in his voice when he spoke. "I've been waiting a long time to hear you say that."

"I've wanted to say it for a long time, but I was too scared. I'm not scared anymore."

She pressed herself again him and brought his head down for a deep drugging kiss. Alex lifted her off her feet and swung her around. Julia threw her head back and laughed.

He set her on her feet and kissed her again. “Is Ava with the Stewarts again?”

“Yes, she’s staying overnight and spending all day tomorrow with them.”

He grinned down at her. “That’s good. Since I’m not about to let you leave here tonight, are you sure you don’t want to move your car so the neighbors don’t see it? Someone’s going to notice that it’s been sitting in front of my house all night. People will talk, you know.”

“Let them talk. I’m in love, and I don’t care who knows it or what they say. As long as you love me too, that’s all that matters.”

“Sweetheart, that’s no problem at all.”

A word about the author...

Jana Richards has been making up stories since childhood, but she was in her thirties before she began to put pen to paper. She loves writing romance fiction because of its message of hopefulness and its steadfast belief that love makes people better human beings.

When not writing or working at her day job as a bookkeeper, Jana can be found reading, gardening, spending time with her family or tearing up her favourite golf course. Jana lives in Manitoba, Canada with her husband Warren.

Visit Jana at http://www.janarichards.com

Thank you for purchasing
this publication of The Wild Rose Press, Inc.

If you enjoyed the story, we would appreciate your letting others know by leaving a review.

For other wonderful stories,
please visit our on-line bookstore at
www.thewildrosepress.com.

For questions or more information
contact us at
info@thewildrosepress.com.

The Wild Rose Press, Inc.
www.thewildrosepress.com

Stay current with The Wild Rose Press, Inc.

Like us on Facebook

https://www.facebook.com/TheWildRosePress

And Follow us on Twitter
https://twitter.com/WildRosePress

www.ingramcontent.com/pod-product-compliance
Lightning Source LLC
LaVergne TN
LVHW020531100826
845148LV00010B/1425